I pulled my weapon and stepped into the C-130. The small windows were covered with rain, leaving the unlighted interior a darkened tube. The noise from the turbine engines was thunderous, a high-pitched scream that caused the deck to tremble under my feet.

He moved fast, coming out of the shadows and attacking before my eyes were adjusted to the darkness. I sensed a blur of motion as he kicked the gun from my hand. I ducked as the hatchetlike edge of his hand sliced above my head. That one would have given me a sore throat of the worst kind. He was confident. He had relieved me of my weapon. I heard him laugh as he advanced toward me, arms circling, fingers rigid for a lethal strike.

Then he was on me.

Praise for Robert Coram's
KILL THE ANGELS

Robert Coram

DEAD SOUTH

A SIGNET BOOK

SIGNET
Published by New American Library, a division of
Penguin Putnam Inc., 375 Hudson Street,
New York, New York 10014, U.S.A.
Penguin Books Ltd, 27 Wrights Lane,
London W8 5TZ, England
Penguin Books Australia Ltd,
Ringwood, Victoria, Australia
Penguin Books Canada Ltd, 10 Alcorn Avenue,
Toronto, Ontario, Canada M4V 3B2
Penguin Books (N.Z.) Ltd, 182–190 Wairau Road,
Auckland 10, New Zealand

Penguin Books Ltd, Registered Offices:
Harmondsworth, Middlesex, England

First published by Signet, an imprint of New American Library,
a division of Penguin Putnam Inc.

First Printing, June 1999
10 9 8 7 6 5 4 3 2 1

REGISTERED TRADEMARK—MARCA REGISTRADA

Printed in the United States of America

PUBLISHER'S NOTE
This is a work of fiction. Names, characters, places, and incidents either
are the product of the author's imagination or are used fictitiously,
and any resemblance to actual persons, living or dead, events, or locales
is entirely coincidental.

BOOKS ARE AVAILABLE AT QUANTITY DISCOUNTS WHEN USED TO PROMOTE
PRODUCTS OR SERVICES. FOR INFORMATION PLEASE WRITE TO PREMIUM
MARKETING DIVISION, PENGUIN PUTNAM INC., 375 HUDSON STREET, NEW
YORK, NY 10014.

For Royce and Betsy Hayes,
who have the best front porch in the world

ACKNOWLEDGMENTS

Thanks be to the staff of the Georgia Police Academy, particularly Don Sparry, who teaches an extraordinary course on Interviews and Interrogations. Don is one of America's foremost experts in the law enforcement use of Neuro-Linguistic Programming, and his course is the foundation for much of this book.

Thanks to Lt. Col. James M. DePaz, who, at this writing, commands the U.S. Army Criminal Investigation Laboratory at Fort Gillem, and to his investigators, the most professional to be found anywhere in the federal government. Any mistakes herein are not theirs, but mine.

At the DeKalb County Police Department, thanks to Sgt. Joe Fagan, officers Leon Mitchum and Steve Wright, and the others who revealed the arcane subtleties of Buford Highway.

A special thanks to Grady "Himself" Thrasher, who granted access to the peaceful kingdom of Sunnybank.

Finally, and most important of all, hosannas to Ginger Barber, a descendant of blockade runners who carries on the tradition.

1

I was sitting there doing CPR over a bottle of beer and keeping my eye on the two guys in the corner.

Neither man belonged in the bar.

One was about forty, slender, average looking except for the little tortoiseshell glasses and the bow tie. He probably was the first man in history to come into Mustache Mal's wearing a bow tie; one of those droopy paisley jobs, burgundy with little blue swirls that matched his button-down blue shirt and set off the gray of his suit.

Bowtie smiled too much. He wanted to be liked. He never looked his companion in the eye for more than a second, and, unless he was pushing up his glasses, which kept sliding down his nose, he kept his hands clasped in his lap. His body was rigid.

The other guy was Chinese, younger than Bowtie by maybe ten years, but clearly the power player in the duo. He was wearing a beautifully cut black sport coat and a black shirt that had a stand-up collar and a black button at the throat that looked like a piece of costume jewelry. I wouldn't wear that shirt on a bet. But it looked good on him. He was an elegant son of a bitch; elegant and smooth. His eyes were black and bottomless like two pools of oil. He was maybe five-nine, not a big guy at all, but with those eyes no one was going to give him any trouble, not even in Mustache Mal's. He was smoking one of those long thin little cigarettes and blowing smoke in Bowtie's face.

The Chinese guy was relaxed and kept his eyes locked on Bowtie the same way a cat keeps its eyes locked on a mouse. He frequently interrupted Bowtie's conversation.

Even Buster the waiter showed a reluctant deference toward the Chinese guy. And Buster, who also acted as bouncer, was a snarly hulk who weighed about two forty on the hoof. That night Buster was serving beer with a bandaged left hand. The bandage was dark and soaked and not from beer.

People like Bowtie and the Chinese guy usually don't go in Mustache Mal's. For that matter, people like me don't usually go in there. I'm the only black man I've ever seen in there and I almost had my butt kicked the first time.

This good old boy sauntered up to me, planted his feet, rolled his shoulders and grinned. "What the fuck does some . . . somebody like you want in here?"

That was close enough to the N word for me to jump in his face and say, "I want some cracker to take a swing at me, because there's going to be a movie of the week about what happened to his sorry white ass."

For the next five seconds we stared at each other. Then somebody laughed and said, "Hey, Movie Star, you two grab a beer and forget it." That set the whole bar to laughing. The good old boy grinned in relief. He had looked into my eyes and realized he was a heartbeat away from getting his bony ass kicked.

I went back to the bar and lit a cigar. Few things piss off a cracker more than seeing a black man smoke a cigar.

Mal thought I was a crook. He looked at me and

saw a guy wearing lug-soled work boots, jeans, and a wrinkled plaid shirt. All topped by a camo hat with a BASS logo on it. Yep, gotta be a crook, and not a very bright one at that.

Crooks like this place. Mustache Mal's is low, unpainted, decrepit, seedy, and set back off Buford Highway; clearly a hangout for people on the windy side of the law. This place would have to burn down and be rebuilt in order to be upgraded to a blue-collar bar.

I sit in here two or three nights a week and look down the row of pale-faced, gimme-hat-wearing bozos slumped over the bar and I wonder how empty a life can be. Except for *TV Guide* and the labels on beer bottles, these guys never read. They come to a cheap bar, eyeball cheap whores, and buy cheap dope. They order hamburgers served by a waiter with a suppurating hand wound. They drink PBR from the can and then go pee in the parking lot.

White people are weird.

I looked toward the corner. Bowtie and the Chinese guy were drinking beer out of glasses. Where did Mal find glasses?

I watched the two guys closely. Their faces were lighted in the tiny lamp on their table and I knew their conversation was reaching a critical point.

Something about the way the Chinese guy carried himself, maybe it was the way he looked around as if he owned the joint, made me wonder if he was on the Job.

Bowtie stood up and leaned over the table, shaking his head and pushing up his glasses. He was taller than I had thought, a little over six feet. Looked to be around forty. He had the gaunt body and finely chiseled face of one of those overbred white aristocrats. The Chinese guy stood up and dropped his cigarette in Bowtie's beer. I almost laughed. These guys are

supposed to be the model minority and he was acting
like Bogart.

He reached into his pocket and pulled out a stack
of bills and thumbed through them, then slid a twenty
under the ashtray. With a tight smile and a derisive
half-bow, he gestured toward the door. Bowtie
walked away.

Buster's eyes snapped toward the table. He saw the
twenty and nodded to Mal.

Mal watched the two guys walk toward the door.
"You guys come back," he said in a not very convinc-
ing tone.

I motioned for Mal to bring another beer. "I'd
rather have a bottle in front of me than a frontal
lobotomy," I said.

Mal stared and I thought for the hundredth time
what an ugly specimen he was: hair as thick and greasy
as a kitchen mop and a face so covered with beard
that only piggy little eyes and wet droopy lips are
visible; a real flat-liner.

Mal didn't get my joke. But then, I've only told it
to him a dozen times. I knew from Mal's stare what
he was thinking. In addition to believing I was a crook,
he thought I had the potential to become a smart-
mouthed nigger. That's the worst kind, you know.

I keep an eye on Mal when I'm in his bar. He's
always talking about having a "come to Jesus meeting" with people; that's his signal to Buster. When he
says those words, a customer is about to have his lights
put out.

I sat there another hour memorizing faces and doing
overheards, eavesdropping on people who were plan-
ning everything from their next drinking party to how
to rob illegal aliens. Just doing my job. And not liking
one minute of it.

A bar is the best place in the world to watch people

lie to one another. I include myself in that. People think I'm just another customer. That's good, because I'm a cop working undercover.

I don't like working U.C. in a redneck bar. I'm a homicide cop in Atlanta. But I stepped on the toes of an engineer from Universal Aerospace Technologies who had the juice to get me transferred. My major says I'm lucky I wasn't fired. But I don't see it. The Universal guy was a jerk.

Anyway, I've been exiled.

You watch TV and you see cops drinking and smoking and cursing and playing good guy–bad guy with suspects. Andy Sipowicz is always knocking somebody around in the interrogation room. TV cops are poorly educated, rumpled, hang out in bars and are always on the prowl for women. Many of them are divorced and have kids who won't talk to them. They have no goals. They are psychological basket cases who saw Mel Gibson in *Lethal Weapon* and think they have to live in a trailer and, for fun, eat their service weapons.

Let me tell you something. You got to have it all together to do this job. I'm working my way through this vale of tears as best I know how. My role model is Henry Louis Gates, the chairman of the African-American Studies Department up at Harvard. Skip Gates. He's also a staff writer at the *New Yorker* magazine. I started reading his stuff when I was working on my masters degree at Emory. Black professors there called him "His Skipness."

You see something strange about a black cop in Atlanta who idolizes a Harvard egghead? Well, His Skipness says there are thirty-five million black people out there, which means there are thirty-five million ways to be black. I don't like these ideological bullies like Louis Farrakhan or Elijah Muhammad who say, "This is what you got to do if you are black." And all this back-to-Africa stuff and Afrocentric movement doesn't work in the real world. Who wants to go back to the Sudan and use goat piss for cologne? I'm for air-conditioning and tailored suits. I'm for what works in the real world. I'm for what Skip Gates represents.

Look at how the man dresses. Listen to him. He talks white; no, he talks better than most whites. He made it in the white man's world, being himself, doing his thing, writing magazine articles and books as easily as most people write letters.

I'm from the outback, just as he is. I grew up in Albany, Georgia, and he grew up in a West Virginia mill town. A ridge-running hillbilly nigger grew up to be king of Harvard. Can you believe that? I love this country.

What he did in the cloistered halls of Harvard, I want to do on the bloody streets of Atlanta.

I don't smoke. Well, I don't smoke cigarettes. An occasional cigar is different. When I drink, which is rarely, I drink Scotch. I almost never use profanity. I think this good guy–bad guy nonsense a lot of cops still use is terribly outdated. The Supremes have ruled it to be coercive, TV has ruined it, and it just plain doesn't work. The one place where I am like a lot of other cops is on the domestic front: I am divorced and have a daughter that my dear sweet and wonderful ex-wife does not allow me to talk to.

As you might have gathered, I care about my appearance. When I was working Homicide I wore dark suits, white shirts, shined wingtips and bow ties. I dressed like a middle-aged white banker. Two reasons for that: One, my goal in life is to be successful in the white man's world. By dressing like white men, I am seen as more like them. I keep my dignity because I know where I'm going. The second reason is that I simply like to dress up. By attending once-a-year sales and with careful shopping, I buy clothes that otherwise I could never afford.

So there I was hanging out in a sleazy bar, nursing a warm beer and getting lung cancer from cigarette smoke.

I don't like this bar, I don't like the people who come in this bar, I don't like dressing this way, I don't like beer, I don't like cigarette smoke, and I don't like this assignment.

I looked at the door through which Bowtie and the Chinese guy had disappeared. A powerful dynamic was working between those two. I read it in the Chinese guy's eyes and in Bowtie's fear.

I ordered another beer. An hour later I was about to leave when I heard a siren coming north on Buford Highway. Seconds later there were two more coming from the other direction. They were flipping modes, going from wail to yelp to high-low. Both stopped across the road, no more than a half-block away, down near Asian Square and the El Toro Restaurant and the Han Motel and the gun store. People in the bar tensed and looked up.

"Relax, people," Mal shouted. "The storm troopers ain't coming in here."

A few people laughed nervously. Mal straightened his black leather vest like he was Peter Jennings straightening his suit coat and said, "Those are the sons of bitches that led the charge at Waco and Ruby Ridge."

Applause.

"The same people who hung Richard Jewell out to dry."

Applause and whistles. "They walk in my door and there will be a come to Jesus meeting."

More applause and whistles.

But Mal had exhausted his cop-hating repertoire.

He nodded once emphatically, took a sip of beer, and squinted around his dingy little kingdom.

As I walked to the cash register to pay my bill I passed the table where Bowtie and the Chinese guy had been sitting. A thin little cigarette floated in the beer like a white cork.

I head another siren and I knew it was on a fire and rescue unit, very distinctive because it sounded like a screaming baby. The wavering signal and the blaring horns told me it was weaving in and out of traffic. Then there was the angry growl of the big engine and I saw the strobing lights through the windows.

I paid Mal and stared toward the front window. Mal misunderstood. "Want to use the back door?" Mal looks after his customers. And somebody is looking after Mal. Mal knows in advance when the plain-clothes guys from licensing are coming in and he puts a lid on the dope and prostitution. Surprise raids by the uniforms do no better.

"It's okay. I'll just slide on down the road." I heard another siren and guessed it was an ambulance. Judging by the number of units responding this was a possible 48. I felt a moment of anxiety. By the time Homicide got there, the crime scene would be so walked over that the detectives would be lucky to find the body.

Mal handed me my change and nodded knowingly as I turned away. He thought I was running from the cops. When this assignment is over I am going to bust this place, take away the liquor license, and put Mal in jail. In the process, I might accidentally bounce Mal's pointed head off a few walls. If anyone ever needed some street-level law enforcement, it's Mal Merkin.

Let me tell you something. There are unwritten but inviolate rules that guide policemen. Some rules have ecclesiastical weight, such as "When in doubt about a case, always climb the money tree." Some are practical, such as, "When you see an ATF agent running, you better be in front of him." And some are just common sense, such as "When you're dealing with a bad guy, never cut him any slack." One day Mal will learn that I'm a cop. If I don't go back and clean up his act, he will never appreciate the majesty of the law.

I opened the door and looked down Buford Highway toward the Han Motel. An ambulance pulled up followed by an unmarked car with a blue light on top; DeKalb County Homicide. Another blue light was racing south on Buford. No siren. I knew Mal had his beady little eyes on me so I stood there as if I were hiding, watching the blue light coming up the road. The driver was blowing the horn and trying to get the Saturday night crowd out of the way. I was right; it was a 48.

Another marked car, siren on and blue lights flashing, pulled in behind the van. I saw a white shirt at the wheel: a supervisor. Two uniforms lifted the yellow crime scene tape so the van and the supervisor could go under.

No one can contaminate a crime scene quicker than a supervisor. A rookie uniform will put his hands in his pockets and not move because he knows that he knows nothing. But a supervisor knows everything. He will pick up evidence and move things around, I was collecting fiber once at a homicide and a supervisor flicked cigarette ashes on the carpet and said, "There's some more evidence, young detective."

I sighed. My orders were specific: stay away from all crime scenes and any place where I might be identified as a police officer. That is, unless life and limb were at stake.

But I had a gut feeling this involved Bowtie and the Chinese guy.

I walked toward my car.

It was time for me to put on my cape and jump out of the phone booth.

2

Buford Highway is a bizarre and frantic place. It begins somewhere in northeast Atlanta in a tangle of
expressways and access roads, crosses Lenox Road
and then arrows up into DeKalb County and begins
to assert itself, a wide four-lane crowded by apart-
ments and gas stations, discount malls, car dealerships,
transmission shops, flea markets, pawnshops and
neon-crested restaurants from a dozen countries.

Anyone who thinks Atlanta is part of the Old South
should come to Buford Highway on Saturday night.
In addition to a dozen or so ethnic groups, the white
bread crowd from downtown drifts into the restaurants. Good old boys from outlying counties slick
down their hair and gas up their pickups and come to
Buford Highway looking to buy or kick some ass. And
the mood along Buford becomes so tight it hums and
sizzles and crackles like a high-tension power line.

I got in my old Ford Explorer and pushed across
north-bound traffic on Buford and turned left. Three
blocks later I turned right, another right and parked
a half-block from the rear of the motel.

It was hot and humid, one of those cloying oppressive nights when people want to punch each other out
just to relieve the tension.

The Han Motel was U-shaped, with the open end

of the U facing away from Buford Highway. I walked
across the back parking lot. A uniform guarded a door
to one wing of the U. From his posture and his antsy
movements, this was not a run-of-the-mill Saturday
night killing.

I coughed. I wanted the uniform to see me. There
was little light back here. This was the sort of motel
where patrons rent rooms by the hour. The uniform
couldn't get a good look at my face but he could see
I was black.

He put his right hand on his service weapon, stuck
his left hand out front, palm facing me and said, "Stop
right there. Hands where I can see them."

I held my hands wide. Too many black cops wearing
civilian clothes have been shot for me to do anything
other than exactly what the young officer ordered.
Driving home from Buford Highway in the early
morning hours, I've been stopped twice in the past
week for DWB—driving while black.

The law may not be on the books, but it is a law.

The uniform glared. "What can I do for you?"

"Send over your supervisor. I'm a detective. Working U.C."

"Show me some I.D."

"Would I carry I.D. if I'm undercover? Get your
supervisor."

Now I had annoyed the baby cop.

"You armed?" he growled.

In my sock was a six-inch ballpoint pen; one of the
most dangerous weapons imaginable if you know how
to use it. "No gun."

He pointed his finger and said, "Don't you move."
Eyes locked on me, he leaned into the microphone
clipped to his epaulet. A moment later a big guy in a
white shirt with gold badge stepped out of one of the
rooms and looked me up and down. Or tried to. The

only light was down at the other end of the hall and my cap was pulled low. Two suits—homicide detectives—stood beside him, shoulders rounded, peering at me like a couple of belligerent tortoises.

"That's Major Hutt," the baby cop said. He flicked his forefinger in a motion for me to move forward.

"First name Jabba?" The uniform's face remained blank for a moment. I heard a reluctant chuckle as I passed.

The major had one of those red-splotched faces that white folk get after twenty years of hard drinking. He was one of the fattest cops I've ever seen. His belly started somewhere around his chin and dropped outward at a forty-five-degree angle then cut sharply back in a straight line toward his belt buckle. He hadn't seen his feet in fifty years. I sensed from his belligerent posture and from his basilisk gaze that he was not your neighborhood Officer Friendly.

Let me tell you something. This business about fat people being jolly and good-natured is a myth. They've been picked on for years and they hate themselves every time they look in the mirror. Fat people are meaner than Baptists.

"Who the fuck are you?" the major rumbled. It sounded like a distant volcano about to erupt. I expected the top of his head to pop open and fire and brimstone spout through the ceiling. "I don't have any undercover people working here."

I kept my hands in sight, stayed against the wall and waited until I was close. I motioned for the major to step away from the two detectives. I didn't want them to see my face. They slid their hands inside their coats as the major stepped forward.

"The umbrella man."

It sounded stupid. But when my major had me transferred out here, he and the DeKalb chief agreed

that if I ever had to identify myself to a DeKalb officer, that's how I would do it.

He stared. "I been briefed on you."

I waited.

"You from Atlanta." It was a statement.

I nodded. "Sergeant C.R. Payne. APD Homicide."

DeKalb undercover people usually are fresh-faced
recruits who can't find their backsides with both hands
and a search warrant. They have two attributes: They
look too young to be cops and no one on the street
knows them.

The major was surprised that the umbrella man was
a homicide sergeant. His eyes were wary. Nobody
likes it when a U.C. guy from another jurisdiction
comes into his territory. "What do you want?"

"You got a forty-eight."

He nodded slowly. "Yeah. A doozy. We're waiting
on a video tech to shoot the crime scene."

"Major, could I ask you to describe the victim?"

The two detectives were beginning to relax. But
they kept their eyes on me.

The major stared. "Why? You know something?"

"I might."

He waited long enough to let me know he had his
doubts. "White male. Late thirties. About six feet two;
one sixty."

"How was he dressed?"

"Like a skinned mule."

"Clothes in there?"

"Hanging in the closet." The major was trying to
figure out what I wanted.

"Would you describe them?"

"His clothes?"

"Yes."

"Gray suit. Blue shirt. Bow tie. Black shoes. Expensive. He wasn't a dirt bag."

"Personal belongings?"

"Watch. Ring. Wallet. Cell phone."

"Money?"

"Couple hundred dollars. Wasn't a robbery."

"Glasses?"

The major paused. "Yes."

"Tortoiseshell?"

"That the same as horn-rims?"

"Yes."

His eyes narrowed. "In the pocket of his suit. How'd you know?"

I didn't answer. I was thinking about Bowtie and the Chinese man.

The volcano emitted a threatening rumble. "I know you're working undercover. But since you already stuck your nose in this case, you got to come inside and talk to my homicide detectives."

"Major, whose crime scene is this?"

He knew what I was asking. In many jurisdictions homicide detectives rule supreme at a crime scene. But sometimes the ranking officer is in charge.

"Homicide."

"In Atlanta if a superior officer has compelling reasons to do so he can take over a crime scene."

He bowed up. "That's not special to you people in Atlanta. We do that, too."

"Major, because I'm undercover and because of the information I can provide, I'm asking if you will take over this crime scene."

He stared at me for a long moment and then looked over his shoulder at the two detectives. "They've seen your face."

"They know I'm black, that's all."

"They will raise hell."

"Major, I'm asking if you will clear out everybody but the M.E. until after we talk. Put them in an inside room and shut the door. I'll talk to you and you can pass it on to Homicide."

He shook his head. "That's not good enough."

"That's as good as it gets, Major. You got problems, go to your chief. He's the one who put me here." I paused. "Besides, it's not that much better than the airport."

"What was that?"

"Nothing, sir."

As the major said, he had been briefed. He grimaced. "Never seen a crime scene like this before. It's a bitch kitty." He stared at me. "You going to cause me a bunch of grief?"

"Major, I'm here to help."

I stood in the doorway and got an overall view of the crime scene. Then I closed my eyes, sniffed, and listened. The dead want to tell what happened. The souls of the recently departed linger for a while to assist in balancing the scales. Homicide cops come to a crime scene ready to look and listen and feel. With some cops, it's twenty years' experience. With me, it's more. I hear. Maybe it's a voice from the other side. I don't know.

But I do know that I am never more filled with the impulse of life, never more alert and intuitive, than when I am with the dead.

What I heard here, what I felt, were two things: first, and most powerful, was a lingering, almost ineffable feeling of an ancient evil, a seasoned and pervasive malevolence. And then there was a clean purple outrage.

The medical examiner stood patiently. He was an old geezer who didn't care if syrup went up to a dollar a sop as long as he put in his eight hours. The major was another matter. He had homicide detectives and tech people and uniforms jammed in another room thinking he was a loon for letting someone from another jurisdiction roam around his crime scene. A crowd of gawkers was out front bellying up to the crime scene tape. And the media slugs were out there clamoring to exercise their divine right to every scrap of information.

I took a deep breath and approached the body. I glanced down at the orange shag carpet.

"Lovely. Wonder who the decorator was."

The major glared.

The carpet was so trampled by the major and the EMT's that there was no chance of my stepping on the perp's shoe prints. The bed was turned sideways; clearly not where it was supposed to be.

"This the way you found it?"

"Yes."

Bowtie was lying on top of the covers, arms parallel to his sides, fingers closed. I walked to the edge of the bed.

"You move anything? Touch anything?"

He paused.

"What did you move?"

The doctor held up an evidence bag. "These were in his hands."

"Hold onto those for a moment."

I leaned over.

Flat white objects, oval in shape, translucent with a deep warm soaplike luster, were wedged into Bowtie's eye sockets, giving him the blank stare of something in a museum storage room. A white device of the same material was shoved into his nose.

I leaned closer. A slight bruise had formed on his throat.

"Doctor, tell me about his throat."

The M.E. looked at me in surprise. "Not many lay-men would have seen that."

"I'm not a layman. I'm a city of Atlanta homicide detective."

"No offense. Right now I'd say the cause of death is a crushed larynx. Until I do an autopsy I can't be certain. I palpated his throat and there appears to be an internal fracture of both the thyroid cartilage and the hyoid bone." He paused. "He has an object in his throat that appears to be of the same material as the one you see in his nasal passages. I believe they were inserted after death."

"Crushed larynx. A slow way to die."

"Slow and agonizing. The blow to the throat, which probably was done with the edge of a hand or a blunt instrument, can cause a cardiac rhythm disturbance. That triggers a vagal response and he goes into some-thing like cardiac arrest. At the same time the injured tissue in his throat begins an immediate swelling, blocking his breathing passage."

"He's dying of a heart attack and asphyxiation at the same time?"

"Possibly." He paused, looked at the major then back to me. He spoke cautiously. "There's also a small carved piece on his tongue." He paused again. "Shaped like a cicada."

I turned and stared. "A what?"

Sometimes my responses are so eloquent. But what do you say when the M.E. tells you a homicide victim has a carved cicada perched on his tongue?

"A cicada."

"Let me see that evidence bag."

The M.E. handed me the plastic bag. Two cylinders, each a milky white and about the size of a pencil stub, were inside.

"What are they?"

"You tell us," the major said.

I twisted the bag around and studied the two pieces.

"You superglue these?"

The major shrugged. "No."

Even through the plastic the two objects had the same soaplike luster as the pieces covering Bowtie's eyes and in his nose. What had appeared to be cylinders I could now see were intricately carved pieces. "Pigs."

"What makes you so certain?" the major asked in his everyday querulous rumble.

"Major, I grew up in Albany. In Southwest Georgia. Farm country."

"You oughta know, then."

The M.E. spoke. "Detective?"

"Yes."

"Look at his ears."

"Got a light?"

He handed me a tiny flashlight. A small round object was deep in Bowtie's ear. It was white. I looked at the M.E. "The other ear also?"

He nodded. "And his penis."

My eyebrows jerked. I moved toward the end of the bed and leaned over.

I grinned at the two men. "The stories I hear about you white people are true."

The major's mouth went as thin as a couple of razor blades pressed together.

"You a Baptist?" I asked.

"What?"

"Never mind."

I returned the light to the M.E. He reached out with a gloved hand, picked up Bowtie's penis, and pointed it in my direction. He turned on the flashlight. A round white object distorted the urethra. The M.E. walked his fingers down Bowtie's penis for several inches, squeezing. "The object stops about here. It appears to be about four centimeters in length and about five millimeters in diameter; size of a cigarette butt."

"He was not alive when this happened?"

The M.E. flipped Bowtie's penis aside. "The discomfort would have been significant."

Understatement of the year.

I looked at Bowtie's left hand. He wore a wedding ring, not that it means anything. "Any idea what happened? This a homosexual attack?"

I knew the answer before I asked. But I wanted the M.E.'s opinion.

"No. Too neat. Too clean. Too organized."

I thought about the timing. Bowtie had been in Mal's little more than an hour ago. He had been killed and the body found in a very short time. "Who reported this?"

"The manager. A Chink. Said a woman rented the room late this afternoon. Paid cash. We already checked. Bogus name and address."

"Who found the body?"

"The manager. Said she was walking back to the Coke machine and the door was open."

"Body temp?"

"Still normal."

At 70 degrees ambient temperature, a cadaver loses about 1.5 degrees of body temperature per hour.

"Postmortem lividity?"

"Not yet."

I looked closer at Bowtie. The pale bloodless appearance that occurs about a half hour after the heart stops was just beginning.

Everything I saw reinforced what I knew: Bowtie had been killed in the last thirty to forty-five minutes.

"Any cars in the parking lot you can't account for?"

"No. There are only two and they belong to guests."
He looked around. "Why anyone would want to come
to this shit hole, I don't know."

"You'll find the victim's car up the road at Mustache Mal's."

The major nodded. "You're gonna have to talk to
me, Sergeant."

I turned to the M.E. "What do you think happened?"

"It's speculation at this point, but my scenario is
that the victim knew his assailant; knew him well
enough that he was not alarmed by the perp's being
close to him. The victim was killed by the blow to the
throat, undressed, placed on the bed, and the objects
were inserted into the body orifices." He looked at
me. "I don't believe he was killed here."

Makes sense. It was probably done in a car while
the two men were sitting side by side. But why, unless
Bowtie was gay, would he come to a sleazy motel with
some guy he was having a disagreement with? Maybe
he thought they were driving into the parking lot to
talk.

I studied the body.

"Why did he bring you here?" I mumbled. "Why
did he put you on display like this?" My eyes walked
along the body, searching, probing, wondering. "There
is some sort of ritualism or symbolism here. Eyes,
nose, ears, mouth and penis."

"One more," the major said.

"One more?"

"Roll him over."

I looked at the M.E. in disbelief. He nodded. "Every
orifice has been plugged and with objects that—since
they fit so well—are apparently designed for that purpose. And there's one other thing, Detective."

I did a quick count. "There's no place left."

"Not that," the M.E. said. "The white objects."

"What about them?"

"I went to a convention of pathologists last year in Southeast Asia. I'm certain the objects are jade."

I waited.

"Imperial jade. Very expensive."

"Tax deductible?"

"What?"

"The convention in Southeast Asia?"

The good doctor looked at me as if I'd just come in on a turnip truck.

I'm jealous. Cops don't have tax-deductible trips to Southeast Asia. We meet at some Mexican joint and fight over the check.

I stared at Bowtie's body. I always look for the simplest explanation. I believe in Occam's Razor: The most obvious answer often is the right one. But there is nothing simple or obvious about the jade. I've never seen or heard of a victim having jade inserted into every body orifice.

What did it mean?

The major rumbled. "This puppy went into the next world with what the doc says is a fortune shoved up his ass. Now, young sergeant, I don't want to hold you up longer than necessary from your secret squirrel stuff, so tell me what you know about this victim."

3

I told the major what I had seen at Mustache Mal's and was about to leave when there was a knock on the door.

The major walked across the room, talked to someone for a moment and was handed a two-page computer printout. He studied it then shook his head. "Now I'm really in the shit." He handed me the printout. "What would a smart cop from Atlanta do?"

DeKalb County has one of the most sophisticated law enforcement computer networks in the country. Before I arrived at the crime scene, a detective had scanned Bowtie's prints into a notebook computer then connected his cell phone to the computer and sent the prints via modem to the Georgia Bureau of Investigation.

Alarm bells went off at the GBI. The victim was Richard Morris, thirty-eight, an engineer at Universal Aerospace Technologies, the big defense contractor about twenty miles north of Atlanta.

I felt a slight chill, almost as if I had been given a psychic warning. A case involving a Universal engineer is the reason I am no longer in Homicide.

A brief bio was attached to Morris's file. He had a security clearance beyond top secret and more degrees than a thermometer: graduate of Bowdoin with a major in Asian Affairs, engineering degree from MIT, and a master's in international business from Wharton. His wife, Susan, also had a master's degree. They lived in Pine Hills, no more than a couple of miles away, and had two boys, eleven and twelve, enrolled in Westminster, the most exclusive private school in Atlanta.

But what caught my attention was an attachment saying any incident involving Morris should be immediately reported to J. Stanford Godbey, president of Universal; to a representative of the Joint Chiefs of Staff, and to the undersecretary of state for Asian affairs.

What kind of engineer was this guy?

What was he doing dead in a cheap motel room with a fortune in jade in his body? And who was the Chinese guy who had been with him an hour before his death?

"Your officers taken a statement from the manager?"

The major shook his head. "Doesn't know anything. Damn immigrant. Can't speak ten words of English."

"You said a woman signed for the room. Did the manager say who she was?"

"Said she was Oriental."

"Oriental?"

A Chinese does not refer to fellow Asians as Orientals.

"That's what she said." He looked around. "I hate this fucking case. A dead engineer with jade in his ass. Washington and the State Department. Jesus, Joseph, Mary and the blue-assed donkey."

"Major, did she say what country?"

"What country what?"

"The woman who rented the room. Did the manager say what country she was from?"

"Yeah. Another Chink."

My gut feeling had been right. The Chinese guy had

planned to bring Bowtie here. This was a premeditated homicide involving a Universal engineer with ties to the Pentagon and the State Department.

I was out here working Buford Highway and knowing things can't get any worse when suddenly the heavens parted and I'm handed a case that can get me out of cheap bars and into expensive suits; back to Homicide, back to Atlanta. I'd be crazy not to pirate this case. I have nothing to lose and everything to gain.

I took a deep breath.

"Major, I'm going to do your department a favor and take this case. Can you give me until noon before you contact Washington?"

He looked at me as if I had taken leave of my senses. "This is a DeKalb case."

He didn't seem as territorial as he might have been.

"Your chief and mine agreed that if I obtained unique knowledge of a case that I would be given authority to work it. My discretion."

That was stretching the truth. But I knew what was going through the major's mind and I was trying to make it easy for him. First, it is DeKalb's case and DeKalb does not give up jurisdiction to Atlanta. On the other hand no local jurisdiction wants to work a homicide involving national defense issues. No local jurisdiction wants to be involved with Pentagon spooks and State Department suits looking over an investigator's shoulder, throwing their weight around, second-guessing every move, just waiting for something to go wrong so they can blame the locals for incompetence. To DeKalb, this case is fraught with peril. It is a quagmire into which careers will be sucked down and lost forever.

But to me it is as if the bright golden ring of opportunity has been placed in my hands. This is my chance for redemption. What are they going to do to me? Put me in jeans and send me to work sleazy bars on Buford Highway?

I can see in his eyes that the major would love for Atlanta to take over the case. That way, when it turns sour Atlanta will take the heat. But the major can't seem too anxious.

He shook his head. "We don't need any help from Atlanta."

"Major, as you know, your chief granted me certain discretionary powers while working U.C. out here. Could I suggest you run this by him?"

The major stared at me for a long moment then pulled his cellular phone from his pocket. He walked across the room and stood in the corner showing me his back.

After about five minutes the major clicked his phone off, dropped it into his pocket, and turned. He nodded in pretended doubt and reluctance.

"You got it. This is your crime scene. But my chief says he can't wait until noon to notify Washington and tell them Atlanta has the case. He says eighty-thirty or nine o'clock is as late as he can go. He wants you to notify the family."

DeKalb was dropping this case as if it were a hot rock. I will make it easy. "I want to be the one who informs the Universal president."

Done and done.

I turned toward the M.E. "When can I have your report?"

The M.E. looked at the major. They had worked together long enough that the major's nod spoke volumes. He turned to me. "Monday morning."

The major and his chief wanted this case, all of it, dumped on me before my superiors could back out.

I turned to the major. "What about the workup by your people?"

"That you can have this afternoon."

"Photos, videotape, crime scene report?"

"Everything. But you have to canvass the neighborhood."

"Okay. And before anyone forgets it, bag the victim's hands. I want the room and everything in it printed. As soon as your people are through, I want this crime scene locked down. It is not to be returned to the manager until I say so."

"No trouble there. The Chinks don't fuck with us on Buford Highway." The major grinned and pulled at one of his chins; I think the third one. "Not like wetbacks. Lean on one of them and they mule up on you with this *'no hable Inglesia'* shit. You put an ass whipping on one of those boys and they learn English in a hurry. It ain't perfect you understand; not nearly as good as mine, but enough that they can tell me what I need to know. They—"

"You got an artist who can sit down with me and do a composite of the Chinese guy?"

"When you want him?"

I thought for a moment. "Ten o'clock. In the parking lot."

"You got it."

"I need a hundred copies."

"I'll light a fire under his ass. You'll have them mid-afternoon."

I looked around the crime scene again. "Major, I need to be on the road. Can your people finish?"

"You bet."

"I'm out of here." I checked Morris's address on the computer printout—Lenox Crest, a cul-de-sac off Shady Valley—and walked through the parking lot toward my Explorer. Considering the hour and the way I was dressed, it would be prudent to call Mrs. Morris before I arrived. I reached under the dash where I had hidden my cell phone, called and told her that I was an undercover police officer and that I would be there in ten minutes. Official police business. I pulled the black wallet containing my badge from under the dash, stuck it into my shirt pocket, and flipped the badge down. My picture I.D. I stuck in my pocket.

Susan Morris was about five feet nine inches tall with her blond hair cut in a crisp pageboy. She was dressed in slacks and a blouse and, unlike many tall women, stood pine-tree straight, adding inches to her height. She was a chic and sophisticated woman; very much in control. Except for her eyes. Her eyes were filled with apprehension.

I took a deep breath. Being a police officer involves a lot of unpleasant experiences. None brings more pain than notifying someone a family member has been killed. It is particularly painful when, as in this case, the family members are well-educated, upper middle class, and utterly unacquainted with the world in which I live.

I told Mrs. Morris as gently as I could that her husband was dead; no details about the jade and nothing about the Chinese guy. She looked at me as if there had been some terrible mistake. Then she whimpered once and bit her lip. She did not cry. She would control her grief around a stranger.

"Mrs. Morris. Do you mind if I ask you a few questions?"

"Come back to the kitchen. I'll make some coffee."

I don't like coffee. Never acquired a taste for it. But I'll put a lot of milk in it and manage if it will help her talk to me.

A dog was curled up on the floor in the kitchen; a

shaggy mutt with long black and brown hair and, almost comically, one white stocking. This dog had descended from every dog that ever lived. She seemed almost out of place in this elegant house until she raised her head, looked at me with the most love-filled eyes imaginable, thumped her tail twice on the floor and plopped back into peaceful dreams of a mutt who lives in doggy heaven.

"Great dog."

Mrs. Morris smiled. "That's Annie. Orphan Annie. I found her in front of Harris Teeter's. I went up there to buy a few things one evening and she was on the curb with a broken leg. She was wagging her tail, begging people to pet her."

"You went to buy groceries and brought home a dog with a broken leg?"

She shook her head as if she couldn't believe it herself. "She cost me a fortune in vet bills. But the boys love her. Richie loves her."

Her hands were shaking as she busied herself. "Go ahead with your questions. It's all right."

There are reasons we ask certain standard questions of a victim's family. Most homicides are committed by people well known to the victim. Friends and family members do most of the killing.

I took a deep breath.

"Mrs. Morris, did your husband say where he was going tonight?"

She paused. "No. He said he had to go out for a brief business meeting. He said he wouldn't be late."

"He often have business meetings on Saturday night?"

"No."

"Did he say who he was meeting?"

She looked away. "No."

"Your husband was an engineer at Universal?"

She closed a door leading into the house. Her back was to me as she poured coffee grounds into the filter and flipped the switch. I waited. Why was she delaying answering such a simple question?

"Yes. But his job is selling aircraft." She corrected herself. "His job was selling aircraft."

"What kind?"

She made herself busy with the coffeepot. "The F-twenty-two."

"Is that the one they call the Raptor?"

"Yes."

"Who are his customers?"

She turned around. A wry smile was on her face. "The F-twenty-two costs around two hundred million dollars a copy. That's an unofficial figure."

"For one airplane?"

"Yes."

"He sold to governments?"

She nodded.

"What governments?"

She turned back to the coffeepot.

"He works . . . he was working with several."

"Any one in particular?"

She shrugged and made herself busy wiping the spotlessly clean countertop. When she spoke, her voice was casual. "The Chinese."

There are moments in a homicide investigation when a question, oftentimes a boilerplate sort of question, opens a door and gives the detective a glimpse of the promised land. This was such a moment. I suddenly knew that I was up against the Chinese government. But I gave nothing away to Mrs. Morris. I simply nodded and asked, "Big sale?"

"The largest in the history of Universal."

"How much?"

"Eighty billion dollars."

My eyes widened.

"Plus the . . ."

I waited. "Yes?"

"It's all very complicated." She took down two mugs from the cupboard. "What do you take in your coffee?"

"Milk, please." I waited a moment. "There was something else you were going to say?"

She opened the door of the refrigerator, took out a container of milk, and turned to face me. "I don't know how much of this I am supposed to talk about."

As gently as I could, I said, "Mrs. Morris, did your husband have any enemies?"

Her eyes filled with pain. "No. None. He was . . . he—it's so hard to speak of him in the past tense— he was a kind and a sweet man. Everyone liked Richie. He was so smart." She bit her lips. "He was a good person."

"Then the reason he was killed could have something to do with his work."

She thought for a minute. "What do you want to know?"

"What were you going to tell me earlier?"

"It's very complicated. There was a technology exchange involved. It was business dealings, it had nothing to do with his . . . with Richie's . . ."

"What is a technology exchange?"

"The Chinese wanted a side agreement allowing them to buy fifty million dollars' worth of equipment from Universal. They wanted to be able to do the maintenance and future upgrades on the F-twenty-two in China and not have to send the aircraft back to Universal."

"Is that unusual?"

"It depends on the country." She looked toward the door leading to where her sons were still sleeping. This woman was a thoroughbred but the shock of what had happened was beginning to sink in. I was losing her.

"What was the position of our government?"

"The White House was in favor. The Pentagon was opposed. State was involved."

"State?"

"The State Department. They were neutral. They had no position either way."

"Which means they favored the sale?"

She looked at me sharply. "Yes, I suppose so."

"Why was the Pentagon opposed?"

"They are concerned about certain technologies going to China. They believed the equipment the Chinese wanted to buy would enable them to . . . to build other things."

"Such as?"

She paused. "Rockets."

"Rockets?"

"Rockets."

"You mean . . . ?"

"I mean intercontinental missiles. I'm not telling you anything I shouldn't. This was in the paper, not the local paper, *The New York Times*."

"These missiles can carry nuclear warheads?"

"Nuclear. Thermonuclear. Chemical. Biological. Of course."

Not only was I up against the Chinese government, but the government had a quiver filled with weapons of mass destruction.

4

She touched the handle of the coffeepot, one of those unconscious little gestures people do when they are about to add more information. "The Chinese already have that capability. But the new equipment would significantly upgrade their technology."

I tried to digest this. I'm used to people killing each other over women or drugs or for a few dollars or just for the sheer hell of it. But eighty-billion-dollar contracts and fifty-million-dollar side agreements and rockets that can carry atomic bombs are out of my line. I had to keep focused on the basics. This was a homicide; a homicide with high stakes, but still a homicide.

She opened a cupboard and began searching.

"What's the status of the contract? Is it about to be signed?"

"I believe so."

"What did your husband say about this?"

"He was very excited in the beginning. But then the Chinese brought up the side agreement and made it a condition of the sale. He began having doubts."

She reached into the cupboard. "Here's my pitcher."

"Please. I'll pour from the container."

She sat the milk carton on the counter. An open

notebook was there under the telephone. She picked up a pen and began doodling on the pad, heavy black lines. A tight, forced smile was on her face. She was having a difficult time controlling herself.

In an effort to keep her with me, I pointed toward the carton. "I have a pitcher just like that in my house."

She smiled weakly, dropped the pen and turned to the coffeepot. She cupped her hands near the top of the pot as if to draw warmth from it. The bubbling noises ceased. It was ready.

"Was it the Pentagon that caused his doubts?"

She shook her head and looked up and to her left then down to her left. "That was part of it. Richie is . . . was very patriotic. But his reason had more to do with . . . with things he discovered about the people he was dealing with."

She was not telling me everything. In fact, she was withholding something very important.

"The Chinese?"

She nodded.

"Did Universal know your husband was opposed to the sale?"

She snapped her head toward me, started to say something, then changed her mind. She spoke sharply. "He had reservations. Questions."

The idea of her husband's opposing the sale seemed very sensitive.

"Did Universal know?"

"Yes." Again she looked down and to her left. There was something she was not telling me. I would come back to that later.

"If the Pentagon was opposed to the sale and if your husband—the man who made the sale—had . . . reservations, Universal was in a bind."

She nodded as she poured the coffee. She filled my

cup almost to the top. Not much room for milk. "Do you know anything about what has happened to the defense industry since the end of the Cold War, about the JSF contract, about our relations with the Chinese?"

"No, no, and no."

"It doesn't matter. Universal was giving Richie a big promotion and an enormous bonus. There were many meetings with the Pentagon and with the Chinese."

To me, the last two sentences seemed unconnected. But to her they were connected. I made a mental note.

"Did your husband ever go to China?"

"After the Chinese tied the aircraft sale to the equipment purchase, he went over several times. He wanted to separate the two."

"The sale and buying the equipment?"

"Yes."

"What did the Chinese say?"

"They refused."

I thought for a moment. "He ever bring you any jade?"

She looked at me, surprised. "How would you know that?" She held up her right arm, the coffeepot still extended, and pulled the sleeve of her blouse back, revealing a circular white bracelet. "Richie brought this back from his first trip. It was a gift from the Chinese. He said they knew our anniversary was coming up." Her eyes teared. "It's imperial jade. He brought back some other pieces for me, along with books about jade and its role in the history of China. Wonderful books."

She was turning to replace the coffeepot when the phone rang, a loud shrill jangle. She dropped the coffeepot, shattering it, and gasped as the hot coffee splattered across her ankles.

Her face twisted into a quick grimace of pain as she grabbed the phone. "Hello."

She closed her eyes. "Oh, hello, Stan." She paused. "It's okay, Stan. I'm up."

She nodded. "Yes. I know. The police have already told me."

Stan? Who was Stan? Who was calling her to tell her about her husband? How did the caller know?

She nodded again, her eyes still closed. She had a very intense way with the telephone. She leaned into it as if straining to pull out every word. "Not yet. He said they don't have any idea."

Stan must have assumed she had been informed of her husband's death by telephone. He did not know I was here.

I stood up and moved around the counter to pick up the shattered coffeepot. She motioned for me to sit down.

"What would the police ask me about?"

I held up my left forefinger, tapped my lips in a motion of silence and shook my head. She was a quick study. Her eyebrows raised and her eyes became fixed on me.

"Should I call you?"

Her eyes remained locked on me. "I didn't know it was classified." Her lips trembled. "Even if it concerns Richie's death?"

She nodded. "I'll refer them to you."

Her eyes closed. "No, Stan, I haven't begun to think of that. The boys are still asleep. I haven't told them. I'll make those plans later."

Tears were sliding down her cheeks.

"Later this morning. About ten or so. Not now."

She nodded. "Thank you. I'll see you then. Goodbye."

She hung up. "Stan Godbey. He's coming by later."

The name rang a bell. "J. Stanford Godbey? President of Universal?"

"Yes." She stared, measuring me. "Why didn't you want me to tell him you are here? You said you are a police officer."

I walked back around the counter. "I am. But it would be better for the moment if he didn't know. I have to ask you to trust me. Did he say how he knew of your husband's death?"

She was still studying me. "No. He said I should not talk to the police."

"Why?"

The president of Universal had not been notified that Morris was dead. The big question was how he knew.

"He said national defense issues are involved and that all statements should come from Universal." She wiped her eyes. "I'm so confused." She looked at me imploringly. "I'm sorry about the coffee. I'd offer to make another pot but I have to tell my sons. I have to call my family."

I stood up. "Of course. Forgive me. I'll leave." I looked at her.

"Yes?"

"I have to ask you one more question. We always ask this. Were you and your husband having marital problems?"

She shook her head and laughed a quick mirthless laugh. "No. We've talked about that. We never had the problems that most people seem to have."

"Have you noticed any behavioral changes on his part lately?"

"No."

"Okay. Thank you." I stood up and patted my shirt pocket. "Mrs. Morris, I don't have a card with me. Could I write my number on your notepad?"

"Yes." She handed me the pad.

"If you lose the number, just call the police station and ask for me. My home phone is on here, too. You need anything, or you have any questions or if you think of anything else you want to tell me, please call."

"Will you find whoever did this?"

"I'll do my best."

"Mr . . . ?" She looked at the notepad.

"Payne. Sergeant C. R. Payne. My name is Caesar Roosevelt, but everyone calls me C.R. As I said, I'm a detective with Atlanta."

"I'm sorry. Sergeant Payne, I'm opposed to the death penalty."

I nodded. I knew what was coming.

"My husband was a good man and a good father. Whoever did this deserves the death penalty."

I nodded again. I'd heard it before.

She was crying as she closed the door.

As I drove away, I couldn't help but think what a class act this woman was. She was everything my former wife imagined herself to be but was not. I had been married two years when my wife inherited about $200,000; not a lot of money, but enough to make her unsatisfied with being the wife of a cop.

That was three years ago. Enough time that the divorce itself doesn't bother me. It bothers me that she won't let me talk with my daughter who is now four years old. And it bothers me that my former wife handled the divorce the way she did.

She sent me a fax.

She notified me by fax that she was divorcing me. She didn't give any reason. Just said that she was moving to California and taking our daughter. She did it one morning when she knew I would be on the firing range all day. I called in about 4 p.m. as I was driving home, and one of the detectives said I better come in. It was shift change time, so the evening watch got to read what everyone on the day watch had already read. She had changed the locks on the house and hired a security firm to keep me out.

It was two weeks before I could get my clothes, and only then because my lawyer got into the act.

Mrs. Morris would never behave like that.

5

"Mrs. Godbey?"

"Yes."

She sounded faintly disappointed, almost as if she had been hoping it was someone else.

"This is C.R. Payne. I'm sorry to be calling so early, but I need to speak with Stan. Is he available?"

Mrs. Godbey paused. I could almost hear her mind clicking through the memory banks. She thought I was someone who worked for her husband. Being a good corporate wife, she prided herself on knowing his senior people, at least those on a first-name basis with him. But executives were always coming and going from the home office in California. Or I could be someone she met at a party and simply didn't remember.

J. Stanford Godbey, a major deity in Atlanta and environs, was not at home. Mrs. Godbey said he was "at the plant" in the same tone of voice someone would say, "He is in heaven."

Sunday morning, 7:00 A.M.—the time I usually go to bed—and the guy is at work. No wonder he's president. I mentally recomputed my course to go to Universal.

"The switchboard is closed, you know. Do you have his private number?" she asked.

"Not with me. I'm in my car."

She gave me the number. She couldn't have been more cooperative. I never cease to be amazed how often people at the top have the nicest manners.

I took a chance. "He doesn't usually go in on Sunday. Is there a problem?"

"Yes, there seems to be, Mr. Payne, although I don't know what it is. Stanford received a phone call in the middle of the night and dashed away." She paused. "Will you be seeing him?"

"I'm on the way there now."

That cinched it for her. If I was going to meet her husband on Sunday morning, I must be one of his intimates. An even warmer note came into her voice. "Perhaps you would do me a favor. I don't like calling him at work when his secretary is not there. Would you please remind him to call if he's coming home soon and I'll fix his pancakes."

"I'll tell him. Thank you for your help."

"You're welcome, Mr. Payne."

The woman makes me want to work on my manners. Well, not my manners so much as my mouth. Sometimes I'm too quick with the one-liners.

I turned off I-75 onto Delk Road. A few minutes later I passed over U.S.-41. The fence that surrounds the giant Universal complex came into view on my left. In World War II this was called Bell Aircraft and it turned out hundreds of B-29 Super Fortresses. The locals called the big defense plant "the bummer plant."

Universal holds a place in the minds of Georgians somewhere up there between the sixth and seventh layer of heaven. First, it is a big defense plant, and Georgians love any place that makes weapons to kill the enemy, any enemy. Our briskets boil with pride when we see pictures of Universal aircraft taking part in military operations around the world. Second, Universal keeps a lot of people off the unemployment rolls; as many as thirty thousand people worked here in the glory years. The employment today is about half that on assembly lines producing the C-130 and the F-22.

I drove several miles with Universal on my left. The official name of the facility is Air Force Plant No. Six. The plant is unusual in that it is co-located with two large military bases: Dobbins AFB is at one end of the runway and Naval Air Station Atlanta on the other. Universal takes up everything else.

I turned into the gate and drove through several large parking lots and around the west end of the building to park in a VIP parking place in front of the administration building. A black Lexus with tinted windows was backed into the adjacent space.

Daylight was beginning to ease up over the low hills east of the runway and overhead I could see a thin layer of clouds pushed by a west wind. When the wind is out of Alabama, anything can happen, none of it good. The clouds would break apart by mid-morning and start building. By early afternoon we would have heavy thunderstorms.

I picked up my cell phone and called the number Mrs. Godbey gave me. The big mules, men like Godbey, expect visitors to have appointments. But here's another inviolate police rule: It's hard to say no to someone sitting in your parking lot.

The security guard put on his stern face when I stepped out of the Explorer. I don't blame him. People judge you by your appearance. He saw a black guy in jeans and boots parked in a VIP parking space. As I approached, he saw I needed a shave. It was a good thing I took of the BASS cap.

I badged him, told him I had been working an

undercover operation all night and that J. Stanford was expecting me. He made a brief call.

"If you'll sign in, Detective, I'll take you to Mr. Godbey's office." He paused. "I want to see Mr. Godbey's face when you walk in."

I signed the big book. Mine was the only name on the page. "Quiet shift?"

"Yes." The guard glanced at his watch. He had been working since midnight and was anxious to get home. He handed me a clip-on visitor's badge with a big V printed on it and the notation "Escort Required," then motioned over his shoulder for me to follow. We walked into the heart of the building and turned right down a long hall.

We were about to go up a flight of stairs when I glanced through an open door on my right and saw, through the windows overlooking the parking lot, a slender dark-haired man in a black coat striding rapidly toward the VIP parking spaces. He was wearing sunglasses and looked vaguely familiar. I was about to go to the window for a closer look when the guard said, "This way, Detective." He was halfway up the stairs waiting for me.

At the top of the steps I looked down Mahogany Row, the quiet and elegant offices of Universal's top management. The first door on the left had a small brass nameplate: "Raymond Vandiver." Under the name in smaller letters was written "Executive Vice President." I stopped. I recently had dealings with Mr. Vandiver.

I easily won the first round.

He won the second even more easily. He had me transferred from Homicide.

Two battles don't make a war. My time is coming.

The guard was getting antsy. "Down here."

Another minute and he opened the door to a suite

of offices on the right. We walked through the empty outer office, through a smaller inner office and finally into an office that appeared to be about half the size of a grocery store.

J. Stanford Godbey was what you would expect from the president of a big defense contractor: slim, brushed-back white hair, big smile and wearing a navy suit even at this hour on Sunday morning. The man had style. He also had eyes you could strike matches on.

Black people are particularly attuned to the eyes of white people. Their eyes give us an instant and reliable indicator of what they feel about us.

J. Stanford looked right through me.

Let me tell you something. I know my weaknesses. I have two big ones. The first is that I am not good at accepting criticism. Every time a superior officer criticizes me, I hear my old man screaming, "You're a sorry nigger and you ain't never gonna amount to nothing. You're sorry as gully dirt. Just plain sorry."

But my big weakness is that I have too much respect for white people who have accomplished a lot, people like J. Stanford. I've thought about this and I believe part of the reason is the insecurity I feel in coming from deep southwest Georgia, a flat, desolate, sun-baked, godforsaken part of the state that even people from other parts of Georgia ridicule.

Another reason, and I have to be careful with this one lest you misunderstand and think I am making excuses, but we—that is, black people—have been on the receiving end of generations of prejudice. It's genetic. No matter how educated I am or how many cases I've solved, I see an accomplished older white guy, a big mule, and he says something or does something and the first thing I think is: "If he's white, he's right."

This is not good. It hurt me badly on my first big case several years ago. I thought I had learned a lesson. Then I walk into Godbey's office and it boils up as fresh as ever.

It's crazy. Intellectually, I know that. But I'm in jeans and boots and I feel grungy and I know J. Stanford is looking at me and thinking I personify every stereotype he ever had about black people.

I wonder what His Skipness would do in a situation like this.

J. Stanford stood up and walked around his desk. It was an enormous desk with a big leather daddy chair and a cherry credenza. I noticed a lingering odor of cigarette smoke but there was no ashtray anywhere. I glanced over to the side where several chairs and a low table were grouped. Three skinny little cigarette butts floated in a Styrofoam cup half-filled with coffee. Another cup, also half-full, sat across the table.

"Good morning, Officer," Godbey said with a smile that lowered the room temperature about ten degrees. He stuck out his hand. It was soft and surprisingly small and he pulled it back quickly. "Welcome to Universal."

"Thank you."

His smile widened as he took in the way I was dressed. "You Atlanta police officers dress differently from the way police officers up here dress."

I pushed down the feeling of intimidation. Of inadequacy. Nonverbal clues are the major way we make a first impression and I'm not doing well.

"Been working all night, sir. Under cover." He nodded at the guard and motioned me toward the corner where the chairs were grouped.

"Sit down, please, and tell me what I can do for you. You said on the phone this was official police business.

Urgent, you said." His smile tightened. "You're a bit out of your jurisdiction up here, aren't you, Officer?"

"It's detective, sir, and I'm investigating a homicide."

I sat down. The soft leather chair was warm. Someone had been sitting here a few minutes earlier. I leaned forward and put one hand around the cup containing the floating cigarette butts. Also warm.

"Let me have those," Godbey said, picking up both cups and carrying them across the room. "I see by your expression you do not like cigarettes. Well, neither do I. Usually I smoke cigars." He looked over his shoulder, paused, and added, "Fine cigars."

I nodded.

"Can I get you a cup of coffee?"

"No, thanks."

He sat down across from me and patted his open palms on the arms of the chair. "A homicide you say? Tell me what that has to do with Universal."

I wanted to ask him two or three open-ended and nonthreatening questions in order to find his truth zone and then I would bore in. But my experience with Raymond Vandiver was still very much with me and I didn't want to repeat that debacle. Plus, I felt ill at ease with J. Stanford. So I would use other, less direct, interview techniques.

I opened my notebook and took my pen from my pocket before I answered. "Sir, the victim is one of your employees."

He stared straight into my eyes. Not much of a reaction. But then he already knew of the death.

"The GBI says you are to be notified in the event anything happened to him. His name is Richard Morris."

"Morris is dead? Good God. What happened?" He leaned forward, still not moving his eyes from mine.

He called the victim Morris, not Richard Morris or

Richard or Richie. Morris indicates distance. Yet Godbey felt close enough to Morris to call his wife earlier with expressions of sympathy.

And he was pretending all this was news.

People tend to overestimate their skills in several areas: driving, sex, telling jokes, and lying. Most people, if you were to ask them, believe they can lie and you can't detect it; that they can tell you anything and you won't know if they are telling the truth or not. They might be able to do that with friends. But not with someone who is trained to detect deception.

"Mr. Morris was killed early this morning. Could you tell me what he did here and whether or not he had any enemies you might know about."

"Enemies? Morris have enemies? You must be kidding. One of the most popular people in this plant. If he had enemies, or people who would want to kill him, they were not at Universal."

He didn't answer the first part of the question. And his choice of words about enemies was interesting. I made a note.

"How did it happen?" he asked.

"He was found dead a few hours ago. Now, what did Mr. Morris do here at Universal?"

J. Stanford stared through me for a long moment. People lie by being nonresponsive, with a parried response, a simple fabrication, a complex fabrication, and deception in depth. A pause, especially for such an easily answered question, is a non-answer, a sign of deception. Then he shook his head as if he had been prodded, and said, "Yes. Morris was an engineer here. Didn't report directly to me, but I knew of the work done over there."

"He reported to Raymond Vandiver?"

Godbey's eyebrows rose in surprise. "Yes, as a matter of fact."

Godbey's language distanced him from Morris. "A Universal engineer," rather than "one of my engineers" or "one of our engineers" or even "an engineer." But most significant of all, he avoided all pronouns in referring to Morris.

About ninety percent of the admissions of guilt in a person's statement can be found in the use of pronouns.

"Did he have any special interest or area of expertise?"

J. Stanford smiled. "We're in the aircraft business, Officer . . . Detective Payne. Morris sold aircraft. Very good at it."

He was not responsive to my questions. Every time that happened I could hear the voice of my instructor in the class on Scientific Content Analysis: "If they don't answer, they answer."

"Which aircraft?"

"The F-twenty-two." He said it almost reluctantly.

"Did he have a sales territory?"

"What do you mean?"

"A sales territory."

J. Stanford smiled again. This guy smiled too much. He was as bad as Jimmy Carter. He never took his eyes from mine. A hundred percent eye contact is an attempt to dominate; a sign of deception.

People don't realize what they give away in conversation. J. Stanford was giving up volumes every time he opened his mouth, with how he was conducting himself, and he didn't realize it.

He shrugged. "Wherever people want to buy our aircraft."

"All over America?"

He laughed. "All over the world."

"Was there any special area?"

J. Stanford shrugged and broke eye contact. If a

person holds unusual eye contact and then breaks the contact, the question that caused the break is significant.

"If he thought there might be a big sale in a country, any country, he would, of course, devote more time to that country until he made the sale."

Another non-answer. I don't personalize it when people are evasive. And I don't correct people when they lie. A liar is giving me a priceless gift, the gift that keeps on giving. I let him continue.

When J. Stanford visits Mr. Morris, she will tell him I was there early this morning. Her loyalty to Universal will prevail and she will tell him what we talked about and he will wonder why I didn't call him on it when he tried to mislead me. He will wonder about a lot of things. He will wonder why I did not ask who told him about Morris's death. I want that knowledge to percolate in his soul. I want him to be off balance. I want him to be off balance because of what he says or does, more than because of what I say or do.

"Did anyone have reason to be angry with him?"

He leaned back in his chair. "I said earlier Morris was quite popular. But keep in mind Morris was a salesman for Universal. We're one of the largest defense contractors in the world. England, France, Germany and a half-dozen other countries all have aircraft manufacturers who are not fond of us."

"Why?"

"Our people are good. Our products are good enough that some competitors, both here and abroad, have been forced to sell out, consolidate or even go out of business. Universal dominates the world defense market, Officer Payne." He smiled tightly. "But you wouldn't have any reason to know that."

I nodded. The part of Georgia where I grew up has some of the largest quail-hunting farms in the world.

Everyone calls them plantations. All of them are owned by big corporations or by rich guys like J. Stanford. I wondered if he had a plantation. He sure had the manner.

"When was the last time you had a conversation with him?"

He looked up at the ceiling. "I think maybe it could have been sometime last week, or perhaps it was the week before. I can't say."

That was the most overly qualified sentence I've had thrown at me in a long time.

"About what?"

"Company matters. I'm afraid it was classified."

"Was he working on anything in particular, any large contract?"

"Everything Morris worked on was special. Several contracts were being negotiated." He shook his head. "Again, I'm afraid I can't be specific. National defense issues, you understand."

He leaned toward me. "Have you contacted Washington? The Pentagon and the State Department have interests here, overriding interests."

He was pushing.

"Someone is handling that liaison, sir. But this homicide is the overriding interest."

He smiled.

Let me tell you something. When I want to practice my interrogation skills, I go into the files and look for people who have been convicted of homicide on physical evidence or on the testimony of accomplices but who have never confessed. I study the case file, go back through the evidence, maybe even talk to the witnesses if they are around, and then I go out to whatever prison the guy is in and I interrogate him. My goal is to get a confession out of a professional ball-buster, a guy who has been through the system without confessing, who is in jail either for life or awaiting execution; in short, a hard-nosed professional criminal who has no reason to give me the time of day.

I get confessions out of forty percent of those guys.

Down at Homicide they say I can go into the interrogation room, which we call "the Box," and make a man regurgitate, expectorate, defecate, urinate, and flatulate. They say I can make him do everything but lactate, and I'm working on that. All of which is to say that when it comes to interviewing, I have a gift. Maybe it is because so much in interviewing is based on the involuntary eye movements of the person being interviewed and, as I said, we black people have a lot of experience at reading the eyes of white people.

Whatever it is, when I combine that gift with my training, I will find the Truth. Doesn't matter who the guy is, how educated or uneducated he might be. It doesn't matter how polished or how rough he is; how bright or how stupid.

I will find the Truth.

I tell you that as an aside. My point is that even if I were a uniform a week out of the academy I would know J. Stanford was lying.

Nevertheless, I gave him my Welcome Wagon smile. Smiles reassure the innocent and cause anxiety in the guilty.

"Would you like to change anything you've said this morning?"

"What do you want me to change?"

"Would you like to change anything you've said?"

"I don't think so."

I stood up and closed my notebook. "I won't take any more of your time, Mr. Godbey. Perhaps I might call you again later."

"If you think it's necessary. I want to cooperate. I really do. Although, to be absolutely frank, I don't

know what I could add to what I've already told you."
He paused. "That presupposes, of course, the Pentagon has no objections. You do know this is technically an Air Force installation and that we have very close ties with the Pentagon?"

He did it again. He pushed. This time it broke the spell. If he had been happy playing Lord of the Manor, I might have continued buying into it. But he pushed me twice. It was subtle. But when I am on the Job, when I am investigating a homicide, especially a homicide that will get me away from Buford Highway and put me back downtown, I will not be pushed. I'm like every cop in that respect. Cops can be led. Supervisors, good supervisors, tell us what they want done and then they get out of the way. If they get authoritative, we will mule up on them every time.

"The Pentagon has its priorities and we have ours."
I paused. "You do know that, technically, murder is not a federal offense? The federal government has no authority to investigate a homicide unless it occurs on federal property. Mr. Morris was killed on Buford Highway, which makes it just another homicide. I think you'll also find, sir, that homicide investigations take precedence over making airplanes."

He smiled again. "Even when national security is involved?"

"First, a court must rule that national security is involved. Such cases always attract the attention of the media and you know how the media meddle in everything."

I smiled back at him. We were sitting there showing our teeth to each other like a couple of tomcats. "Most prudent managers prefer to deal with the police rather than fighting it out in the newspapers. Especially since they almost always lose."

J. Stanford's smile disappeared. "Do they now?"

He stared at me for a long moment. He was about to change direction.

"This is an immense tragedy in the Universal family, Mr. Payne. Morris had a very important job here. I hope you find whoever the killer was."

"We will do more than find him, Mr. Godbey."

"Yes. I suppose you will." He stood up and stepped aside for me to proceed toward the door. Then he walked through the middle office and into the reception area. The security guard was standing by the door. J. Stanford nodded at the guard and shook hands again.

The guard looked at me. "If you're ready."

"Yes. Thank you again, Mr. Godbey."

He nodded. "I'm not sure I helped you."

"You were a big help. I learned more than you realize."

While he was trying to figure that one out, I came at him from another direction. "One other thing."

"Yes?"

I smiled. "Your wife wants you to call before you go home. Pancakes."

A dozen emotions flitted across his face.

A few moments later I was at the gate. "Let me have your badge," the guard said. "I'll sign you out."

As I was getting in my car, I wondered what Godbey and his wife were spatting about. Whatever it was, she was trying to smooth things over by cooking pancakes.

Ah, marital bliss. I'd had my share.

I noticed the parking space next to mine, the space where the black Lexus had been parked, was empty. A smoldering cigarette, one of those thin little jobs, was on the ground.

I stopped and stared at the cigarette, remembering

a similar cigarette floating in the coffee in J. Stanford's office.

I remembered the cigarette in the beer last night.

And then it hit me.

The guy in the black coat and sunglasses I had seen walking across the parking lot was the Chinese guy who had been with Bowtie.

My number one suspect was having coffee with the president of Universal a few hours after the homicide.

I used the ballpoint pen in my sock to knock the burning ash off the cigarette. Then I picked the cigarette up in my handkerchief and put it in my pocket.

I thought for a moment and then returned to the guard shack. "Is there a good place to eat breakfast near here? I've been working all night."

The guard smiled. "You and me both, buddy." He pointed east. "There's a couple of good places over on Highway Forty-one across from the main gate at Dobbins. If you're headed back to Atlanta, they're on the way."

"Thanks. Guess you'll be glad to get off and go home?"

He looked at his watch. "Relief should be here in a few minutes."

I looked up at the low scudding clouds. "You on the Job before you came here?"

He nodded. "APD. Twenty years."

"I'm working on my twenty." I looked at the sky again. "I was surprised I didn't see anyone else up there around Mr. Godbey's office. Is he the only one working?"

The guard yawned. "On Sunday morning? You better believe it."

I yawned, mirroring his behavior.

"Well, he's busy. First the Chinese guy and then me."

"You got that right. When I called to tell him you were here, he said bring you up; that the Chinese guy could find his own way out."

I remembered that mine had been the only name on today's visitor log.

"He didn't have to sign in and out?"

The guard shook his head.

He yawned again. So did I.

"Must be a VIP."

"I been here four years. And except for some Air Force generals from the Pentagon, he's the only person I know who comes and goes without signing in and out."

"Comes and goes?"

"Yep."

"Who is he?"

The guard shrugged. "He . . ."

He stopped and glared. "You ask a lot of questions, buddy."

I laughed. "Goes with my job."

"Yeah, well keeping my mouth shut goes with mine."

I looked at his name tag. "Bill Brumby. Well, Bill. May I call you Bill?"

He nodded warily. "That's my name."

"Bill, I don't blame you. It's a good job." I waved. "I'm going to eat breakfast. Thanks for the help."

He nodded again. It didn't matter. I would subpoena him later and put him under oath. He would tell me all about the Chinese visitor.

I was so excited about what I had learned from J. Stanford and from the guard that I didn't look around the parking lot before I left.

I should have.

6

I don't believe in talking about my troubles. Half the people I talk to think I got what I deserve and the other half doesn't give a rat's ass.

Nevertheless, let me tell you something. I don't belong on Buford Highway, I belong in Homicide. All I want is to return to Homicide. Nothing else in police work—not Sex Crimes, not Intelligence, not Special Investigations, not VIP Protection, not anything—deals with the thundering human emotions found in Homicide.

People like firemen because they drive big red trucks and get your cat out of the tree, and people like uniformed police officers because they are handsome and they look good out there directing traffic. But I'm a homicide cop. When I knock on your door, somebody is going to jail.

I see my job as biblical. I search out and bring to justice those angry and rancid souls who kill their fellow human beings. To take a life, to decide when a child, a mother, a father, a friend, or even a stranger, should depart this mortal coil is to assume the role of God.

God frowns on that.

He won't get personally involved in balancing the scales, but He does provide guidance to his foot soldiers.

I am one of God's foot soldiers.

You take a life, you answer to me.

It doesn't get any bigger than that.

Some cops don't have what it takes to work Homicide. They think they do. They angle to get transferred to Homicide and they think their experiences in Sex Crimes or Ag Assaults means this will be a cakewalk. A month later they have ulcers or are budding alcoholics and are begging to be transferred back to where they came from. It's not what you think; not the bodies, not the horror, not the psychological pain at what man does to man. No, it is for the simplest of reasons: pressure. Pressure such as they did not know existed. The lieutenant is screaming, the major is screaming, the chief is screaming, the mayor is screaming, the family of the victim is screaming, the press is screaming; they all want something and they want it yesterday. And many of them want the wrong thing for the wrong reasons.

Doesn't bother me. Compared to my daddy, all these people are amateurs when it comes to applying pressure. I roll with it. I love this job.

There was a time when I wanted to be a cop for a few years and then move into politics. I had plans to become mayor of Atlanta. No more. I could never be as good at anything else as I am at being a Homicide cop. I found that out two years ago on my first big homicide. The perp was a hot shot police reporter and successful novelist, a man who was old money and old Atlanta. He will be an old man when he gets out of jail.

My major says that case made me a little cocky.

Could be. But what he doesn't realize is that my cockiness is an effort to cover up the fact I am sometimes intimidated by fat cat white men.

I mentioned that I got exiled to Buford Highway

because of a little run-in I had with a Universal engineer. What I didn't mention is that I had a brief stop at the Atlanta Airport.

In the Atlanta Police Department, you annoy the brass and you are sent someplace where the brass doesn't have to look at you. It doesn't matter how good you are, the chiefs will banish you to a dead-end beat with the incompetents and the bozos they suspect of being on the take but can't prove it. In Atlanta, that means the airport. Good cops don't like the airport because they are confined to one location, have no city car, and the biggest enforcement challenge they face is telling some asshole to move his Buick.

Here's what happened.

A little over a month ago I was in cop heaven, a Homicide sergeant working day watch with weekends off. On the day in question I was up, which for those of you who don't know squat about cops means the next call was mine. Usually, sergeants are supervisors and don't take calls. But I do. The call came in and I went out to West Paces Ferry in Zone 2; that's Buckhead, Atlanta's high rent district.

Victim was a white male in a three-piece suit. Mid-thirties. He was lying facedown on the lawn. Two bullets had creased his skull and caused a lot of blood and the young uniform who was first on the scene thought the guy was about to die. He called Homicide when he should have called Ag Assaults.

The uniform already had a confession from the victim's wife. She was standing there crying one minute and swearing at her husband the next. Didn't take a rocket scientist to see this was another domestic.

Jack Deaton was the victim's name. Deaton was a Universal engineer who got too friendly with his secretary. He was like the dog playing on the railroad tracks. When a train ran over the tip of his tail, he became so angry he turned around to bite the wheel and got his head chopped off. Moral: Don't lose your head over a little piece of tail. Deaton did and told his wife he was moving out. She took the .38-caliber revolver he had given her to protect herself, chased him across the lawn, and, as he was approaching his new Mercedes convertible, pointed the gun at the back of his head, closed her eyes and got off two quick ones.

So I'm standing there watching the M.E. trying to scrape up pieces of the victim's hair and skin from the yard before the neighbor's dog can get them when this TV slug from Channel 11 drove up.

He leaned across the tape, stuck a microphone in my face, dropped his voice a couple of notches and said, "Officer, what does this do for Atlanta's crime statistics?"

I didn't like his question for two reasons. First, I am not an officer, I am a detective. Second, it was a stupid question. Even for a TV reporter.

I said, "It demonstrates that if husbands keep their pants zipped, they won't become part of those statistics."

The slime went back to his truck, got on the air live and fed the tape. The victim's widow was annoyed— I don't blame her—and filed a complaint. I could have ridden out that complaint. But in the meantime I had gotten on my white horse and asked Deaton's boss, one Raymond Vandiver, to come to my office.

I've been in Homicide a little more than two years, well, really a little more than a year because after my first big case I took off a year to go to graduate school. The point is I've been in Homicide long enough that I don't have many heroes. But guys like Raymond

Vandiver I admire. It's guys like him I model myself after. Professionally, that is.

He walked into the squad room wearing a pinstripe suit, shined shoes and the aura that comes from being at the top of the food chain.

I looked at him through the partially opened blinds of my office. Big guy, six-two and about two-twenty. Late forties. Tanned with a few flecks of gray in his dark hair. I mentally reviewed what I knew about him. Number two person at Universal. Responsible for Sales and Manufacturing. Had a lot of what military people call command presence. That's understandable when you consider he was responsible for the lives of about fifteen thousand people and military contracts valued in the billions.

Then I remembered what I knew about him personally. The guy had the reputation of screwing anything with a heartbeat. Had a thing for the wives of subordinates. Think of a combination Bill Clinton and Ted Kennedy and you begin to get the idea. He had no center.

I took a deep breath. Personal feelings are a no-no in my job.

When I asked Pinstripe to come down and talk, I did the obligatory thing about his having a lawyer present. But he looked at me and saw a young cop making maybe $40,000 a year and he thought if I wasn't a cop I'd be driving a cab somewhere and he figured he would have my black ass for lunch. He said he had nothing to hide and didn't need a lawyer.

Neither of us had anything but contempt for the other. Should be an interesting session.

I stepped into the squad room. "Mr. Vandiver, thank you for coming."

He was all smiles. "Mr. Payne."

I opened the door to the room where we would

talk. Pinstripe nodded as if I was the luggage handler at the Ritz and wrinkled his nose in distaste. He was not impressed. I can understand that.

The Box is twelve feet square and has one window which is covered by a heavy grate that is so high up the wall all you can see through it are the trunks of several scrawny trees and a little piece of sky. The lighting is from harsh fluorescent fixtures suspended from stained and broken ceiling panels. For furniture there is a small desk with collapsible legs and three straight-back chairs: Two are metal with padded seats and one is wooden with no padding. The wooden chair has short legs. A battered trash can sits in a corner.

Academics would say the Box is a low-stimulus environment.

The walls of the Box once were white, but what you notice are the scuff marks and the bashed-in panels and the dirt and the scribbled notes on the wall such as "I love you baby. I don't know what's going on." Dark rust-colored spots also are on the wall and the brown linoleum floor. The spots cause one to become aware of the room's odors: first the astringent tingle of industrial-strength cleaner and then, underneath, the faint lingering odor of blood, vomit, urine, and fecal matter. There is no telephone, no TV, no knick-knacks atop the desk, no ashtray, no bookshelves, no water cooler, no nothing.

In defense of the Box, one thing can be said: It serves its purpose.

"Have a seat, please," I said with a big smile. "I'll be right with you."

I went down the hall, used the bathroom, splashed cold water on my face, popped a lozenge into my mouth and straightened my tie. I took several deep breaths.

It was time to go to work.

*   *   *

When I returned, Pinstripe had walked around the table and sat in one of the padded chairs. He thought the chairs had been placed at random and that it didn't matter where he sat. He sat facing the door, looking at the way out.

He was mine.

Pinstripe graciously motioned for me to take the chair with its back to the door.

I gave him my five-hundred-watt smile and took off my coat. With my left hand I reached around the corner and hung the coat on the doorknob of the adjacent office. Pinstripe took a long look at the nine-millimeter on my right hip.

We never wear weapons when we're in the Box with a suspect or a prisoner. But Pinstripe was neither. This was a non-custodial interview. The only thing keeping Pinstripe there was his ego.

That and the fact he didn't realize the police have far more latitude in interviewing witnesses than in interviewing suspects.

I reached around the door fame with my right hand and flipped a switch. Over the door a red light came on and conversation in the squad room ceased. The other homicide detectives know that when I am in the Box I get temperamental if I hear talk or laughter or any other sound that might be a distraction. The Box is the universe. And until I get the Truth, it is the only universe.

I walked into the room, closed the door and smiled at Pinstripe. Then I picked up the two vacant chairs—one in each hand—and walked to my right. I skidded the wooden chair into the corner and placed the other padded chair in front of it. I pointed to the chair in the corner. "Sir, would you sit here, please?"

Pinstripe brushed imaginary lint from his trousers. "This is fine."

I kept smiling as I pointed to the chair in the corner. "Would you sit here?"

A tiny grimace strobed on and off. "I prefer to stay here if you don't mind."

"I do mind."

Pinstripe started to say something then looked at my face—I was no longer smiling—and decided against it. He shrugged, stood up and strode three quick steps to the corner. He turned the chair so it was facing the door, sat down, crossed his right leg over his left and shot his cuffs. He glanced at his thin gold watch, looked over his right shoulder at me, and said, "Might we begin?"

He was still not aware that I was in charge. I sat down. "Turn around and face me, please."

"What?"

"I'd like you to look at me when I talk to you."

For a second his eyes hardened. No one had spoken to him like that in years. But I was wearing a gun and a badge so he decided to humor me.

He turned around, reached into an inside pocket and pulled out a pack of cigarettes.

"Sir, no smoking in here."

He replaced the cigarettes and pressed his lips together.

I waited. He hadn't recognized me when we met several days earlier and he doesn't recognize me now. He doesn't remember that about eighteen months ago, right before I took my leave of absence, we met at Country Club of the South, where I was working a second job as security in the pro shop. I remember the day because in between making humiliating comments to a caddy, Pinstripe was boasting about getting the club's bartender fired. He ignored me that day.

And now his memory simply couldn't make the connection that the security guy in the pro shop was an Atlanta homicide cop.

"Sir, do you know why I asked you to come down here?"

"Well, yes, of course." He looked up and to his left. "You said you wanted to talk about Mrs. Deaton, and why she shot her husband."

"That's correct. Now, before we begin, I need to get a few administrative things out of the way. Give me your address, please. Zip code first."

For a moment he appeared puzzled. Again he looked up and to his left as he recalled his zip code. He gave me his address.

I thought I had his truth zone. But I must be sure.

"Tell me about your dog."

"What . . . ?"

"You do have a dog?"

"Yes, I have a dog but . . ."

"Before we get started, tell me about him. I'd like to know."

He glared, looked to the left again, then back at me. "My dog is beautiful. Short hair. Big ears. A corgi."

I was right. His orientation is left. His preference is visual. Now that I know where he goes to find the truth, I will know where he goes to tell a lie.

I smiled approvingly and pulled my chair a bit closer. "Tell me about Mrs. Deaton."

"Where do you want me to begin?"

"At the beginning."

"What do you want me to talk about?"

He uncrossed his legs. Good. No one ever confessed to anything with his legs crossed.

"Everything you believe to be important."

"I believe I did in our earlier telephone conversation."

"Would you do it again, please." I pushed my chair closer. Our knees were almost touching. I was sitting with my left leg to the side and my right knee pointed at his groin.

He put his right foot against the leg of my chair.

"Move your foot, please. This is my chair."

"I apologize, Officer Payne." He smiled and leaned forward to pat me on the shoulder. I pushed his hand aside.

"Don't do that, sir. Please keep your hands to yourself. And it's Detective."

"What?"

"I am a detective. An officer wears a uniform."

He snorted and tried to push his chair back. But it was against the wall. "I need to go to the bathroom." I stayed close, so close he couldn't cross his legs again.

"After we finish."

"I'd like a cigarette."

"After you tell me what you have to tell me."

"You know what happened."

"Yes, I do. I know exactly what happened. But I want you to tell me."

"It is very sensitive. I would want it treated in confidence."

"Tell me what happened."

He looked at the ceiling. "It's cold. Can you turn the air-conditioning down?"

"No."

Pinstripe slid his tongue over his lips, raised his eyes to his left and then down and to his right. I knew what he was thinking. It was as if it were written across his forehead. He came down here on his own. He is not being treated as he thought he might be. But he is in too far to back out. He has to see this thing through to the end. He thinks he can stay in charge. I'm a simple black cop.

He took a deep breath. A long sigh eased from his lips. Then he told me how he had met Elaine Deaton at a party for Universal's top executives, how they had been attracted to each other, how they became intimate, how he hired a secretary—actually she was a bimbo whose main job was to divert Jack Deaton's attention away from his wife by screwing his eyes out—and how Jack Deaton, poor bastard, confused a great piece of ass with undying love and told Elaine he was divorcing her. This convoluted little urban saga culminated when Mrs. Deaton chased her husband across the yard, pointed a pistol at the back of his head and tried to blow what few brains he had into the neighbor's yard. Now Mrs. Deaton was awaiting trial on aggravated assault charges.

Pinstripe knew I talked with the secretary-bimbo and that she had told me the whole story. He probably suspected I had telephone tolls showing all the calls from his office phone to Jack Deaton's home, calls made during the day when Jack was working a few doors down the hall. He didn't need a lawyer to tell him there was nothing I could charge him with.

I listened without interrupting to his version of the sordid tale. The rate, pitch and volume of his voice was constant. He spoke calmly, never pausing, going straight through the story as calmly and dispassionately as if he were giving a briefing to a group of civic officials.

When he finished, I was silent for a long moment, nodding slowly in understanding. Then I spent more than an hour going back over what he had said, tugging and worrying with every detail, watching Pinstripe slowly become more and more agitated, watching him begin leaning toward the door, watching his body react to the increasing fermentation going on inside his head.

Innocent people do not carry guilt. But when you commit a crime, the guilt is heavy and cannot be put down. A fearful and terrible battle goes on inside a man when he commits a wrong and sets about to conceal it. He forces it deep, far out of sight, and tramples it into the darkest recesses of his being and he believes it is gone and that he is safe. But the wrong is indelible. It is alive. And like some ancient creature entombed under mountains of rock, it needs only heat and light, poking and stirring, to feel the impulse of life and to fight and struggle to break free, to surge upward toward the light. The greatest military battles in history are nothing compared to the battle that goes on inside a man's soul when this happens.

I am the man who makes it happen.

You see, the guilty want to tell the truth. They really *want* to. They *need* to. That is a difficult thing for civilians to understand. But the guilty can be free only by telling the truth. Sometimes you have to show them the way. I was about to show Pinstripe the way.

"Would you take a polygraph test about all you've told me?"

He tossed his head to the side and tired to push his chair back, to get away from me. But he was against the wall and had no place to retreat. "Must you sit so close? Move away."

"I want to hear every word you say."

"Why should I take a polygraph? You can't charge me with anything."

"You wanted her all to yourself, didn't you?"

"Who? Elaine? Mrs. Deaton?" He looked up and to his right and for a moment his knees spread slightly. In that moment I split him; I slid forward until my right knee was between his knees and about a foot from his groin. "I had nothing to do with her killing her husband. I didn't know she was going to do that."

"You wanted to end the affair but she didn't."

He looked up and to his right. "I didn't want to end it."

He was lying.

"Does your wife know what was going on?"

Pinstripe inhaled sharply and scratched his nose. He looked down and to his left and then to his right. His lips trembled. He tossed his head again.

"Does your wife know what was going on?"

I reached down with both hands and gently pulled his knees farther apart and slid both of my legs between his and he never noticed that my knees were inches from his groin. I slid closer. Our noses were almost touching.

"Does your wife know?"

"You're not going to tell her?"

"No. You are."

He was breathing rapidly. The whites of his eyes, not just on both sides of the pupil, but above and below the pupil, were visible. His left heel bobbed up and down at about a hundred taps a minute.

"You're a deacon at First Baptist Church." I hammered my closed fists, forefingers extended, toward his testicles. His carotid pulse was racing and throbbing.

"How did you . . . Yes . . . Why do you . . . Why do you say that?" He scratched his nose rapidly. The rate and pitch of his voice was changing and he was pausing between sentences, within sentences, and no longer sounded confident.

"You're a member of Country Club of the South. You play golf there." Again I hammered my fists. He repeatedly licked his lips. He looked over my shoulder toward the door, leaned farther in that direction, and suddenly belched. Loudly.

"Why do you . . . How is this . . . What . . . ?" His voice trailed away. Now I could smell him. The

perspiration of a man under stress does not smell like
the perspiration of an athlete who had just run a mile.
A fetid odor, the odor of guilt and sin and pain, oozed
from every pore.

"You're the president of your Chamber of Commerce and a member of the Governor's Round
Table." Again with the fists. My eyes were locked
on his.

He farted, a loud and prolonged fart, and never
changed expression. He did not realize what was happening; he did not realize that stress was causing uncontrollable internal reactions. Truth was becoming
insistent. The great battle was raging within his soul
and within his body. He had no control over what was
taking place, no knowledge, no understanding. Truth
was alive and fighting its way to the surface and Pinstripe was reduced to a role less than that of a
spectator.

"I'm telling you I'm not guilty of anything."

"I know what you're telling me and I know what
you're not telling me. You are not telling your wife,
your church, your country club and your political
friends that you were fucking an employee's wife. You
are not telling them that you acted as a pimp for the
employee. You're not telling them that you set him
up. You are not telling them that you broke up a
family and caused a woman to shoot her husband.
And you are not telling them you are the reason that
the woman is in jail."

His carotid pulse was jumping. His diaphragm was
convulsing.

"How does it feel to be responsible for a man being
shot?" My voice lashed him. "How do you sleep at
night knowing what you did?"

A deep and protracted belch puffed Pinstripe's lips
apart. The odor of fear was in his warm breath.

"Have you prayed for forgiveness? Has God forgiven you for adultery? For causing a murder?"

Retching noises were coming from his throat. His head was tossing from one side to the other.

The birth of Truth was imminent. Truth needed only a soothing balm to ease the final passage.

I leaned forward, put my hand on Pinstripe's shoulder and spoke to him softly and compassionately. "You didn't want any of this to happen."

He shook his head and looked at me like a penitent child.

"You never planned this. You never expected it."

Again he shook his head.

"You didn't mean for Elaine to shoot her husband. You are a powerful executive. You think for yourself, but you can't think for Elaine. Everything would have been okay if Elaine hadn't become emotional. Wouldn't it?"

Tears formed in the corners of his eyes. He nodded in agreement. The retching sounds were closer together. Then suddenly Pinstripe's face sagged and he looked old.

I rubbed his shoulder and kept my voice soft and low. "You must feel terrible about what took place that day. You are carrying a big burden. I know you want to lay your burden down. I know you want everything to be all right. Don't you want to lay your burden down?"

I pushed lightly on his shoulder as if signaling him that now it was his turn to talk.

He nodded. "Yes."

"Are you about to be sick? It will be okay."

He looked at me.

I stood up and continued to rub his shoulder.

"Hurry."

"Tell me what happened. Tell me in your own words. Then you will be okay."

His face was contorted. "It . . . it was an accident," he wailed. "Elaine is so pretty. I wanted . . . I just wanted to be with her. It wasn't serious. I just wanted to see her a couple of times a week. Nobody would know. Nobody would be hurt. Jack wasn't supposed to fall in love with that woman. Elaine . . . Elaine wasn't supposed to shoot him. I don't want people to know about this. I never meant for this to happen. Any of it."

He shook his head in disbelief. "All I wanted was to spend a few afternoons each week with Elaine. Then . . ."

I caught the trash can with my toe and slid it in front of him. He leaned over and seized it with both hands and vomited uncontrollably.

The Truth was out.

Pinstripe sighed and took his monogrammed linen handkerchief from his pocket. He wiped his mouth, blew his nose, and looked up at me.

I waited a moment until he settled down.

"There's nothing I can charge you with, Mr. Vandiver. You are free to go about your business. But before you leave, I want you to understand something."

He looked at me. Curious. Wary.

"I'm a homicide detective," I said softly. "I see more pain and misery in a week than most people see in a lifetime. I see the absolute worst of human nature. Every day I deal with the muck at the bottom of the gene pool. But I have to tell you something."

I paused and leaned over until I was in his face. The odor of vomit was strong. "Your adultery, your selfish and reckless adultery, caused the shooting of a good man and put his wife in jail. Of all the muck

I've ever had to deal with, of all the low-life just plain
sorry no-good butt-wipes I've met or will ever meet,
you are at the head of the line."

"I had nothing to do with that."

"You're a sorry son of a bitch."

He stared at me, slowly folded his handkerchief, and
stood up. He stuck the handkerchief in his pocket and
smiled tightly.

I kept going. "I'm sending copies of this case file
and what I know about you to your preacher, to
Country Club of the South and to the governor's office. I would send it to your wife but I'm going to let
you sweat that one out, because sooner or later she
will find out on her own."

Pinstripe was still smiling. "You have made a big
mistake, officer. The mayor of Atlanta is a friend of
mine. A personal friend. You will be seeking other
employment by the end of the day."

"If you can take my job, it's not worth having."

"I can and I will."

I looked him up and down. "You know, I was impressed with you from the first time I saw you. But
today you have proven something to me." I flicked
the sleeve of his suit. "You can cover a pile of cow
shit with a silk handkerchief. But underneath, it's still
cow shit."

He spun away and walked rapidly out the door.

I ran to the door, and as he crossed the squad room,
I shouted after him. "You should name your penis.
You don't want so many important decisions being
made by a stranger."

A few people in the squad room looked up. Pinstripe kept going.

"And it's *detective*," I shouted as he went through
the door.

I sighed and shook my head.

Sometimes I generate more indignation than I can contain.

Pinstripe was not bluffing. He knew the mayor and he tried to get me fired.

The mayor talked to the chief who talked to my major. The major said Pinstripe had committed no crime and that I was not to discuss his personal life with anyone. I was ordered to surrender the case file and told if any copies, or any information from the file, appeared in the media, that charges would be filed against me.

I was not fired and I was not demoted. But I was sent to the airport. Morning watch.

It took only a few days for me to realize I had to do some serious ass-kissing if I wanted to return to Homicide. I wrote a contrite letter to the chief and promised to do anything short of an unnatural act to get back where I belonged.

A week later I got the biggest surprise of my life. DeKalb County, the adjacent county, was having a problem finding undercover officers who had not been burned. DeKalb needed an umbrella man, somebody to float up and down Buford Highway gathering intelligence. The chief decided I was that man.

Buford Highway was not what I had in mind. Reminds me of what my major said. He said every time he thought he knew all there was to know about ass-kissing, somebody came along and changed the rules.

My major is a good guy. He said my job was simple: hang out in the bars and restaurants and be my usual smart-ass self. I should listen, observe, and write good reports. He said this could be my stepping stone back to Homicide. So I agreed.

Not that I had a choice.

7

Thunderstorms rolled across Atlanta late Sunday morning, big boomers filled with lightning and thunder and rain so heavy that the bright summer morning turned to twilight. Within minutes after each storm the sun leaped into a clean blue sky and the sidewalks oozed rising clouds of steam while the gutters overflowed with tumbling sun-sparkling waters. A half hour later the skies would darken and there would be another storm and the cycle began all over.

During the storms I sat in my Explorer and planned the investigation. This case is crucial to me. After I identified myself to the DeKalb major, I can't work U.C. anymore on Buford Highway. This case is my ticket back to Homicide.

Three things about criminals you can usually count on. First, bad guys often come back to the area where they committed the crime. Second, criminals know what other criminals are doing. And third, there is always one more potential witness, one more person to interview.

Major Hutt was as good as his word. I had the crime scene report, photos and video. The police artist had finished what I thought was an excellent likeness of the Chinese guy. Later this evening or early tomorrow morning I would pass out copies to the media. I had shown the composite up and down Buford Highway and gotten not a single hit.

I called a friend at Homicide and had him check the computers for crimes similar to the homicide on Buford. Taxi drivers, delivery truck drivers, prostitutes, hotel, restaurant and bar employees all must be interviewed and shown the composite. Then I called both DeKalb and APD Intelligence and got the names of convicts on parole, violators on probation and convicts discharged in the past six months who lived on or near Buford Highway. Not nearly as many as I feared. Only several dozen. One of them might know the Chinese guy.

I'm working as hard and as fast as I can. And I'm working without a net. Because when my major discovers tomorrow morning that I have taken over a DeKalb homicide, he will raise hell. I plan to be so far into the case by then that the DeKalb chief will laugh and hang up if anyone asks him to take it back.

I made a list of the people I needed to interview, including someone at the Pentagon and an expert on jade. I don't know anyone at the Pentagon and I sure don't know an expert on jade. But I will find them.

When it was not raining, I canvassed businesses around the Han Motel. I figured the employees who had worked Saturday night might be working the same shift Sunday. It was slow going. Few people spoke more than passable English, and my Vietnamese, Laotian, Cambodian, Gujarati and Spanish are nonexistent. The Russians were impenetrable. Talking to a Russian is like talking to a surly clam.

On television cop shows there is always a witness. A homicide could take place in the middle of a national forest sixty miles from the nearest farmhouse and there would be a Boy Scout troop and a scoutmaster-preacher camped out fifty yards away. I wish that

would happen just once in my life. I want a homicide
scene with witnesses, preferably a priest and a gaggle
of nuns who happen to be standing on the corner. In
reality, a detective is lucky if he can find a one-eyed,
partially deaf, mentally defective drunk who speaks
English.

It was mid-afternoon and another storm had passed
over and I was standing in the parking lot of the Han
Motel thinking about what I had learned so far—nothing—when I noticed through the big plate glass window that the manager was watching a local TV station.
She wouldn't speak more than a half-dozen words to
me but she was watching local television.

I walked across the parking lot to try again. I
pushed open the door just as the broadcast was interrupted by a blaring voice: "This is a special news
bulletin."

Then the anchor who had been at the Deaton crime
scene came on. I'd recognize that empty suit anywhere. I shook my head. A Chinese motel manager
in Atlanta watching Channel 11. This is where she gets
her knowledge of America.

Then the TV guy had my undivided attention:

"The body of a Universal security guard has been
found in a guard shack at the sprawling defense plant
near Marietta. The body of the fifty-two-year-old
guard was discovered about eight a.m. today by another guard arriving at work. Cobb County Homicide
officers said the guard apparently had been struck in
the throat with a hard object. The Cobb officers said
the guard who discovered the body reported seeing a
late-model black Lexus exit the main parking lot on
Delk Road as he entered.

"Repeating this breaking story, a Universal security
guard has apparently been murdered. Cobb police

want to question the driver of a black Lexus. We'll have more details at six p.m."

The Chinese manager was speaking as she turned away from the TV. "This is one more mean town, you know." She looked up and recognized me.

"Oh, fuck," she said.

Her English was improving.

I laughed and turned around. I had to get on my cell phone and call the Homicide division of the Cobb County Police, the jurisdiction where Universal was located.

As I dialed, I wondered why the security guard had been killed. The Chinese guy was in J. Stanford's office when I suddenly popped up on he radar screen. He waited in the parking lot to get a look at me, the cop who would be investigating the homicide. He saw me talking to the security guard, remembered his previous trips when that guard was on duty, and realized he had at least one vulnerable spot. He killed the guard.

I told the Cobb detective I was working on a homicide involving Universal and I wondered what he might have on the security guard's homicide that he had not given the media. We never tell the media slimes everything. We always hold back the important stuff, the guilty information known only to the perpetrator.

"I can give you several things."

"Okay."

"He knew the guy who did him."

"What tells you that?"

"He let him get close."

"How close?"

I don't know why cops play these games. You would think two cops talking would have a shorthand system that would enable them to slice right to the point. But, no, we have to parcel information out, a piece at a time, in response to direct questions.

"Close enough to reach up and jab him in the throat and drop him."

It *had* been the Chinese guy.

"In the throat?"

"Yeah, some kind of karate stuff." He paused and I heard papers shuffling as he looked at his notes. "The M.E. says the cricoid cartilage, whatever the fuck that is, was crushed and the vocal ligaments collapsed into the rima glottis. Jesus, I hope I don't have any of those things in me. Probably took him a couple of minutes to suffocate."

"That from the M.E.?"

"Yep. Said the perp knew his anatomy. Got the guard right in the goozle."

"What else?" He would hold the good stuff for last.

"Well, his body was crosswise in the security guard shack; almost as if it was laid out a certain way."

"The perp was staging?"

"The body wasn't lying in a crumpled heap, or in a corner the way you would expect. It was laid out across the floor of the guard shack. The perp dropped him then placed him a certain way."

"Why?"

"Who the hell knows?"

I thought for a moment. "Can you send me a copy of the crime scene photos?"

"Later today."

"What else?"

The Cobb detective chuckled. "Found a watch at the scene. Didn't belong to the victim. He had his on. Besides, this one was too expensive for a security guard. Brand I never heard of. A Baume and Mercier."

I won't even begin to tell you how he pronounced that.

"Belongs to the perp?"

"Probably. We've had instances like this before when two people are fighting or scuffling and a watch band breaks or, if it's an expansion band, it gets pulled off. Owner never realizes it."

"Any distinguishing marks?"

"We're looking at it. We'll shoot it with a microlens and I'll include the pictures in the stuff I send you."

"What else you got?"

The detective chuckled. "You ain't gonna believe this."

I knew it. He was saving the best stuff for last.

"Try me."

"He had something in his hand."

"The victim?"

"Yeah. He was holding something. Weird."

"Holding something," I repeated.

"I never saw anything like it before."

I took a shot. "A pig?"

Silence.

I instantly regretted opening my big mouth.

The detective exploded. "How the hell did you know that? You been talking to somebody up here?"

I laughed. "You mean he really had a pig in his hand?"

"Don't gimme that. A Universal guard has been killed. FBI and Air Force investigators are flying in, arriving at Dobbins later today to take over my case. If you know something, I need to know what it is."

I should have thought of that. The feds have authority to work homicides that occur on government installations. In addition to wanting everything I have on

Bowtie, now they will demand everything on a related homicide.

"Okay. But you mentioned a pig. Was there only one?"

"Yes." He paused. "How many should there have been?"

I ignored him. "What was it made of?"

"Some kind of green stone. It had been carved into the shape of a pig." He chuckled. "We didn't know what it was. Finally, one of the body snatchers, some gomer from the country, said it was a pig."

"Any other objects like that found in or near the body?"

"What do you mean?"

"Have the M.E. check all the body cavities."

The Cobb detective paused. "Man, you people down there in Atlanta got some weird garbage on the street."

"Tell me about it."

"Okay, I showed you mine. Now show me yours. Tell me what you got."

I told the Cobb detective about the Richard Morris homicide and the jade objects found in his body and then I told him about the interview with J. Stanford.

After hanging up, I realized three things: First, I had to keep some information for myself. Second, this case was going to be a lot more complicated than I had originally thought. Finally there was the sudden and almost overwhelming realization that here I am, a black guy from Southwest Georgia investigating a homicide involving one of the world's most powerful defense contractors. The Pentagon and State Department and possibly the Chinese government are players. FBI and Air Force investigators are flying in.

I wondered if I might be in over my head.

8

Monday morning and I had on a suit. His Skipness would be proud of my appearance.

I stood in front of the mirror in my bedroom and took a long appreciative look. It's been so long since I wore a suit to work. I've missed it.

The navy suit, white shirt, and the bow tie—navy with white polka dots—made me feel like an Atlanta homicide cop again. I adjusted the knot of the bow tie until it was smooth and the tie lay perfectly level. Then I backed up and looked at myself; adjusted the squared-off white handkerchief in the breast pocket and smiled.

"Caesar Roosevelt Payne, you have pulled a Thoreau," I said to the mirror. "You have come in out of the woods."

The Mont Blanc pen was in my shirt pocket and my city-issued S&W was on my right hip. I checked the contents of my black-leather briefcase. One of the extra plastic ballpoint pens I pulled from a pocket of the briefcase and stuck inside my left sock.

The ballpoint is far more versatile, lethal and surprising than most people realize. By clutching it in a hammer-grip, you can jab upward into someone's heart before they know what you're doing. It is equally powerful when held in dagger grip or when you brace the butt of the pen against the palm of your hand and steady it between your ring and middle fingers.

It's true what they teach you in high school: The pen is mightier than the sword.

I took a final look at the man in the mirror. Dirty Harry said a man has got to know his limitations. He was talking about the bad guys. A homicide cop has no limitations. A homicide cop is the closest thing to Superman on the face of this planet.

Intermittent thunderstorms were still rolling across the city so I picked up my white Burberry raincoat and threw it across my shoulders. It looked like a cape.

I headed for the door, ready to fight some crime.

The phone rang.

"Payne."

"Detective, this is your major."

This was not a social call.

"Yes, sir."

"You've stepped in it big time."

"Sir?"

"Up to your neck, Detective. You put yourself and this department on Front Street."

"I'm not sure I follow you."

"Don't play innocent with me. You are in it over your head. You can't even see daylight. You are gasping for air."

"I'm beginning to get the picture."

"No you're not. You are awash in it. Lost. Even your mama can't help you now."

"You're talking about the Buford Highway homicide?

"Hell, yes, I'm talking about the Buford Highway homicide. I received a call from the chief. He said he received a call from the DeKalb chief advising him you had taken over the investigation."

"That is correct."

"You just waltzed in there and took over a De-Kalb homicide?"

"I thought the situation justified it."

"You're the umbrella man. You're supposed to be out there doing a good job and impressing the chief so I can bring you back to Homicide. Then you go and pull Atlanta into a case like this. The chief wasn't off the phone with DeKalb five minutes and the feebs call. They landed at Universal yesterday like it was a Normandy beach. They're talking State Department, the Pentagon, and national security issues. They want everything you got on the Buford Highway case. They say it's related to the death of the security guard at Universal. You're supposed to be working undercover. What in hell made you jump into that case?"

"I saw bright lights in the sky. And then these little people ran out of a spaceship and told me to do it."

"Don't be a wise ass with me, Payne. You're run out from under my protection. The mayor got a call from the attorney general. Detective, I'm not talking about the attorney general of this state, I'm talking about the attorney general of the United States of America. The mayor called the chief and the chief gave me the word. Detective Payne, do you know what the word is?"

"Not yet, sir."

"The word is that you will cooperate fully with the FBI."

"Or I'll be back at the airport?"

"You got it. And you'll be in the bag, mister; not a detective."

"How long do I have?"

"The chief is getting one ball squeezed by DeKalb, one by the attorney general, and his ass kicked by the mayor."

"A vivid picture."

"How vivid is this? The chief wants this case solved in a forthright manner. Forthright, Detective."

"How much time do I have?"

The major took a deep breath and paused. His voice softened. "Not long. You'll be okay as long as Washington and Universal stay calm. They start raising hell and you're history. Atlanta will drop you like a used rubber."

"I'm glad my employer is so loyal. Makes my heart sing with joy."

"You brought this on yourself."

"Do I get the resources I need?"

"You don't get a city car if that's what you're asking. Officially, you're still the umbrella man."

"I'd rather drive my own car. At least it works."

The Atlanta Police Department has probably the junkiest cars of any police department in America. Half the cars in Homicide are in the shop and there is no money to repair them. Those on the street are prime candidates for the junkyard. Detectives regularly spend their own money on minor repairs.

"What else do you need?"

"Whatever it takes."

The major sighed. "I'll do what I can. For as long as I can. But the truth is, Payne, you're on your own."

"Your job on the line, too?"

"I didn't say that."

"Yes you did."

"You'll be working out of Homicide. But don't get the idea this is permanent. If you don't give me a perp soon, your ass is in the wind."

"I hit the street with a singing heart."

"Go see an Agent Harde, FBI Special Agent Streighton Harde from Washington. He's supervising the Universal homicide investigation. He's waiting for you at the Atlanta field office."

The major hung up.

I had opened the front door of my house when the phone rang again. For a moment I considered not answering it. But it could be the major. I put my briefcase on the table and picked up the phone.

"Payne."

"Goddammit, Caesar Roosevelt Payne, why did you release that composite this morning when you could have done it last night on my time? Now the airheaded piss fucks will use it on TV when it should have been in the paper first."

I'm going to stop answering the phone if this keeps up.

"Well, Kitty, don't get any on you."

She laughed; a loud, free and unfettered laugh.

Kitty O'Hara is the crime reporter for *The Atlanta Constitution.* About two yeas ago she and I met during my first big case, which turned out to be her first big story. Then I took a year's leave of absence to get my masters at Emory. About the time I finished, she won the Pulitzer Prize and then went to Harvard for a year on a Nieman Fellowship. She has been back only a few weeks and is ravenous for a big story.

"I heard you were back in town. I've been expecting to hear from you."

"I would have been back sooner, but after my Nieman I went on a cruise."

"Have a good time?"

"Only got laid twice; once by the captain and once by the crew."

"Sounds as if you're okay."

"My therapist says I am. I don't know."

I looked at my watch. "What's the matter?"

"Payne, they got me working for a woman. My cluster leader is a woman. That's not good."

"Cluster leader?"

"She is the supervisor for those of us who cover the courts and law enforcement. A bitch on wheels."

"Whatever happened to sisterhood?"

"She's too busy calling meetings. She spins around in her chair and lines all of us up and talks to us like we're village idiots."

Kitty laughed again. "I got off to a bad start with her. She's intimidated by my Pulitzer so she goes to great lengths to tell me how much I don't know. This morning while she was roaming around the newsroom collecting all of us for a meeting, I went to her computer and changed her screen saver. She sat down facing us and behind her the screen saver popped up."

"What did it say?"

"It said, 'I fart when I eat lettuce.' Everybody else fell off their chairs laughing. I sat there straight-faced. I think that's why she suspects I did it."

"Welcome back to the big city."

Her humor suddenly disappeared. "Payne, I needed to break that story. You can't imagine the grief I am catching. Why did you give that story to the piss fucks?"

"I'm not a Harvard person as you are, but by that obnoxious phrase I assume you mean the stalwart lads of television; the source from which seventy percent of the people in America get their news. And inherent in your statement is the belief, on someone's part, that you control the police department. Am I right?"

"Payne, we are southwest Georgia buddies."

Kitty is from Edison, a little crossroads town about forty miles west of Albany. We are the same age.

"Is the illustrious Pulitzer Prize-winning reporter

suggesting that the Atlanta Police Department show favoritism to the print media?"

Kitty snorted. I could picture her; a thatch of blond hair that looks like a haystack caught on the edge of a tornado, tomato-red lips shaped like a Cupid's bow, eyes that are harder than they should be and a body that can cause cardiac arrest.

"Damn straight, that's what I'm suggesting. Hey, remember me? I just got back in town. People in this town forget you in a week. I've been gone a year."

"I haven't heard your name since I've been back."

"Payne, don't screw around with strong women. We got half the money and all the tootie. Don't force me to tell you what I really think."

"You didn't just do that? Fooled me."

"I need to know why you're working a DeKalb homicide and I need whatever you can tell me about the Universal case. My sources in Cobb say they are connected. I know the feebs are in town working the Universal case."

There was no need for me to play games with Kitty. She was not like one of those TV slimes who could ooze along for a week on raised eyebrows. Kitty was the best reporter in Atlanta. She had covered what she called the cop shop since before I became a police officer. She knew more officers, both in Atlanta and surrounding jurisdictions, than I did. Plus she and I had a history. Too much of a history.

I thought quickly. When I am working a homicide case, I follow standard investigative techniques. The difference is that I cast a much wider net than some detectives. I want to know everything about everything that is remotely connected to my case. That is the distilled essence of success in this and every other investigative agency: know every thing about every thing and then put all the pieces together.

Kitty could help me. Newspaper reporters are like delivery truck drivers or taxi drivers or waiters. They talk to a lot of people. They can ask questions without raising suspicions.

"Do two things for me and we might talk."

"How about, 'Do two things for me and we *will* talk'?"

"I have to go. I'm late."

"I'm running a story based on what I have."

"I'll look for it."

"Okay. Okay. What do you want?"

"I need some background on Universal."

"You're not working the Universal case. Why do you need this?"

"I ask the questions."

"Okay. What do you want?"

"Corporate history. Corporate morality. Same stuff you would look for if you were doing a long piece on Universal. Something that might indicate which rocks I should turn over."

"Corporate morality." She laughed. "That'll be a short piece of paper."

"I also need a name in Washington."

"What sort of name?"

"A think tank sort of person, a Pentagon insider, someone who knows the defense industry."

"You got a big one, don't you? This is not just another homicide. That dead engineer was more than an engineer. How was the security guard involved?"

"Kitty, I can get this information some other way."

"Okay. I'll call our bureau chief up there. But I want an exclusive. I don't want you to do like you did with the composite and release it on TV time."

"Sunday is a slow news day, Kitty; You taught me that. If I had released it yesterday, it wouldn't have the visibility it will get on the Monday evening news.

My job is to catch whoever committed the homicide; not pander to the media."

"I hate it when TV gets a story first."

I looked at my watch. "Kitty, I have to go. We have a deal?"

"We have a deal."

"Call me when you have something."

"Payne?"

"Yes."

"Can we talk about . . . ?"

"No. That never happened."

"I was there."

I hung up. The phone was ringing as I left. I ignored it. Mustn't keep the FBI waiting.

9

There were two of them and I knew from the get-go they were bad news.

Streighton Harde, the older guy, was the stereotypical feeb, a white guy in a white shirt wearing a gray suit with the buttons buttoned. He had the impassive eyes of a tiger shark, the beefy body of a weight lifter on the edge of going soft, and the official FBI manner, which is to say he was supercilious, overbearing and generally obnoxious.

His partner was a black guy about my age, dressed like Harde and with the same eyes. I've seen black guys like him before; not often, but enough to recognize them instantly. He and I are alike up to a point; both of us are black and young and ambitious. The difference is that I have my dignity. He has never had dignity and that makes him dangerous. I won't get any secret handshakes and brotherhood stuff from him. I am fighting to get over in the white man's world and he is a lobotomized dweeb; a bureaucrat with a badge, a black man who hates black people.

Now the feeb and the dweeb are about to start double-teaming me.

Doesn't matter. I'll put on my Mormon underwear and whip their asses.

"Thank you for coming, Detective," Harde said, his

flat eyes staring unblinking into mine. "I'm Special Agent Streighton Harde with the FBI and this is Will Jackson, who represents the Air Force's Office of Special Investigations."

I shook hands with both of them then turned to the black guy. "Are you military or civilian?"

"Civilian." He smirked. "Why? You one of those affirmative action babies?"

"No. Are you a former black man?"

We understood each other.

Black people who are angry about being black usually handle their problem in one of two ways. They hate their selves and their blackness and become white niggers. Or they hate society and everybody in it. Jackson was the former.

Harde waved his arm toward a cluster of chairs in the corner of his office. "Gentlemen, shall we sit down?"

I sat down first. Bad mistake. Each of the feds sat on the arm of a chair so they could look down at me. Both had their coats open so I could see their federal badges and their guns.

Oooooohhhh.

Harde got straight to the point. "Agent Jackson and I represent the U.S. government in the matter of the recent homicide at Air Force Plant Six." He paused and his eyes bored into me. "Universal."

He was playing My-pecker-is-bigger-than-yours, letting me know he was a federal agent and that Universal was an Air Force installation. Now comes the part where he reminds me I am a lowly city detective.

"We understand you've been working undercover in the local bars and we were reluctant to pull you away," Harde said. "Our people asked the A.G. to call your mayor. He did and the mayor was kind enough to allow you to chat with us."

I had to play with him.

"A.G.?"

Jackson stared at me, a lazy smile tugging at the corners of his mouth. "Attorney General." He leaned closer. "Of the U.S. of A."

"Lions and tigers and bears, oh, my."

Harde frowned. "Gentlemen. Please." He turned his baby blues on me and flipped them to high beam. "We wanted to talk with you because we also understand that this past weekend you took charge of a homicide in which the manner of death was essentially the same as that of the security guard at Air Force Plant Six."

"You think the two are connected?"

The two of them almost looked at each other in disbelief. "We are exploring that possibility. We thought you could help us. Let's start with the manner of death."

"There were similarities."

They both leaned toward me.

"Similarities?" Harde asked, incredulity in his voice.

"Both died after being struck in the throat. Beyond that I don't know enough about the security guard's case to say with any certainty that he died in precisely the same way. I talked with the investigating detective briefly."

I did not mention the medical examiner's report that I had in my briefcase.

"Forget the security guard," Jackson said. "We'll take care of that case. Tell us what you have on your victim, a Mr. . . ." he looked up in the air as if searching for the name, ". . . Morris I believe."

"Not much. As I mentioned, he died from trauma to the throat. His larynx was crushed by what might have been a martial arts chop at the throat. And . . ."

"Might have been?" Harde asked.

"It's a guess. I don't know for sure. But someone who knows enough about human anatomy to strike at that point is probably trained in one of the martial arts. He might have used his hand. Could have been a blunt instrument. I don't know."

I was talking too much. The only way for a person being interviewed to control the interview is to say as little as possible; give them nothing to work with.

"What else?" Jackson asked.

"What do you mean?"

"Were there any other similarities in the deaths of the two men?"

"Again, I don't know anything about the security guard's death other than what I told you. I have no basis for comparison."

Harde leaned closer. "You were the last person to see the security guard alive."

"Probably. Other than his assailant."

He and Jackson stared at me. I ignored Jackson and looked at Harde. "What's your point?"

"I have no point. I'm saying that judging by the time you signed out on the security guard's logs and when his replacement appeared—a matter of perhaps eight minutes—you were probably the last person to see him alive."

"I couldn't say for certain that no one else stopped. But, again, you are probably right."

"Did you see anything at the crime scene that could be used as evidence?"

I thought of the cigarette butt and the DNA that could be obtained from it. "When I was there, it was not a crime scene and I wasn't looking for evidence. I was tired and wanted something to eat."

Jackson leaned over. "You were one of the last people to see this Mr. Morris alive also."

"Other than his assailant. And maybe someone at the motel. I don't know."

Harde interrupted. "Did you see anyone in the parking lot at Universal as you left? Anyone at all?"

I let them stew for a good thirty seconds. I pursed my lips and looked at the ceiling as if trying to remember.

"No."

"A car? Did you see a car moving toward the security guard's post as you were leaving?"

"No. The parking lot was virtually empty. A car here and there. But none were moving and I didn't see anyone sitting in a car." Almost as if it were an unimportant afterthought, I added, "But there was a television story about a black Lexus being seen there."

"Not very observant, are you?" Jackson asked.

"I'm not a federal agent."

"You saw nothing?"

"As I said, I was tired and wanted something to eat. I saw nothing." I raised my eyebrows. "Did I miss something? Did you federal boys"—I looked at Jackson when I said "boys"—"come to town and find something I missed?"

"The security guard's logs," Jackson said. "Let's talk about those."

These guys were good. They had to have practiced this double-teaming technique. Good change-up, too. It probably worked for them with almost everyone they interviewed. But I've done more interviews than both of them combined and I know the technique better than they. This is the first time I've been on the receiving end and I have to admit there is a certain intimidation factor when two federal agents are in your face. But nothing I can't handle.

I nodded. "What do you want to know?"

"There are no other names on the logs that indicate

anyone visited the administrative offices of Air Force
Plant Six after you were there."

"Or before I was there."

"Correct."

They waited.

So did I.

"Did you talk with the guard as you were leaving?"

"Briefly."

They waited.

Harde leaned closer. "Detective Payne, you can vol-
unteer information, you know. Don't wait for our
questions. You know where this is going."

"The guard indicated to me he was tired, that he
had a slow night, and that he was anxious for his replacement to arrive. I had been up all night. I asked
him if there was a restaurant nearby where I could
get breakfast."

"You keep talking about looking for a place to eat,"
the dweeb said. "But you live here."

"You guys are from out of town. Cobb is not a
place that smiles on black folk. Besides, I don't live
in Cobb County. I live in Atlanta."

There was a brief pause. Harde stood up and turned
away from me, toward the window, and pressed his
hands into the small of his back as if he were tired.
His voice was casual, too casual, when he asked the
next question. "Did you talk about anything else?"

I believe in cooperating with brother law enforcement agencies. But these guys don't feel right. When
the FBI and the Air Force, neither of which has a lot
of experience investigating homicides, come flying into
Atlanta and take over a homicide case that Cobb
County could handle far better, then I wonder about
their agenda.

I shook my head. "He said he was retired from APD
and I told him I was working on my twenty years."

Harde spun around. "How did that come up? If he's tired and you're hungry, how did you wind up talking about his career?"

Harde was good. Any explanation I could give him would only make it worse.

I shrugged. "Both of us had been up all night. Both of us were tired. It was just chitchat while I signed out."

"Tell me about the jade," Harde said, changing pace again.

"My victim had jade pieces in every body orifice and was holding a carved jade pig in each hand. I understand from Cobb County that the security guard had a carved jade pig in one hand."

"That signify anything to you?" Jackson asked.

"Not a thing. I didn't even know it was jade until the M.E. identified it. There must be some significance but I don't know what it is."

"Must be? Why do you think the jade is important?"

I looked at him. "Two reasons. First, the M.E. said that it was worth a fortune. I want to know why someone would leave a fortune in my victim's body. Second, and this is the big reason. The jade was important to the perpetrator. That makes it important to me."

Harde stepped in. "Agent Jackson is not so much concerned with the simple existence of jade at the crime scenes as he is about what the jade indicates to you about the perpetrator."

Time to play with them again.

"Jade is synonymous with China. I wondered if the perpetrator might be Chinese, or someone who has spent a lot of time in China."

A quick tightening in Jackson's face and the feigned indifference of Harde told me I had hit another hot button.

"Chinese?" Harde asked. "Most jade comes from

Myanmar. Why should it signify anything to do with China?"

"Are you an expert on jade?"

"Do you have anything specific that links this homicide to China?"

Good technique. The man was not to be diverted.

I shook my head. "It's conjecture. The perpetrator may not be Chinese. As I said, it might be someone who has spent a lot of time in China. My victim traveled to China frequently in the past year."

They did it. They made me slip. I was on guard to prevent it and they still made me give up something I had not planned to reveal. They probed and circled enough that just when I thought I was ahead of them, I gave up something I shouldn't have.

"Do you think that is significant?" Jackson asked.

I shrugged. "Probably not. He sold airplanes. The president of Universal told me he went all over the world. Wherever governments wanted to buy."

Another looked passed between the two feds.

"Governments?" Harde smiled. "Do you think a foreign government might be involved in these homicides?"

"Governments buy Universal airplanes. Nobody else can afford them."

The feds didn't want to plant ideas in my head so they dropped that line of inquiry.

Harde nodded. "Anything else you want to mention, anything we might have overlooked?"

"No. I wish there were more I could tell you but at this point I can't."

I don't believe I said that. The only good thing about that is that the two feds haven't had the training to catch it.

Harde stood up. Jackson followed. The interview was over.

"Thank you for coming by," Harde said. "The mayor indicated your cooperation would be ongoing, that you would remain in touch with us. Would you mind making an extra copy of all your interviews and reports and faxing them to me?"

He pulled a card from his pocket, underlined the fax number, and passed it to me. "That is in Washington, but copies will be forwarded immediately to me."

"Washington?"

"We're working out of the Atlanta field office. But the fax will reach us quickly."

"If the chief has no objections, I'll be glad to."

Jackson smiled. "The chief has no objections."

"And you will send me copies of whatever information you discover relating to the security guard's death?"

Harde nodded. "Whatever information we have that we believe might be relevant to your investigation, we will of course pass it along."

I didn't say anything. But I thought of a south Georgia expression: In a pig's ass.

10

When I came out of the FBI offices at Century Center, it was raining. Again. It was early June and already we were into the rainy period; brief but violent thunderstorms raced out of the west, the skies clashed and banged like some cosmic bowling alley, tons of water were dumped on the streets, and then we had an hour or so of brilliant sunshine before it started all over again. The temperature was in the high eighties and the humidity turned the city into a sauna. Life was a race from one air-conditioned space to another.

Nothing good ever came out of Alabama.

I sat in my Explorer in the parking lot and opened my black leather briefcase. In the leather-bound notebook I began making notes of the conversation with the feeb and the dweeb.

The crux of their questions and the real reason they wanted to talk to me was to find out if the security guard had mentioned the Chinese guy or if I thought the perpetrator might be Chinese.

They know who he is. And what he is.

He left jade at the crime scenes for a reason.

I looked at my watch. Morris's funeral was in twenty minutes.

I was at the Cathedral of St. Philip, the big Episcopal church on Peachtree Road, in fifteen.

Cops like funerals. You can learn a lot at funerals. I wanted to know who came for Richard Morris's send-off to the next world.

J. Stanford was there, of course. He sat with Mrs. Morris and her two sons on the front row.

Except for a few rows in the rear the church was full; a lot of young people as well as the expected middle-aged crowd.

As the preacher spoke I understood why. Richard Morris had taught Sunday school and was active in the Boy Scouts. Turned out he also was a descendant of a family that had come to America on the *Mayflower* and settled later in Houlton, Maine, where they operated what for two hundred years was the largest potato farm in the state. The family had given their country two U.S. senators, a governor and several prominent academics. This guy was as close as it gets in America to being an aristocrat.

The *Mayflower* bit was nice but it's not all that impressive. My people came over on a boat, too.

I sat alone on the back pew. J. Stanford stood up and walked to the pulpit. When he turned around his eyes were drawn to my face. For a split-second he didn't recognize me, probably because I was in a suit instead of a plaid work shirt. Little cognitive dissonance going on there. His eyes widened for a second. He pulled a stack of cards from his pocket and placed them on the lectern.

His eulogy sounded as if it were written by the Universal public relations staff. And he still had problems with how he referred to Richard Morris. You would expect warm and personal remarks in a eulogy, comments that humanize the deceased and cause everyone to remember him fondly. But J. Stanford distanced himself from the dead man.

"Friends, we gather here today to remember a man

who was a husband, a father and a valuable member of the Universal community. Richard Morris was all that and more. I knew Richard Morris well."

For a moment, J. Stanford faltered. He was remembering that last Sunday morning he told me he hardly knew Richard Morris. He looked up and began ad-libbing.

"Actually, Richard Morris reported to someone else. But Richard Morris's work was well known to all of us on the senior management team."

He droned on. Several times Mrs. Morris tilted her head, almost in bewilderment. This was not what she expected.

She was not alone in her reaction. From the back of the church I noticed several people looking at each other with raised eyebrows. Others whispered to each other.

J. Stanford never referred to Morris as "my employee" or "my friend" or "my associate." And he never referred to him as "Richard."

In an instance where criminal activity has taken place, it is crucial how people refer to the victim. This is especially true in homicide cases. In a statement, if a person changes the way he refers to the victim, the point at which he changes is crucial. For instance, if he refers to the victim several times as "my friend" and then, when the time line of his statement closes with the time at which the victim died, he begins using "mister," then he is removing himself both from the victim and the crime.

J. Stanford was consistent. He referred only to "Richard Morris," which creates distance. He was doing that because of me. For a moment I almost wished I had not come to the funeral. This was not fair to Mrs. Morris.

After the funeral I stood **up** and moved to the rear wall of the church, watching faces.

I saw my old friend **Pinstripe** stand up from the row behind J. Stanford and **Mrs.** Morris. J. Stanford held his arm for a moment **and** whispered something and then Vandiver's eyes darted toward me. He kept his eyes on me as he edged through the crowd.

"Mr. Vandiver," I said as he approached. I don't like saying "mister" to such people, but I'm going to be interviewing him and I believe in displaying professional courtesy. I reached out to shake his hand. He ignored me.

"Why are you here?"

"Official police business."

"Stan Godbey told me you went to see him. I thought you were out at the airport." He smiled.

"I'm in charge of the investigation into Mr. Morris's death."

"You don't conduct murder investigations in church. Have some consideration for the family."

"I'd forgotten what a strong family values man you are."

He glared.

"By the way, Mr. Vandiver, I'll be giving you a call. Since Richard Morris worked for you, I need to talk to you."

"There's nothing I can tell you."

He could have said "yes" or "no" or "I don't know anything" or "I'll be glad to help" or a host of other things. But he said, "There's nothing I *can* tell you."

"It's routine, Mr. Vandiver. We wouldn't want it said I neglected part of the investigation, would we?"

"The mayor is still my friend, Officer Payne."

"We all need friends."

"I'm not coming to your office."

"I'll come to Universal."

"Fine." He turned away.

"By the way."

He turned around. "Yes."

"It's Detective. I wish you would remember that."

I was walking through the front door when I saw Mrs. Morris. She was talking to J. Stanford and a group of sleek men and women I assumed were either top Universal types or friends. I nodded briefly in her direction. She held my eye a fraction of a second longer than I expected.

I made a mental note to call her this afternoon.

I turned on the air conditioner in the Explorer and pulled the cell phone out of my briefcase. The sun was out and so much steam rose from the ground and the sidewalks that the church parking lot appeared to be covered by a low-lying fog. I interrogated my answering machine and watched people mill around the parking lot.

Kitty had left a message. Said it was important.

My eyes were locked on J. Stanford and Vandiver as I called Kitty. The two top guys at Universal were standing away from the crowd, huddled closely in an intense conversation. Both were smoking cigarettes. I smiled. When I saw cigarettes in the coffee cup in J. Stanford's office, he told me he smoked only cigars.

"Kitty, Payne. What do you have for me?"

Wrong question. I knew it the moment it left my mouth.

"You know what I got for you, big boy."

"Don't call me boy."

"I meant it in a nice way."

"You left a message on my machine that you had the information I wanted. Care to share it with me?"

"I got the stuff on Universal. That was easy. I called

our Washington bureau on the Pentagon thing. The bureau chief was out. But I'll have a name tomorrow."

I kept my eyes on J. Stanford and Vandiver. "What do you have on Universal?"

When Mrs. Morris walked out of the church, the two Universal executives talked with her for a moment. She hugged both of them and walked away holding hands with her sons.

J. Stanford and Vandiver watched Mrs. Morris. J. Stanford tilted his head toward her as he said something to Vandiver. Vandiver looked at her disappearing back for a moment then turned to J. Stanford and nodded.

"Where are you? I'll bring it to you."

"Don't have time, Kitty. Tell me what you have." I pulled out my notebook and took the Mont Blanc pen from my pocket.

"I don't mind."

"Kitty."

"It's sort of technical."

"Hit the highlights. Fax me the whole thing later on. Send it to me at Homicide."

"I'm glad you're back over there."

J. Stanford jabbed his finger at Vandiver's chest. Vandiver nodded and flicked his cigarette into the bushes. The two men turned and walked toward the parking lot.

"It may not be full-time. A lot depends on this case."

"What was a Universal engineer doing in a cheap motel on Buford Highway? He catting around?"

"Kitty."

"Okay. First, Universal's place in the universe. It has one quarter of the Pentagon's annual fifty-billion-dollar procurement budget; far more than any other defense contractor. Add in other customers and the company has annual revenues of around thirty billion, which is almost as much as the defense budget of the United Kingdom. Put another way, Universal's annual revenues are comparable to all the defense spending of Africa and South America combined."

It took a moment for that to sink in.

"Universal is bigger than many governments."

"You got it."

"Keep going."

"I'll summarize a *Wall Street Journal* piece of several years ago; an op-ed piece written by a freelancer here in Atlanta. The thumbnail version is that the Georgia plant began production of the C-one-thirty Hercules back in the fifties and that it was one of the greatest aircraft ever built by anyone anywhere."

"Okay."

"Since then they've gone to hell. There was an airplane called the LASA-sixty; they made two models and canceled the program. The JetStar was a four-engine fuel guzzler that had to be re-engined—whatever that means—and was obsolete when it rolled out the door. Two models of the VX-four-A Hummingbird crashed, ending that program. Then there was the C-one-forty-one, another fuel guzzler that required major structural modifications before it could do the job."

"How have they stayed in business?"

Kitty laughed. "There's more. Their next airplane a the C-five-A, the airplane that made cost overruns famous. It had parts that fell off in flight and cabin doors that cost more than seventy-four thousand dollars. Those airplanes cost somewhere around a hundred and seventy million dollars each and average flying about fourteen hours a week. He says it is the most expensive and least utilized transport in history and is aviation's greatest hangar queen."

She paused. "What the fuck's a hangar queen?"

"An aircraft that spends more time in maintenance than in flying."

"Hell, that's me. I'm getting where I need lots of maintenance. Here's an investment tip: buy stock in L'Oreal, Revlon, Maybelline, Cabot's, Elizabeth Arden, Clinique, Chanel, Vidal Sassoon and Jack Black."

"Why Jack Black?"

"After using all that other stuff, I have to have Jack Black."

"Okay. What else?"

"The former president of Universal died unexpectedly about three years ago; hit a bridge abutment. He didn't drink so there was some speculation about what happened. Godbey replaced him. His mandate was to make Universal a player. Soon afterwards the company not only got the F-twenty-two contract but became a finalist in the contract of the century, the two-hundred-billion contract for the Joint Strike Fighter, the JSF."

"Hold on a minute." I was trying to recall something. Last Sunday morning Mrs. Morris asked if I knew about the JSF and what was happening in the defense industry.

I remembered one of the inviolate rules of police work: When in doubt, climb the money tree.

"Look for stories about contracts, what's going on in the defense industry that is changing the business, who is profiting, who is complaining, where and how Universal fits into the big picture. Can you do that?"

"For you, Caesar Roosevelt Payne, I will do anything." She paused. "Anything."

I laughed. "You sound like the dialogue in a cheap novel."

"I know. But I keep hoping that since we are both

from southwest Georgia that you will give in." She paused. "Again."

Sometimes I think it is the goal of half the black men in America to go to bed with a white girl. A pretty blonde. Which is why I stay away from white women. I am not a stereotypical black man and I will not become one. I have too much at stake. I gave in once; it was several years ago when Kitty and I were drinking and celebrating how I had solved my first major case, a case that sent a prominent reporter to jail for life.

I gave in once. But it won't happen again. Ever.

"This is a big help. Thanks."

She got the message.

"Just remember, no more of this shit about releasing stories on Monday morning for the TV stations. This one is mine. Right?"

I looked up as Mrs. Morris drove past in a dark gray Suburban. Both hands were on the steering wheel and she was leaning forward. Her oldest son sat beside her. He was now, at twelve, the man of the house. I felt sorry for him. For the next four or five years, formative years when a boy should be a boy, he can never do what his mind tells him he should be doing. He has to be the man of the house.

I was about to turn back to my notebook when a black Jaguar eased past with Pinstripe at the wheel. He didn't see me because I was under the shade of a big oak and the windows of my Explorer are heavily tinted. He stopped at the edge of the parking lot and looked around. This guy was about to do something he didn't want anyone to see.

He was speaking into a cell phone as he turned the corner and fell in behind Mrs. Morris.

"If it is at all possible, I will release this on your time. You'll have an exclusive."

"I'll have that name for you in the Pentagon tomorrow. And I'll get the stuff on the defense industry in the next day or so." Her voice turned casual. "I'll drop by your place and go over them with you."

"I have to go, Kitty. Thanks."

I fell in a half block behind Raymond Vandiver.

11

Pinstripe was hanging back two cars behind Mrs. Morris as she drove north on Peachtree Road. I was two cars behind him.

Vandiver had his cell phone pressed to his ear. He stayed on Peachtree at the Peachtree–Roswell Road split and began leaning from side to side to see each street sign he passed.

That gut feeling was back.

Something was going down.

From my briefcase I pulled out my geek box, the little electronic organizer in which I keep my telephone numbers. I entered the code word "Sowega," an acronym for Southwest Georgia, to pull up a hidden menu. Then, staying close behind Vandiver's Jaguar, I called my friend in the security department of the telephone company.

"Lee, this is C.R. Payne. I need a phone number fast. A cell phone."

"The party uses us as a carrier?"

I hadn't thought of that. There were two or three carriers that could be used. But Richard Morris was a New England aristocrat, probably conservative. My guess is that he would go with the oldest and largest phone company.

"Probably."

"Give me a name."

Richard Morris had a special Universal cell phone. How would Mrs. Morris list her phone?

"Check for Mrs. Richard Morris."

I heard his keyboard clicking.

Just then a black Lexus passed me and accelerated rapidly. The Lexus had tinted windows.

I gasped and pressed the accelerator but he was still pulling away. Because of the dark windows and the overcast sky I could not see inside the car. Mud obscured his license plate.

"Got several Richard Morris's. Know the home address?"

"Lenox Crest. I don't recall the number."

"That's okay. Unlikely there are two people with the same name on the same street."

Pinstripe was talking rapidly into his cell phone and looking at the Lexus, which now was in the lane next to him. I leaned forward. There was a ball antenna, a tiny but highly effective car phone antenna, atop the Lexus. I'd bet my pension that whoever was in the Lexus was talking to Vandiver on his cell phone.

"I have a residential listing but no cell phone for Richard Morris or Mrs. Richard Morris."

I tried to remember the computer printout from that night in the Han Motel. I had always called her Mrs. Morris. What was her first name?

"Susan, I think. Try Susan or Susie Morris."

The Lexus stayed alongside Vandiver.

Vandiver pointed toward Mrs. Morris's car and talked rapidly. Then he listened for a moment. I saw him stiffen and his head turned before he caught himself. He nodded and began punching another number into his cell phone. He talked rapidly for a few seconds then punched in another number. The Lexus accelerated and pulled up two cars behind Mrs. Morris. Vandiver had turned left at the next light.

The Chinese guy had seen my Explorer last Sunday in the Universal parking lot and had probably made a mental note of the license plate.

"I have a Susan Morris."

"Bingo."

He read it. I copied it quickly.

"Thanks, Lee. Got to go. Bye." I punched in her number. It rang several times. Please let her cell phone be on and let it be with her. I saw her turn to her son in the front seat. He looked down.

"Pick up the phone," I muttered.

Suddenly a movement in the mirror caught my eye. A gray car accelerated rapidly out of traffic. I saw a hand reach out and place a blue light atop the car. The light began strobing.

Mrs. Morris's oldest son leaned toward her. She put a cell phone to her ear.

A siren began screaming behind me. Now the car was close enough I could see it was a G-car. The feeb and the dweeb. Where the hell did they come from? Did they follow me when I left Century Center?

Why the siren and blue light? Feds didn't work traffic. They can do a felony stop but not a traffic stop.

An Atlanta squad car pulled in beside them, blue lights flashing. Now the feeb and the dweeb have assistance from an Atlanta uniform. I was trying to watch the Lexus, talk to Mrs. Morris, and watch the two cars in the rearview mirror.

Mrs. Morris turned on her blinker indicating she was about to turn right on Lenox Road. I was getting busy.

I turned up the volume on my police radio.

I heard a soft "Hello" in the cell phone.

"Mrs. Morris, this is C.R. Payne."

A pause. "Yes." She sounded confused. She turned right on Lenox Road.

"Mrs. Morris, can you hold for one minute?"

I dropped the cell phone and picked up the police radio. "This is forty-one twenty-four. I am in my personal vehicle in pursuit of a possible suspect in a homicide case. A uniform is behind me with his blue lights on. Advise that unit to back off."

"Stand by," came the laconic voice of the dispatcher.

I dropped the radio and picked up the cell phone. I was weaving through traffic at high speed.

"Mrs. Morris, I'm in a car behind you but I'm about to be pulled over by the police. A man in a black Lexus is two car lengths behind you, one lane to your right. Do you see him?"

Now the Atlanta cop had his siren on. He was on my bumper. Doesn't he listen to the radio?

Up ahead, the twelve-year-old boy in the front seat turned to look over his right shoulder. He twirled toward Mrs. Morris, pointing over his shoulder.

"My son sees him. What is this about, Detective? Why are you following me? And why are the police stopping you?"

"Get away from that Lexus. The man in there . . . You have to get away."

Now the blue lights from both the FBI car and the Atlanta squad car were flashing and their sirens were making so much noise I could hardly hear. A blue light blitz was going on behind me. If I didn't stop soon, the Atlanta car would call for assistance and another marked car would come sliding out of a side street driven by some young hot dog trying to make his reputation.

My radio was blaring. "Forty-one twenty-four, the uniform officer says he is assisting the FBI in a stop. You are advised to pull over."

"Put a supervisor on the radio. I'm pursuing a possible suspect in a homicide investigation. Tell that uniform and the feebs to discontinue pursuit."

"Forty-one twenty-four. You are advised to pull over."

I threw the radio down and picked up the cell phone.

"I asked you who is in the Lexus, Detective Payne?"

"I believe he's the man who . . ." I stopped. The Lexus suddenly turned left across two lanes of traffic and up a side street.

"He just turned off. I want you to wait for me. I'll be a couple of minutes."

"Wait? Why?"

"Mrs. Morris, I have to stop. I will call you back in a few minutes." I pulled off to the right, jammed on the brakes and jerked the Explorer to a stop atop the bridge at the MARTA station. I jumped out, took off my coat and held up my badge as I went steaming toward the two cars. I was trying to decide whether to take on the three of them one at a time or all together. I think all together.

The Atlanta cop, followed by the two feds, came forward. The feeb was putting his cell phone in his coat pocket. The Atlanta cop's face was grim. He didn't like it that I waited three blocks before stopping. Then he saw the badge and recognized me and turned to the two feds.

"What's going on here?"

"Thanks for the assistance, Officer." Harde said smoothly. He looked down the side street where the Lexus had turned.

I held up my hand for the feeb and the dweeb to stop. I turned to the uniform. "What the hell do you mean putting a blue light on me?"

He motioned toward the two feds. "These federal

officers called me on a city frequency to assist in a traffic stop."

He stepped between me and the feds. "You didn't tell me I was in pursuit of an Atlanta detective."

"It didn't matter," Jackson said. "We're federal officers and we wanted to talk to him."

The young officer glared. "The FBI lives up to its reputation."

"Go back to your duties," Harde said.

"One day you'll need a favor. I hope I'm there. Asshole."

Harde waved him away.

"Officer," I said.

The young officer turned around.

I put my hand on his shoulder. "Not your fault. You did the right thing."

He nodded. "Thanks, Detective." He looked at the two feds. "Bastards."

I turned to Harde and Jackson. "You got about ten seconds before I whip your ass. Make them count."

Harde gave me his tough look. "You are supposed to keep us up-to-date during this investigation."

"I'm doing that."

"We believe you're withholding information."

"Tell me what I am withholding."

"Make sure you update us daily."

"You stopped me for this?"

Harde looked at his watch and nodded toward Jackson. The two men turned and walked toward their car.

"That's it? That's it? You stopped me for . . ." And then I got it. All they had wanted was to keep me from following the black Lexus.

"Hey, Jackson."

He turned.

"I was right. You're a former black man."

He laughed and got in the car.

12

I drove rapidly through Pine Hills toward Lenox Crest. I tried to call Mrs. Morris but she did not answer her cell phone.

I turned onto Lenox Crest. I didn't really expect to see the black Lexus. Nevertheless, I checked all the driveways.

I paused a moment on the walkway of Mrs. Morris's home. It had been dark the morning of my visit and I had not noticed the flowers. The yard was bordered with pink hydrangeas, yellow coreopsis that waved in the breeze like wheat, red vinca, cone flowers, and tall purple wands of cosmos. A few day lilies bloomed, exotic hybrids and not the ditch lilies that so many people in Atlanta seem to believe are the sine que non of a proper garden.

Suddenly the door opened and she was there. "I heard your car door." Her brow wrinkled. She wondered why I was standing in her yard doing nothing.

"I was admiring your flowers."

"Why did you want me to wait? Come inside and tell me what was going on back there. You frightened me."

Annie, tail wagging and head bobbing, raced out the door to lick my hands and beg to be petted.

"Annie, back inside," Mrs. Morris said. She opened

the door and I followed her inside. I had decided to tell her exactly what happened. Everything. From the beginning.

"The man in the black Lexus was following you."

She stopped in the middle of the living room. "Who is he?"

"I believe it was the man who killed your husband."

"You know who he is?"

"No. I only know that he is Chinese."

Her hand went to her throat. Her eyes widened. "How do you know that?"

"I saw your husband the night he was killed. In a bar on Buford Highway."

"You never told me that."

"He was with a young Chinese man."

Her eyes widened.

"They left the bar together about an hour before your husband's body was discovered."

"The Chinese man. What does he look like?"

"About thirty. Five-ten. Slender. Hair combed straight back. Sharp dresser."

She stared. Her lips were pressed together.

"You know him, don't you?"

She turned away. "You are certain he is involved in Richie's death?"

"I saw the same man a few hours after I left your house that morning. He had been in Mr. Godbey's office at Universal."

She shook her head.

"He was wearing the same clothes I had seen him in a few hours earlier when he was with your husband."

She stared, not speaking.

"Mrs. Morris, you heard about the death of the Universal security guard?"

"Of course."

"He was killed the same way your husband was killed."

She looked at me a long moment. "There are some things I haven't told you."

"I know."

The words tumbled out. "Several weeks ago, one Saturday morning, Richie left to have a cup of coffee with someone. He didn't say who. He only said he was meeting someone at a little restaurant on Buford Highway. It was business. About ten minutes after he left, Stan called. He—"

"Stan Godbey?"

"Yes. He was terribly anxious, which is unusual. Stan is so self-possessed. But he just had to talk with Richie and he said Richie didn't answer his cell phone. For some reason, Richie had forgotten his phone. It's a special phone that Universal gave him; all conversations are scrambled. It's a satellite phone. He takes it everywhere. But he forgot it that morning. Stan asked where Richie was and I said he had gone to meet someone for coffee, but I didn't know where. He wanted Richie to call him as soon as possible."

She paused, remembering.

"After Stan hung up I realized where Richie might have gone. Richie likes . . . liked Cuban coffee. So I took his cell phone and went to that little Cuban restaurant at the corner of Buford and North Druid Hills."

"The Havana Sandwich Shop?"

"Yes, Richie was there. He was sitting with a Chinese man. The man you described. I gave Richie his phone and told him he should call Stan. The Chinese man laughed. Richie thanked me and stood up to walk me to the door. He tried not to show it, but I think he was disturbed that I was there. He wasn't going to introduce me to the Chinese man."

"What happened?"

"Before we could walk away, the Chinese man stood up and introduced himself. He was very urbane." Her eyebrows knitted. "Richie was surprised. He stared at the man as if he couldn't believe it."

I asked the million-dollar question. "What was his name?"

"Andy Fung."

Bingo.

"Andy?"

She smiled. "I said the same thing later. Richie said it was a nickname. He said Andy came from a very influential family in China. He grew up in America and has a degree from Georgia Tech."

"Your husband told you that?"

"Not in the restaurant. It was later."

"Did this Andy Fung drive a black Lexus?"

"I don't know."

"What does he do?"

"He works for the Chinese government. He represented China in some of the F-twenty-two negotiations; mostly on the side agreement. Richie had been briefed on him and was very wary, almost afraid of him. He said I should forget I had ever met Andy."

"What else do you know about him?"

She paused. "Because of Richie's job I've met enough intelligence agents, military and civilian, that I can recognize them when I meet them. It doesn't matter what nationality they are, there is something about them that one can pick out. Andy was some sort of agent."

"Did your husband tell you that?"

"No. He did not want to discuss Andy. It was something I picked up on."

"Was that the only time your husband ever met Andy Fung?"

She stared at me, eyes filled with tumbling, conflicting emotions. She was wringing her hands. "Give me one moment, please." She walked toward the rear of the house. Several moments later she returned and handed me an envelope.

"This is a letter Richie wrote Stan Godbey three weeks ago. In it he tells Stan that if the Chinese deal is consummated it will bring immense harm to this country; that it will enable China to take a great technological leap forward, and that unless Universal resigns the contract he will take his information to Senator Sam Perry."

"The chairman of the Senate Armed Services Committee?"

"Yes. Richie met the senator once and had tremendous admiration for him."

I read the letter.

"What caused him to write this?"

"He wouldn't discuss it. He said it would be dangerous for me to know."

"What did Godbey do when he received the letter?"

"He returned it. He wanted Richie to think about it for a while. Then, if Richie still felt the same, he would accept the resignation."

"Did your husband discuss this again with Mr. Godbey?"

"Yes. Stan called him last Saturday afternoon, the day . . . the day he was killed, and asked if Richie had given the matter more consideration." She paused. "I've said this to you before, but you must find someone who can brief you on what has happened to the defense industry since the Cold War ended; the JSF contract. It is crucial to your understanding the dynamics of all this; of why Richie was killed."

"I'm talking with someone in the Pentagon in the next few days."

She looked at me with an expression approaching pity. "You have no idea of the power of the people you're up against."

I almost told her about my Mormon underwear, but for once I held my tongue. "What did your husband say when Mr. Godbey called?"

"Richie said his mind was made up, that he was more convinced than ever of what he had to do."

"What did Godbey say?"

"Richie didn't tell me. But late that afternoon he said he had a meeting to go to that evening."

"Just a few hours before he went out?"

"Yes. Usually he told me a week in advance when he was going out in the evenings. He was a very organized, very methodical person. He was very thoughtful of the boys and me."

"You think Godbey sent him to the meeting?"

"Yes."

"Who was he meeting?"

"Usually when Richie met someone for a drink or dinner, he gave me their name. But when he was meeting Andy, all he said was that he had to meet someone. That's how I knew. Because he never told me."

I nodded. She had just stated a fundamental truth about human nature.

"So you knew he was meeting Andy Fung last Saturday night?"

"Yes. And if you want to know why I didn't tell you when we first talked, the answer is simple. Detective Payne, when I say my husband sold aircraft, that is the truth. But it is not all of the truth. Everything he did had the highest security classification. Far beyond Top Secret. Much of the equipment and many of the capabilities of the F-twenty-two are highly classified. What is not classified is proprietary with Universal. Billions of dollars are at stake. This aircraft represents the very apex of American technology. Why should I mention an intelligence agent to a city police officer? At the time, it seemed a coincidence. Besides, and in retrospect I realize I was putting too fine a point on the issue, but you didn't ask me if I knew who Richie was meeting. You asked if Richie *said* who he was meeting. He did not."

I nodded. She was right.

"And I'll tell you something else. After you were here last Sunday morning, Stan came by. I told him you had been here asking questions."

I nodded.

She flicked a hand in impatience. "He should have been reassuring me. He should have told me that Universal was doing everything possible to find the person who killed Richie. And he did. But it was almost as if he were performing a duty. He asked me again and again—not just that morning but several times since—about your visit that morning. Parts of it clearly made him nervous. He calls every day wanting to know if you have contacted me again. He keeps reminding me that all information must come from Universal."

She looked at me in anger. "My husband is dead and Stan says all information must come from Universal. I thought you were the investigator. Did he help you?"

"No."

"He said you were incompetent; that you asked silly and irrelevant questions." She paused. "Did you and Ray Vandiver have some sort of disagreement?"

"You might say so."

"You're the person who arrested Elaine Deaton?"

"I am."

"There were stories about Elaine and Ray."

I waited a moment. "Speaking of Vandiver, let's get back to today. Vandiver followed you when you left the funeral. I believe he called Andy Fung."

She looked at me in her cool fashion. "I was wrong and you were right. Universal is involved in this."

I waited.

She turned and began pacing. "Stan Godbey has been in our home. He was here that morning after Richie was killed. He is a friend of the family." She turned and slowly shook her head. "Why? Why?"

The answer was clear to me. I've seen homicides committed for less than ten dollars. Her husband was about to scuttle a project involving national defense issues and worth billions of dollars. But I said nothing.

"I want to know something else. Why was Andy Fung following me?"

Again, I did not answer.

"Does he want to frighten me? To kill me? Does he think I know something?"

I shook my head.

"Whatever the reason, Detective Payne, he will try again, won't he?"

"Yes."

13

As I drove out Ponce de Leon toward my house, the rain started again; a slow steady drizzle pushed by a light breeze. It was the sort of day that reminded me of a dreary winter evening rather than an afternoon in June.

I passed City Hall East, the former Sears building that now is part of city hall. More police officers are in this one building than in any other place in Atlanta. And there are more prostitutes around City Hall East than in any other place in town. I like the symmetry.

I once felt about Atlanta the way Mrs. Morris once felt about Universal. I've done well here, perhaps better than I might have done in many other cities. But this is not Valhalla. Atlanta has a weird side. A prominent cookbook writer in this town has a radio show sponsored by Kaopectate. And this is one of the top markets in the country for Dr. Laura, the radio shrink-nanny who lashes us daily about how we don't measure up to her standards.

This is a town that demolishes its grand old buildings and keeps its dirty and decrepit old taxis. We ignore the wise and considered counsel of our elders and let aggressive street people dictate city policy. Every year we dump millions of gallons of raw sewage into the Chattahoochee River, the source of drinking water for more than half the people in Georgia.

And we have a police chief whose public pro-
nouncements make him sound like a cross between
Chauncey the gardener and Forrest Gump: "The roots
are deep. The plant will grow." That kind of stuff.

All of which explains why I prefer to work at home
when I have paperwork to do.

I turned off Ponce and a block later parked in front
of my house.

Twenty minutes later I had learned that no one by
the name of Andy Fung was listed with the phone
company, Atlanta Gas Light, Georgia Power, the department of motor vehicles, the credit bureau, city di-
rectory, or even with the IRS. Officially, there is no
Andy Fung in Atlanta.

If, as Mrs. Morris says, he is an intelligence agent,
when I contact Georgia Tech and the Chinese consulate, all sorts of bells and whistles are going to sound.
I suspect the State Department will do whatever it
takes to protect this guy.

I need more information before I reveal what I
know about Andy Fung.

The jade is a good starting point.

I turned on my computer, moved onto the net, and
began searching for entries on jade. On the home page
of a man named Yang Boda, I found hyperlinks to a
menu of jade-related topics. In one of those I found
a reference to *Tao Te Ching,* a book by Lao-tzu, and
made a note to buy the book later today.

On a page about antique jade and funeral jade and
the role of jade in Chinese history, I found what I
wanted. After I scrolled through a half-dozen screens,
I realized that no one but a Chinese person could have
killed Morris and the security guard. The riddle of
why jade had been left with two bodies was explained.
A cicada goes underground and is reborn after shed-
ding its skin. A pig breeds quickly, thus increasing the

owner's wealth. The other pieces found on Morris's body were to protect his soul in the hereafter.

The spinach jade found with the security guard is a common type of jade. The imperial jade found on Morris's body was for the exclusive use of royalty. Andy Fung must have considered Richard Morris to be royalty.

I stared at the screen. Jade is synonymous with China. Jade is the symbol of heaven and earth. Fung has some link, or imagines he has a link or a philosophy or connection, with ancient China.

Each time I scrolled the screen I understood more. Now I had access to Fung's dictionary and could understand what he meant when he left jade with a body.

I leaned toward the printer and pressed the Print button. I spoke to the screen. "He believes China is coming into a new age of power, of pre-eminence in the world, a time when the ancient glory is recaptured. And the F-twenty-twos and the rockets they could build with the technology exchange could give him that belief."

Then I saw the name Han and leaned forward. Han was an ancient emperor of China who recaptured Vietnam and led what some historians consider the most glorious period in Chinese history.

Richard Morris was killed at the Han Motel.

I crossed my arms and rocked back in my chair as I considered the screen. The jade found on Morris's body indicated Fung had planned to kill him. But he couldn't have planned to kill the security guard. The jade pig left there was for someone else.

Andy Fung planned to kill again.

Was that why he was following Mrs. Morris?

14

Suddenly there was a pounding at the front door of my house. It sounded as if someone were trying to kick down the door.

I pulled the nine from my holster, walked swiftly on tiptoes across the room and jerked back the curtain on one of the front windows.

Most people are a bit unnerved when they suddenly find themselves staring down the barrel of a nine-millimeter pistol. But Kitty never missed a beat. "That all you got to point at me?" she shouted.

I holstered the nine and opened the door. "What are you doing pounding on my door like that? I almost shot you."

She brushed past me. She was wearing a very short skirt and a tight blouse. Her hair, which usually looks like an explosion in a haystack, was a bit droopy. Maybe it's the dampness.

"Haven't been here in a long time." She looked around. "You're so neat. It's disgusting."

"Why don't you come in for a minute?"

"Can you smell my perfume? I put on a little extra."

"No."

"We have to talk." She looked around, then sat on the sofa near the desk where I have my computer. "You're working."

She wiggled the mouse to disengage the screen saver and peered at the screen.

"Jade? What are you . . . ?" She spun around. "Okay. What have you got?"

I put my hands on her shoulders and gently moved her aside. I clicked a few keys to bookmark the pages I had been reading and signed off the net.

"This is about the homicides, isn't it? Why didn't I think of getting on the net and researching jade? What did you find?"

"Sit down, Kitty," I said, pointing to the sofa.

She did. She smoothed the sofa on either side of her and smiled. "I remember this piece of furniture. This is where . . ."

"Kitty, I can forgive you barging into my house. But I can't allow you to write about what you see when you invade my privacy. You will not write about the jade. Not now."

She shook her head impatiently. "You know what I do. And you know I work twenty-four hours a day. If you don't want me to write about it, you shouldn't have had it on the screen when I came in."

I stared at her.

She stared back. Then her eyes broke contact. "Okay, I shouldn't have looked at your computer screen. But there's nothing secret about jade. I could have looked it up myself."

"But you didn't."

"Dammit all, Payne, you're always working. You're so damn tight your butt squeaks when you walk."

"And you're such a dirt mouth I bet your mama washes your mouth out with soap every time you go home."

"My mama loves me." She looked away. "I think she does."

"Does all this preamble mean you were unable to get a name in the Pentagon?"

Her head snapped around. "Hey, my boobs are so big they have separate zip codes, but behind them there beats the living breathing heart of the last of the old-time newspaper reporters. To me all things are revealed. The Oracle at Delphi calls me for information. And don't forget, big stud, I won a Pulitzer."

I sat at my desk. "You have a name?"

"The best. A guy in Tac Air, which is a rather infamous little shop of horrors; a bunch of rabble rousers inside the office of the secretary of Defense. This guy is a genius, he knows and understands the defense industry as well as any swinging dick in the Puzzle Palace."

"You have such a way with words."

"You don't like my language, do you?"

"It's your mouth. What you do with it is your business."

She laughed. "You know what—"

"You were telling me about the guy in the Pentagon."

She sighed and rolled her eyes. "Our Washington bureau chief says he was on the cover of *Time* a few years ago; he's one of the most articulate of the Pentagon reformers. That's a little group of anarchists who are trying to change the way the Pentagon does business. These are good guys, patriots, true believers, not fat-assed bureaucrats."

She paused. "Did you know the day is coming when women will evolve eyes in their breasts?"

I looked at her in bewilderment. "Why are you telling me this?"

"That's so we will be able to look men in the eye."

I couldn't help it; I laughed. "What's this guy's name?"

"I like it when you laugh. His name is Franklin Spinney. Everyone calls him Chuck. Our bureau chief says he is the single smartest guy in Washington. He wrote a book called *Defense Facts of Life;* it knocked the Pentagon on its ass."

"Will he talk to me?"

"He's expecting your call." She reached into her huge purse. I knew she carried a stainless .357 Magnum in there. She had a permit. She groped around a moment, then pulled out a piece of paper and handed it to me.

"Kitty, thanks for the name and number. I need to call this guy now. If you stay, you have to agree not to use anything you hear. Otherwise, you have to leave."

"After I got the guy's name and number?"

"You knew the rules up front."

"I'm going to get it all, anyway."

"You may. But not now. At least, not from me." I waited.

She snorted. "Sweet Jesus in the valley. Okay."

"Okay, what?"

"Okay, I won't use anything I year." She looked at the wall across the room.

I punched in the numbers.

Chuck Spinney's voice was loud and clear, the voice of a man who has given countless briefings in large rooms, and there was the sense that laughter was never far away. Once we got past the introductions, he said, "So what do you need?"

"I'm investigating a homicide that occurred in Atlanta. The perpetrator, I believe, also killed a Universal security guard."

"You think Universal is involved in two homicides? You're going to hose Universal?" There was glee in his voice.

"Along with the Chinese government."

Kitty turned to look at me.

I shook my head.

"The PRC? When you launch, stand by for second-ary explosions."

"I just do my job."

"You really are going to try to hose them." He laughed. "How can I help?"

I told him.

"You have to start at the beginning," he said. "Reagan years. Evil Empire. Tremendous defense spendup." He paused. "A spendup is a lot of dollars but not many weapons. Now let me go back a little farther. You have to understand that the Pentagon is a moral sewer dedicated to using other people's money to feed the predators in the military-industrial complex. You with me?"

This guy talked straight. "I'm with you."

"I'm with you," Kitty mouthed.

"The special needs of defense contractors carry more weight than the needs of our soldiers or the rights of taxpayers. You still with me?"

"Singing from the same page, brother."

"Okay. I'm gonna answer your question. But you have to know this first. The Cold War was good for defense contractors. They all got well. Then all at once the Cold War is over. The Evil Empire is broken up. You know what that meant to the defense industry?"

I remembered that Mrs. Morris had made a com-ment about the tremendous changes in the defense industry. "A lot of big changes."

"You got it." Spinney laughed. "Hey, I love it when I talk to a smart guy. Consolidation; that's what hap-pened. Used to be a dozen or so, maybe more, really big defense contractors. Know how many there are today?"

"Not that many."

"Three. Universal, Lockheed, and Boeing. Raytheon is out there, but it's not as big as these guys. Universal is the largest weapons supplier to the Pentagon. Now, you know how much we spend annually on defense?"

"No idea."

"The last unclassified figures I saw were somewhere around two hundred and sixty-five billion. That's billion with a *b*. Now listen to this: Russia spends maybe twenty billion. It's so bad in Russia that soldiers are selling blood to buy food. Iraq, Syria, and Iran each spend about three billion; Libya maybe one billion. China spends about thirty billion but that number is climbing rapidly. What does all this tell you? It tells you the U.S. is spending almost three times the total defense dollars as all our possible enemies combined."

"Why?"

"That's the point. We got a weak president who's afraid to take on the Pentagon and the military-industrial complex because of his personal baggage. Remember, he's a draft dodger who didn't inhale. So he lets the defense industry run wild. He even let the Pentagon subsidize the Lockheed-Martin merger, something that both Nixon and Bush refused to do. Then the Pentagon brings in Clancy's Clowns and—"

"Who?"

"Those people who read Tom Clancy. They carry two or three guns in their cars; they're all for a big military. Half of them think they were in Special Forces. Wackos."

I laughed.

"That's the same president who recently lifted a twenty-year ban on selling F-sixteens to Latin American countries. You think that one didn't make the defense industry happy? We'll be selling them F-twenty-twos in a few more years. And—"

"Tell me about China and the F-twenty-two."

Kitty reached into her purse and pulled out a notebook. I shook my head and waggled a finger at her.

"I just remembered something," she whispered.

I shook my head. She tossed the notebook back into her purse, crossed her legs and arms, and pouted.

"The Chinese have figured us out," Spinney said. "Their philosophy is simple: We let you into our market, you give us technology. If you don't, others will. China is the only country that will not allow the U.S. to verify that acquired technology went to its intended destination. China has diverted supercomputers to military use. Back in 1995 they diverted stretch presses to a military aircraft plant in Nanchang. They violated a government-to-government assurance on that one. When we called them on it, they said fuck you and kept on trucking. They are cold, manipulative, and utterly contemptuous of the West in general and the U.S. in particular. They are convinced that America is on the decline and that within twenty-five years they will be the world's only superpower."

"They play hardball?"

"In China the line between the military and non-military production is blurry at best. The Chinese army owns some twenty thousand corporations. They know how to treat us, but we don't know how to treat them. We don't know if they represent a thriving emerging economy where American business, like Universal, has an enormous opportunity, or a potential military threat and economic competitor."

"Which is it?"

"Listen, we sold F-sixteens to Taiwan, the ROC. That pissed off the Chinese So now we are about to sell the Chinese F-twenty-twos. They get unpissed and Universal gets eighty billion dollars."

"What do they want with the F-twenty-two and how can they afford eighty billion?"

"You need to rephrase both of those questions. It's not that they want the F-twenty-two all that much; it's that we need to sell it to them. As for affording it, we will lend them the money the way we do Israel and Egypt, then forgive the loans. We're talking heart-throb issues here."

"What do you mean we need to sell it to them?"

"You know how much the F-twenty-two costs?"

"About two hundred million a copy up front. That figure goes down, depending on the production run."

Spinney paused. "You're a cop? How do you know this stuff?"

"Keep going."

"Well, you're right. But first, let me tell you about the F-twenty-two. It's called the Raptor, probably because it preys on the American taxpayer. It is supposed to be the death ray. It was designed to defeat a fourth-generation Soviet fighter that will never exist."

"Because the Evil Empire broke up."

Kitty stared and mouthed "Evil Empire?"

"Right. So we are stuck with this big fat fighter that is supposed to be stealthy, but may not be; supposed to have a supersonic cruise, which is a detriment because of all the gas it will suck; and is supposed to have fancy electronics to mask its radar emissions, and we'll have to wait and see on that one."

"You're saying it may not be all it is advertised to be?"

Spinney laughed.

"What will it be used for?"

"The crucial question. How the fuck can you task an aircraft that cost two hundred million a copy? You going to send it on ground support missions so some guy with a twenty-dollar AK-forty-seven can knock it down? You going to send it up against a Sukoi costing one tenth as much? Not likely."

"But if the Chinese buy a lot of them . . . ?"

"The unit cost could come down to a hundred million dollars or so a copy for us. We could buy more. The more China buys, the more we can afford to buy."

"How does that tie into the JSF contract?"

Again Spinney paused. "You know, you need to come up here and talk to some of these D.C. cops. They could learn from you."

I laughed.

"The contract for the Joint Strike Fighter is a two-hundred-billion-dollar contract; the contract of the century. I saw in a newspaper where it was as if Coke and Pepsi were playing winner take all for the world cola market. Except we are not talking colas here. And you know who the defense contractors are bidding on this project?"

"Universal, Lockheed, and Boeing."

"The only three out there. And you know what, there's a good chance this contract may never be issued. The three contractors know that."

"Not enough money?"

"Exactly. Congress may never agree to this one. Or it might be for far fewer dollars. Maybe less than one hundred billion."

"So, the F-twenty-two might wind up being as big a deal as the JSF."

Kitty slumped down on the sofa and uncrossed her legs. Her dress rode higher. She looked around the room as if she hadn't noticed.

"Maybe bigger. The Chinese are buying eighty billion dollars' worth. That's good for them. And we get to buy more than we could otherwise afford."

"You make it sound like a done deal."

"That's the first dumb thing you've said. Of course, it's a done deal. We're climbing Mount Motherhood here."

I laughed.

"Listen. Not many people know this. But in the last twenty years more than a hundred thousand Chinese students have attended universities in America. This is not a cultural exchange program. It is something that has brought about a technology shift."

"I don't understand."

"Do you know the expression *cheng di yu?*"

"No."

"Chinese for 'fish at the bottom of the ocean.' In intelligence circles it means a sleeper, a long-term agent. Many of those students work for Chinese Intelligence. Under the cover of academe, they are sucking us dry. And we are helping them."

I thought of Andy Fung. My decision not to immediately rush over to Georgia Tech and to contact the Chinese embassy once I learned Fung's name was a good one. If Spinney is correct, inquiries will cause what he terms secondary explosions.

"So what are you saying?"

"I'm saying the U.S. and China are in a feeding frenzy and the F-twenty-two contract cannot be stopped."

"Not my job to stop defense contracts. My job is to arrest people and send them to court, where their fate is decided by twelve people too stupid to get off jury duty."

"Hey, I like a skunk fight better than most. But these people play for keeps. You don't realize what you're up against."

That's the same thing Mrs. Morris said. It's beginning to annoy me. Why does everyone think Universal is a steamroller and I'm roadkill?

"No. They don't know what they're up against."

He laughed. "An Atlanta cop? No offense, but what can you do?"

"I can do anything. I wear Mormon underwear."

Kitty laughed. "Not for long."

15

Kitty was reluctant to go. But I sent her on her way after reminding her that nothing she had seen on my computer or heard in the conversation with Spinney could be used in a story.

"I just heard one side of that conversation," she said. "The stuff about China and the F-twenty-two I'd like to hear more about. What the hell's an Atlanta cop doing mixed up with China and jet airplanes?"

I wanted to tell her I was wondering the same thing. Instead I said, "In good time, Kitty. Not now."

She paused on the top step. "What if I get it from someone else?"

"You mean take what you learned here and get someone else to talk about it and then quote them?"

She shrugged. "It's done all the time."

"Is that your idea of professional ethics?"

"Sometimes you can be a real shit."

"It's my good side coming out."

She flounced down the steps. "I'll be back."

"Okay, Arnold."

I closed the door. The conversation with Spinney lingered in my head. It hadn't occurred to me that J. Stanford's career was on the line. He has to consummate the Chinese deal; the deal that will make Universal the biggest stud hoss in the defense pasture.

J. Stanford is one tough old buzzard, a slick, sophisticated, smart, absolutely amoral man who will do what it takes to get the job done; a goal-oriented man, whose goal is to lock up this eighty-billion-dollar contract. I wouldn't say this out loud, but he intimidates me.

The driving force behind J. Stanford is an ingredient common to many homicides: greed. But this time it is greed masked under the banner of national defense.

J. Stanford ordered Morris killed. I think the security guard was a spur-of-the-moment act by Andy Fung that probably scared hell out of J. Stanford because it let him know he had a loose cannon rolling around Atlanta.

There's no way I can bring J. Stanford to the Box; not at this stage, so I'll have to go to him. He and Pinstripe both think I'm some dumb black cop from Atlanta who is so far out of his league that he's almost irrelevant. So he will cooperate.

I'll get J. Stanford in one of two ways: either through MSE techniques or through Neuro-Linguistic Programming. MSE is multiple suspect elimination and is one of the most subtle interview techniques available.

But my favorite, perhaps because so much emphasis is placed on the eyes, is NLP. This is a highly specialized science developed by the CIA about fifteen years ago. It began filtering down to a few state agencies in the last five years. It is ninety-seven percent effective, an extraordinary tool for detecting deception.

Most of us think we communicate through conversation. We place our attention on *what* a person says. But only seven percent of communication is with words. About thirty-eight percent is with voice and fifty-five percent with physiology.

For instance, if a suspect told me, "I didn't say I

stole the money," I would know what he meant by what word in the sentence that he emphasized. Go through the sentence seven times, putting the inflection on a different word each time. You are saying the same thing but you change the meaning every time because you are saying it a different way.

We listen too much to what people say and not enough to how they are saying it.

You can usually tell if someone is angry because he gets loud. Volume is an important barometer of how a person communicates. But also listen to the rate of speech. We think at about 500 words per minute but talk at about 120 words per minute. What people don't know is that when we lie, that rate can drop to about seventy words a minute.

Ever heard someone blurt out something embarrassing, or say something they didn't mean to say? That's because the words went from the thinking rate of 500 words per minute to the talking rate of 120 words per minute without first going through the filter. We all have filters just as we all have our own dictionaries. Usually the Freudian slip is the truth. The correction is the lie.

You might think this is dull stuff. But I'm giving you the secret of the ages here. Put this into practice and it will change your life.

Listen to a person's change in pace and volume. Does he lower his voice, speed up, begin to whisper? Volume, rate and change are the three indicators.

Physiology is how fifty-five percent of our communication is based. That is where NLP comes in. NLP is based on the universally accepted assumption that the mind and body are connected; a set of stimuli on one is manifested in the other. That's one reason eyes are so important. One of my instructors at the Georgia Police Academy said he had never interviewed a deceptive suspect whose pupils did not constrict at the moment of deception.

The brain stores our memories, prejudices, emotions and intuition. The brain also stores whether we are visual, auditory or kinesic. When Pinstripe was in the Box and I asked him about his dog, it was not a frivolous question. A visual person will describe his dog's physical appearance. An auditory person will tell me how it howls. A kinesthetic person will tell me how he feels about his dog—which will be emotional—or how it feels to touch his dog—sensation.

Each of us assimilates information, or best assimilates information, a certain way. A visual person learns best by watching videos or looking at pictures. An auditory person does well in a classroom. A kinesthetic person would be a handyman who is a genius; a man who might never have been to school but who can take an engine apart and modify it to perform better than the engineer who designed it. He learns by doing.

I start out by asking a person neutral questions to determine his orientation, whether it is left or right. If I had asked Pinstripe, "What is your address?" he would have reeled it off without thinking. But when I asked for his address, zip code first, he had to stop and think. People tend to look to their left or right when accessing information. This is involuntary. It's the same thing that happens when you press a button on a computer; it takes a second to access the information and in that second you hear hums and whirs. Rather than asking someone, "What is your name?" I would ask, "What is the name on your birth certificate?"

He looks left or right as he accesses the information, as he retrieves it from the hard disk in his brain. This is unconscious and with most people cannot be controlled.

So two or three questions at the beginning of an interview reveal both a person's orientation—that is, whether he looks left or right to access information—and his preference, whether he is a visual, auditory or kinesthetic person.

A high percentage of people, maybe eighty percent, are left-brained and look to their left when accessing information.

A visual person with a left-brain orientation looks up and to his left when recalling or "seeing" information. The other side of visual recall is visual creation. I don't want a person creating when I ask him a question; creating in this context is lying. Deception is a conscious, creating process, so he turns to that creative corner when lying. Thus, if a typically organized left-brained person looks up and to his left while remembering or recalling information, when I ask him a question and he looks up and to his right, he is lying.

People can control their facial expressions but they cannot control their eyes. NLP is virtually infallible; the two exceptions being long-term drug users and girls going through puberty. A drug user's brain is fried. A girl entering puberty is so dominated by the mad rush of hormones that her brain is on a toboggan ride through the galaxies.

In class training exercises I saw police officers who understood NLP still give themselves away. You have to understand that when you look at the pupil of another person's eye, you are looking at a portion of the brain sticking out for you to observe.

If I ask the typically organized left-brained person a question and he looks down and to his left, he is having an internal dialogue with himself; he is thinking over whether or not to tell me what I want.

If that same person looks down and to his right, this is the kinesthetic or emotional area: "I couldn't stand twenty years in jail" or "She would be terribly hurt."

There are times when I ask a question and the person's head reveals exactly his progression through various internal discussions. It was obvious with Pinstripe when he was in the Box. He looked up to his left to access the information, then he looked down to his left as he debated whether or not to tell me that answer, then down and to his right as he considered the consequences, then up and to his right as he fabricated his lie.

An auditory person, when remembering something heard, turns his head to the side on which he is oriented. If he is creating sound—trying to deceive me about a conversation—he turns his head to the side opposite the normal orientation.

A kinesthetic person, in remembering experiences, always recalls the event through sensation: "I will never forget the feel of the gun in my back."

A person's state is crucial when I am using NLP. His state consists of his voice, his physiology and his visualizations. If I can manage a suspect's state, I can manage his emotions. When you access the emotions, you access the truth. If someone reacts with anger, I don't react to that state, but rather to the state I want him to be in. That changes his state.

You've done this in one way or another, probably without realizing it. If you push someone's hot buttons, you are changing his state. I do it through content reframing, and either reduce an experience or increase it.

When I was talking with the security guard and he yawned, my yawn mirrored his behavior. I was demonstrating to him on an unconscious level that we were alike. In his unconscious mind there was a rapport between us, which is why he told me more than he should have before he caught himself.

With J. Stanford I used another technique. That was a non-interrogative interview. I was not asking him about his guilt in a crime so there were no Miranda requirements. I was only eliciting statements, observing behavior, and noting physical and verbal responses.

When someone lies, he is like a squirrel running up a big oak tree. He's safe in the beginning. But the more complex his lie becomes, the higher up in the tree and the farther out on a limb he goes and the smaller that limb becomes. Pursue him hard enough and eventually he is on a twig hanging over the abyss.

A good example of that is Ted Kennedy at Chappaquiddick. I've analyzed his statement about that incident. If he was telling the truth, his car was traveling at 362 miles an hour—the speed lab tests have determined is necessary to tear the panty hose off a woman and put them in the glove compartment.

16

This has been a difficult case. But now I'm getting a handle on it and I'm about to get aggressive.

Let me tell you something. Every day you see something in the newspapers or on television about some civilian getting mugged or raped or being the victim of a car jacking. The protection industry is based on the fear that civilians have of bad guys.

But if a cop is walking down the street and a mugger steps out, the cop doesn't think, What will I do? How will I get away from this mean man? No, the cop thinks, Oh, goody. Santa got my letter.

A cop has an aggressive mind-set. That is one of the big differences between cops and civilians.

I'm about to stress some people and open up this case. And FBI agent Streighton Harde and his faithful sidekick are prime candidates for stressing. I know how to do it and at the same time see if they are as connected as I fear they might be.

If I can get Harde's cell phone number, I can track his calls. He was talking to someone when he got out of the G-car after the chase up Peachtree. I don't think it was a social call. I think he was talking to Vandiver or Andy Fung.

I can check the time of the calls with the time of the chase, cross-check the numbers of the people he has called and put some of these people together.

I dialed Lee, my buddy in security at the phone company. Lee has a great job. He is a manager of what might be one of the largest intelligence-gathering operations in America. If people realized the technological capabilities of the phone company and realized how the digitized recordings of virtually every conversation are made and how easily they can be accessed, we would go back to sending handwritten notes.

"Hello."

"Hey, partner, what's going on?"

"You tell me, C.R. You're on the street. All I do is sit up here with a computer, trying to track bad guys."

"I need another cell phone number."

"Gimme a name."

"First, let me ask you a question. If a large organization buys dozens, hundreds, of cell phones and parcels them out to employees, are they listed in the name of the organization or of the individual?"

"Is this a private company?"

"No. The FBI."

"Depends on which field office it is, what agent you want, the rank of the agent and the nature of his job. Some field offices have their cell phones listed to the Bureau. Some agents get their own. It varies."

"Okay, a cell phone number for Streighton Harde, that's s-t-r-e-i-g-h-t-o-n and Harde with an *e*."

I heard him tapping the computer keys. "Oooooo-kaaaaay, C.R. Here we go." A long pause.

"C.R., you've done it to me this time."

"What do you mean?"

"You stuck it to me."

"I stuck what to you?"

"This guy is an FBI agent in Washington."

"I told you that."

"Yeah, but that noise you hear in the background

is the sound of falling paperwork. Maybe my ass. Maybe my head."

"What do you see on that computer screen?"

"When I accessed this number it automatically activated special security procedures."

"What sort of procedures?"

"Not only can I not give you any information about the numbers called from this cell phone, my accessing his name automatically notified the head of my department and a vice president who reports directly to the president of the company."

"What are you saying?"

"Within minutes the FBI will know somebody tried to run a trace on one of their boys."

"Can you stop that?"

"It's automatic."

"But they won't know who is asking for this information."

"They know the request came from my computer."

"Can you play with your computer, make it forget this?"

"Not without losing my job."

"Do what you gotta do."

"I will. Sorry." He paused. "I'm going to have to put you on hold for a minute." A moment later he returned to the phone. "Detective Payne?"

"If you call me detective, I guess it's no use asking for this guy's number or who he called and whether or not you can cross-check the numbers?"

Silence.

"I know. Your boss walked in and wants to know who I am."

"That's correct."

"Tell him."

"I already did."

17

Streighton Harde and Oreo were at my house fifteen minutes after I hung up the phone. When they knocked, I stepped outside on the porch.

It was raining and neither had a raincoat. They stood on my front porch dancing around and flinging water and dripping. The FBI agent pulled a handkerchief from his pocket and wiped his face.

"We want to talk with you," Oreo said.

"So talk."

"Inside," Harde said.

"Got a warrant?"

"You've been instructed to cooperate with us," Harde said.

"That doesn't mean I have to invite you into my house."

The two men glared.

"Tell me what you want. I've been very cooperative. I've sent over copies of my case notes."

I should have said "some of my case notes."

"Bring us up-to-date on the status of your investigation. Who you have interviewed, who you want to interview."

"That's in the notes."

"Tell us anyway."

"Why don't you bring me up-to-date on your traffic stop? Let's talk about that some more."

"Why do you think we stopped you?"

"Is this a trick question?"

Very slowly he repeated himself. "Why do you think we stopped you?"

He wants to play. "It could be because neither of you could find your ass with both hands and a search warrant. But I could be wrong. Hey, I'm a simple street cop down here in Atlanta, Georgia. What do I know?"

Oreo spoke up. "That's not what we came here to talk about."

"You always pick the topic of conversation?"

"Where you are concerned, yes."

"I want to know about that bogus traffic stop."

The feeb spoke up. "Can't we do this inside?"

"No."

He pressed his lips together. "Okay, why do you say it was a bogus stop?"

"Because it was bogus."

This conversation was getting circular.

"You said over the radio you were pursuing a suspect in a homicide investigation. Was that this case?"

"Did I say that?"

"You never briefed us."

"It would have been premature."

When I think that the FBI is filled with bozos like this and when I realize that to be working this case Will Jackson must be one of the Air Force's sharpest investigators, then I fear for the fate of the republic.

What they really want to know is if I recognized the Chinese guy's car. They want to know how much I know about Andy Fung.

These guys don't care who killed the security guard. That's not why they are in town. Their job is to make sure the homicides don't reflect badly on Universal and affect the F-22 contract. If this thing blows up, it could, God forbid, force the President to become involved, force him to make some statement about his favorite foreign country—China—that he might not want to make.

"Why is it always a one-way street when locals work with you guys? We are willing to give you whatever it takes to do the job, and you give us nothing."

Harde put on his tough guy face. He took a step forward. Oreo knew his signals. He moved in closer. I closed the space even more by moving forward. "Let's get to the point, Detective," Harde said. "You know why we are here."

"You want to borrow my deodorant?"

"Why did you want my cell phone number?"

"There is not always time to send a fax. I want to reach out and know you are just a phone call away."

"Why didn't you ask me for the number?"

"I didn't know how to reach you."

"You can get me through the FBI field office here. I told you that."

I looked from one to the other. "Is it a federal crime to ask for your telephone number? What's the big deal here? Is your number classified? Hell, if you don't want me to have it, that's okay. I'll leave a message at the local office and hope you get it within two or three days."

Harde looked at me, probing, wondering. "I'll call you every day. You can tell me what you got."

"Okay. But I need to know something. Who do you work for?"

They looked at each other. Oreo grinned.

"What kind of question is that?" Harde said. "I told you I am a special agent with the FBI and Mr. Jackson here is OSI."

"But who do you work for?"

"For the government. What's your point, Detective?"

"What government?"

Harde tilted his head toward the street and he and Oreo stepped away. "Funny guy," Harde said.

"I just want to know who my partners are."

Harde turned toward me and wagged a bony finger in my face. "Be careful, young detective. Be very careful."

Both men pulled their collars around their necks and prepared to dash through the rain.

I looked up and down the street, pretending I didn't see the G-car parked in front of my house. "How'd you guys get here?"

"Why?"

"I don't know. It's just that everywhere you turn up, it's like a Chinese fire drill."

I couldn't help it.

18

The phone was ringing. I looked out the window. Harde had his cell phone to his ear as he walked toward his car. He couldn't leave me alone. I snatched my phone off the cradle and said, "Joe's Whorehouse."

I smiled at the long pause. Zinged him that time. He had no response This guy had about as many original thoughts as Martha Stewart.

"We're having a special today on the wives of FBI agents. Very experienced. But I can't vouch for their health."

I was having a great time. The feeb was so nonplused he couldn't say anything.

"Caesar Roosevelt; what an absolutely extraordinary way of answering your telephone."

I grimaced. It was my Gwendolyn, my former wife who dashed off to California three years ago. She is the only person who ever calls me Caesar Roosevelt.

"Gwendolyn."

"Want to tell me why you answered the telephone in that fashion?"

"It's a long story."

"I'm sure."

Why was she calling? I had heard from her only through her lawyer since that day she walked out. I particularly remember the court order forbidding me to have any contact with my daughter. The woman was angry, and whatever it was she was angry about she was determined to extract the last pound of flesh from me.

"Are you okay?"

"Good Lord, would I have rung you if I were okay?"

"Is Kimberly okay?"

"She is fine. But I didn't call you to talk about her. I called to talk about me. I'm going through a bit of a bad time out here, trying to find myself, trying to move around in this new space I've created for Kimberly and me. It's very difficult."

"I'd like to hear about Kimberly."

"Well, yes, I suppose you would. I have sent her to etiquette classes. She . . ."

"Etiquette classes? The kid is four years old."

". . . knows how to use a fish fork."

I couldn't believe it. The woman was still hung up on fish forks. She used to talk about fish forks all the time. She talked about fish forks as if I didn't know the difference between a fish fork and a pitchfork. I finally realized that a fish fork had some sort of symbolic meaning to her; if a person knew how to use a fish fork, he automatically was the sort of person with whom she might associate. It was the price of admission to her life. It was her single standard in determining the worth of a person, the most important gauge of a person's social skills, a measurement of his family background.

"What else . . ."

"Now, now. Must I remind you about the court order?"

"I would be happy if you told me why you thought it was necessary."

She talked for more than an hour.

About herself.

19

I am an expert on guerrilla warfare. Many black people are. After all, we have to operate in the white man's world. I have no problem with black people who want to put on their Mandela shirts and their sandals and do the Africa thing. Hey, right on. It makes them big in the black world. But it also scares hell out of white people and, as I am ever reminded, this is still the white man's world. And I want to make it in this world; the big world, the white man's world, the only world that really counts.

To be a black man in America is to be like a writer or an actor or a singer from a foreign country. That person might be the most famous writer in Australia or the best known actor in France or the greatest singer in Ireland. But in the heart of every one of them they have not made it until they make it in America. America is the ultimate showcase, and to be a star here is all that counts. So they come here and most of them don't make it and they go back home and they are still big stars, but in their hearts they are failures because they couldn't make it in America.

I can be real black and be a prominent part of the black community. We champion our own. We encourage our own. We applaud our successes and achievements. And that is good. But I want to make it in

America, in the world that offers both the greatest heartbreak and the greatest opportunity.

Much of what Elijah Muhammad wrote and spoke was a bunch of hooey. But in "Message to the Blackman in America," he got it right when he said, "Observe the operations of the white man. He is successful. He makes no excuses for his failures. He works hard in a collective manner. You do the same."

Not every black person agrees with me on this. In fact, most of them don't. But, it's like His Skipness, says: there are thirty-five million black people in America and that means there are thirty-five million ways to be black.

So I'm on the way to Universal to go up against Mister Whitey and prove I can cut it in the white man's world.

The feeb and the Oreo were there when I arrived; sitting in the little conversation corner where J. Stanford and I had talked last Sunday morning. I can't get away from these guys.

Special Agent Harde sat there and nodded. He had on one of those Baptist smiles that made me realize this was going to be a tough meeting. Brother Will eyed me and didn't say jack. He just sat there like a signifying monkey, flexing, trying to act like his white leader.

"Mr. Godbey informed us you were coming by this morning," Harde said. "We wanted to talk to him again about the security guard's homicide so I thought we would sit in on your meeting." He paused like a preacher waiting for the big amen from the congregation then said, "You don't object." It was not a question.

Of course I objected. But it wouldn't do any good. So I said, "Don't interfere with my interview."

"Right," Will Jackson said. He smirked. This guy is

like Maynard Jackson, a former mayor of Atlanta and another former black man. I wonder if they are related. Brother Will wants to be white so bad he can't stand it. But somewhere along the line he realized that short of pulling a Michael Jackson, that won't happen. So he takes out his frustration on black people who remind him that he is still black. I'm going to put him on my list. When all this is over, and after I close down Mustache Mal's, I am going to look up Brother Will and put an ass-whipping on him.

I'm easygoing, but some things jerk my chain.

The FBI agent raised a finger and got the attention of one of the secretaries. "Would you let him know Detective Payne has arrived?"

She nodded and picked up the phone.

I sat there staring at the feds for the next ten minutes. Harde tried to talk about my investigation a few times but I told him I didn't want to go over this stuff but once, that it would have to wait until I saw Godbey.

"I'd advise you to be careful with your questions, Detective. Mr. Godbey is neither a witness nor a suspect. He is president of Universal and a very respected citizen. He has rights."

I opened my briefcase, pulled out the notebook, took out my pen and made a big show of writing.

"What are you doing?" Harde asked.

"I'm writing down what you said. I'm just a city homicide cop. Sometimes those procedure things confuse me."

Harde put on his FBI face.

The door to the sanctum sanctorum opened and out walked my old buddy Pinstripe. He looked through the three of us and kept walking. Behind him in the door stood a very regal middle-aged lady whom I guessed was J. Stanford's secretary. She was white of

course; black ladies are never found as secretaries to
people like J. Stanford. I liked her eyes. She reminded
me of my mother, although, as you might imagine, this
woman was considerably lighter in color.

"Mr. Godbey will see you gentlemen now," she
said. She had a voice like the woman who welcomes
people at the gates of heaven. She was calm and
poised and obviously had been around Universal for
a while. She exuded professionalism.

Harde and Jackson brushed by her without a nod.
I stopped in the door. "My name is C.R. Payne. I'm
a detective with the city of Atlanta. I was out here
last Sunday and didn't get to meet you."

She smiled. "Yes, I heard." She paused. She
reached out to shake hands. "Won't you come in?"

I took a deep breath. The old butterflies came back.
I was wearing my best suit, a dark gray pinstripe, and
my shoes were well shined. I wore a starched white
shirt with gold cuff links. But I was walking into the
barn of a very big mule.

J. Stanford's secretary leaned closer and whispered,
"You don't have to be nervous." She smiled.

"Does it show that much?"

"No."

I walked in, strode up to Mr. Godbey, who had
walked from behind his desk, and reached out to
shake his hand. "Good morning, sir." I gave him a
big smile.

He looked me up and down, nodded in reluctant
appreciation of my suit, and said, "Good morning, Officer Payne."

He continued to eye me. What behavioral scientists
call the Law of Recency was working on him. Even
though we had seen each other from a distance at
Richard Morris's funeral, he was remembering our
first meeting when I wore an old shirt and jeans and

boots. He was having a difficult time reconciling that memory with what he saw today.

"I don't think I will be of much help to you. But I will try."

He had set the ground rules.

I increased the size of my smile until it was approaching watermelon-eating magnitude. Brother Will glanced at me, trying to figure out what was going on.

"I appreciate your time, sir. You were a big help last Sunday when we talked."

J. Stanford smiled at the two feds. "Gentlemen."

I was miffed. I didn't get a smile or a "gentleman." J. Stanford glanced at his watch then motioned for all of us to sit over in one corner of his office.

"Anyone care for coffee, tea, soft drinks?"

The two feds shook their heads. "I'd like a cup of tea," I said.

J. Stanford nodded toward his secretary. "And coffee for me." He would not let a guest drink alone.

The secretary smiled. "Would English Breakfast be suitable, sir? Or would you care for an herbal tea?"

"English Breakfast is fine." One of the few good memories I have of my ex-wife is that she taught me to enjoy hot tea.

As the secretary closed the door, the four of us sat down. I pulled a leather cigar case from inside my jacket.

"Mr. Godbey, the other morning you said you were a cigar smoker. Do you mind if I smoke?"

There was a slight flicker of surprise. But these old white guys do have their manners. "Not at all."

"Would you care for one?" I didn't offer the feds a cigar.

"I have meetings all day, so I'd better not. But thank you."

The two feds looked on disapprovingly as I ex-
tracted a cigar from the leather case.

J. Stanford's eyes widened as he recognized the distinctive red and gold label. "That's a La Gloria. A
pyramid."

"Yes."

"I can't get those," he blurted.

The two feds were puzzled.

"La Gloria Cubana," I said. I turned to J. Stanford.
"I have a supplier here who gets them in Miami and
sends them to me." I lit a match, let it burn for a
moment, then rolled the tip of the cigar through the
flame, put it in my mouth and puffed until a cloud of
sweet smoke wafted around my head. Their heads,
too. "Good cigars. Though not always as consistent as
I would like."

I turned to J. Stanford. "I'd be glad to order you
a box."

He pursed his lips. He sniffed the smoke. He
wanted a box of La Glorias. He really did.

Before he could answer, the secretary returned. She
walked to the table carrying a little silver tray on
which were two exquisite cups and saucers of bone
china and small Waterford milk and sugar containers.
Two small silver pots, steam rising from the spouts,
sat there. Spoons—sterling—and napkins—linen—
were alongside.

The defense industry knows how to serve tea and
coffee.

I smiled at the secretary. "You know, in Colonial
America there was a fascination for all things oriental.
Such as Chinese Chippendale furniture." I picked up
a cup and saucer and examined it. "This is another
example. A Williamsburg pattern called Chinese Flowers. Wedgewood did an admirable job with it, don't
you think?"

The feeb and Little Maynard stared. The secretary smiled and nodded, pleased, as she set the tray on the table. "I chose that for Universal years ago. It is one of my favorites."

"We will pour," J. Stanford said.

"Yes, sir." She turned and walked from the room.

"A very nice lady," I said.

J. Stanford's face clearly revealed what he was thinking: How does some young black guy—he wasn't thinking black guy—know about Wedgewood? He shook his head as if to clear his thoughts. "Yes. She has been here twenty-seven years. About to retire."

He motioned for me to pour myself a cup of tea as he poured his coffee. He held his eyes on me as he picked up the cup. "Detective Payne, you said you wanted to ask about the incident involving Richard Morris. These gentlemen tell me there are parallels in that case and in the death of my security guard, and, further, that you are working together. So I thought we could do this all at once." He sipped his coffee.

I nodded, prepared my tea, took a sip, then took a big puff off the cigar and blew smoke toward the ceiling. He referred to Richard Morris formally but to "my security guard."

I held my open hands toward the two feds. "Why don't we start with your bringing me up-to-date on your investigation. What have you found?"

Harde's lips squeezed together in an effort to control his anger. He glanced at J. Stanford and then at me. "It doesn't work that way, Detective. You go ahead with whatever you want to discuss with Mr. Godbey."

I took another puff off the cigar and blew smoke in his face. "I'm not sure I understand your concept of cooperation."

J. Stanford stepped in. "Gentlemen. I have a great deal of work to do."

I turned toward him. On the spur of the moment I decided not to use NLP with J. Stanford; it's too intense and could be interrupted by the two feds. They might not know what was going on, but they would be able to tell from his demeanor that something was happening. I would use MSE techniques.

"Mr. Godbey, you know why I am here?"

"You said it had to do with the incident involving Richard Morris."

He could talk of the "death" of the security guard. But twice he had referred to Morris's homicide as an "incident."

"Tell me all you know about the murder of Richard Morris."

He looked at me in surprise. "Excuse me."

"Tell me all you know about the murder of Richard Morris."

"I don't believe I know anything at all beyond what I might have told you."

The qualifiers gave him away; "don't believe" and "what I might have told you."

"Who do you think could have killed Richard Morris?"

"It could have been any one of dozens of people. Maybe more. I've thought about that. The defense industry, here and abroad I'm sorry to say, has many people for whom expediency is everything. Morris was involved in very sensitive dealings."

He was making the universe as big as possible. An innocent person would have named several people who could have committed the homicide.

"Why do you say that?"

"Why do I say that? You have to understand our foreign competitors. All these people of all nationalities, most of whom do not share our value system. Some people here in America. It's a strange world we live in."

"Who do you think had the best opportunity to do this?"

"I don't want to get too specific. I don't want to name a competitor or someone from North America or Europe or South America or Africa or Australia. Any number of people would have had an opportunity. I don't know."

J. Stanford was still trying to make it seem anyone could have killed Morris.

"Asia?"

"What?"

Harde shifted in his chair.

"You mentioned North America, Europe, South America, Africa and Australia. You didn't mention Asia. Could someone from Asia have had the opportunity to do this?"

"I didn't mention Antarctica either, Officer. Of course, it could have been someone from either place. Or any other country."

"Antarctica? You think it could have been someone from Antarctica?"

"I just don't know. So many people would have had the opportunity."

"If you were conducting this investigation, how would you do it?"

The two feds looked at each other; grinning at my naïveté.

J. Stanford laughed, looked off to his right and paused. He shook his head. "You really want me to answer that?"

"Whatever you like."

He shrugged. "I would get a list of other defense contractors. Competitors, you know. I don't know. It would be very difficult. The international defense industry is so big. It's a big job you have. I'm just not sure what I would do."

"What do you think are the most important reasons that could have created this situation?"

He shook his head in bewilderment. "I told you about Morris's work and how people in several countries might harbor a grudge. The world is a difficult place today. Beyond that, I don't know." He paused. "These are strange questions, Detective."

Harde nodded in agreement. He was going to wait a little bit longer, until he figured out where I was going, before he interrupted.

Godbey was like most people who have seen a few episodes of a cop series on television. He thinks we use bright lights and get in somebody's face and ask direct questions. And we do once we know the sensitive areas, the areas likely to yield information. We ask those types of questions after we read a person his rights. I think J. Stanford was expecting that sort of question so he could call his lawyer and end the interview.

It is these open-ended, non-accusatory questions, seeming vague and almost dumb questions, that yield acres of information. The beauty of such questions is that the subject is not aware of what he is revealing. He doesn't realize that every word, every qualifier, every phrase, every sentence, gives valuable information to a trained interviewer. Yet, if he were to tape the conversation—and he probably is—he could play it back for his lawyer, who would smile in condescension at what a stupid cop I am. The only thing most lawyers know about interviewing is body language, an outdated technique used only by retired FBI agents who are called up as expert witnesses by prosecutors.

Prosecutors don't know that body language reveals stress, not truth or deception.

Unless a person is trained in a half-dozen interview techniques, the significance of both the questions and the answers is lost. I am guessing that Harde, as a senior FBI agent, has not been required to take any course upgrading his interviewing skills, that is, even if the FBI offered them. Jackson knows nothing of these techniques because the Air Force doesn't offer them.

"What do you think should happen to the person who murdered Richard Morris?"

"Someone who commits murder, or causes a murder to be committed, obviously has pressures on him, problems, needs help." J. Stanford clasped his hands together and slowly shook his head. "Whoever did it needs help."

An innocent person will say the perpetrator should be put in the electric chair, that the book should be thrown at him.

"How do you think this crime was done?"

J. Stanford looked away for a long moment. His lips pursed and he clasped his hands together. He looked back at me and shrugged.

"How would you have done this crime?"

"What the hell?" Harde interrupted.

"I'm trying to figure out how it might have been done. We have the same perp on your homicide and mine. I'm simply trying to learn from Mr. Godbey, to get the benefit of his insights into any possible perpetrators."

Again, Godbey waved Harde away. Middle-aged white guys like Godbey have a lot of confidence.

"This is so far out of my experience. I simply have no idea."

Another bad answer. An innocent person would

come up with several good scenarios for committing murder.

"Mr. Godbey, let me ask you to go back, if you would, to last Sunday when we first talked. Did you work the previous day?"

He nodded immediately. "I work every Saturday."

"You have to remember a lot of details in your work, do you not?"

"Yes."

"You have a good memory?" I puffed on the cigar.

"Very good."

Harde had been about to interrupt. He sensed where that was going. But now it was too late.

"I'm trying to get a picture of what was going on at Universal, everything that might have involved Richard Morris. Could you describe in detail for me everything you did that Saturday until we talked on Sunday morning?"

"What sort of question is that?" Harde asked. "Mr. Godbey is not a suspect."

"Of course he's not a suspect. But I want to better understand Universal so I can get a handle on what might have happened to Morris that night."

"It's okay, Agent Harde. I don't mind answering that question." He smiled at me. "Not much to tell. Went home about four o'clock Saturday. Watered the lawn. Took a shower. Had several drinks—gin and tonic—dinner, TV, brushed the teeth, went to bed, went to sleep. Wife went to bed. Had a lot of things to catch up on so got up early on Sunday—don't remember the time—and came to work. You dropped in." He cast his hands wide. "That's about it."

I puffed on my cigar. J. Stanford knew what time he went home but not what time he got up. He and his wife were having troubles; in fact, they did not sleep together. He left out huge chunks of time. And he never used the personal pronoun.

I took a sip of tea. "Anything you want to add to the conversation we had last Sunday morning?"

"There's nothing to add. I told you everything I could."

"Do you have any further ideas or suspicions about who might have killed Richard Morris or how they might have done it?"

"I think you have a big job, Detective. It's unfortunate for you, as a city detective, but you are involved in a murder investigation in which the guilty person could be from a dozen countries around the world. I wouldn't eliminate anyone from the investigation."

I nodded and puffed on the cigar. "How do you think the person who killed Morris feels today?"

"He feels terrible. Morris was a good man."

"I've noticed some of your reactions during this interview and there are times when you seem worried. A bit anxious."

Harde's eyebrows narrowed.

J. Stanford paused, trying to figure out where the trap was, trying to figure out the point of the question.

"You're wrong, Detective. There is nothing for me to worry about."

I took a final sip of tea and stood up. "That's very good tea, Mr. Godbey, again I thank you for your time and your help. I'll let you know what happens as the investigation continues." I reached out to shake his hand.

Harde and Jackson looked at each other in disbelief. That was the interview? That was all I had?

Godbey nodded. He, too, was surprised. "I would be grateful. Perhaps you could coordinate it through these gentlemen. I'm very busy and I've told you everything I know." He paused. "Several times."

I got the message. Next time I wanted to talk, a lawyer would be involved.

Harde and Jackson looked at me. "Learn anything from your investigation?" I asked Harde.

He nodded. "Informative. If I get anything on the security guard, I'll give you a call."

"Always a pleasure working with the FBI."

"My secretary will show you out, Detective." J. Stanford stepped behind his desk.

The secretary suddenly appeared.

"Thank you for the tea."

She nodded, a slight smile on her lips, then escorted me to the front office, where a security guard waited.

As I signed out and walked toward my Explorer, I smiled and took a big puff off the cigar. I was rather pleased with myself. That was one hell of an interview.

Maybe I'm getting over this intimidation thing.

20

The phone was ringing when I walked in the door.

"Payne."

"Detective, this is your major. Whatever you have planned for this evening, cancel it."

It was six-thirty p.m. Thursday. I hung up my coat and pulled the holster off my belt. "Sure, Major. Nothing going on. I'm just trying to find a perp who has killed two people and who, I believe, has picked out his third victim. The case involves the biggest defense contractor in the world, the Pentagon, China, the FBI and the Air Force. The last two are tugging on my cape. And you got plans for me this evening? Glad to."

The major paused. Then he mumbled, "Universal is the biggest defense contractor in the world?"

"Yes."

"I didn't know that." He was still mumbling. Sometimes he mumbles worse than Columbo. "Well, anyway, fuck Universal and China and everybody else. You got more important things to do."

Supervisors know how to boil things down to the essence.

"I do?"

"Detective, I have been instructed by the chief, and he led me to believe this was coming from the mayor, to tell you to attend a meeting tonight and to take notes."

"Take notes? Take notes? Major, I'm in the middle of—"

"Young detective, this is the Atlanta Police Department, not a democratic institution. I did not ask you for a response. If I did, the only acceptable one is, 'Yes, sir.' You understand?"

"Yes, sir."

I heard paper rustling. "The meeting is downtown. The Marriott Marquis. Seven o'clock for drinks, dinner at eight, speech afterwards. Identify yourself at the door. They're holding a ticket for you. It's black tie optional so you can wear a suit instead of a tux."

"It's a dinner jacket, not a tux, and I have one. Since I have to take notes, I gather the speaker is the reason I'm going."

"Senator Sam Perry is talking to the annual chamber of commerce banquet. Get your ass in gear."

"You want me to go to a chamber of commerce dinner and be there in a half hour?"

"Does that tax your abilities, Detective? You don't have to be there for drinks. You don't have to eat their rubber chicken and Styrofoam bread. But you do have to listen to the senator's speech. That is an order."

He was no longer mumbling.

"This speech have something to do with my case?"

"Detective, you're one mistake away from being transferred back to the airport. You got my ass in a crack. Now, I don't know anything beyond what I told you. I'm simply passing along the wishes of the chief and the mayor."

"The chief doesn't get involved in the details of a homicide investigation. Not unless it's a high profile thing. Everything about this case is classified. The mayor is a bozo. Why does he want me to hear a speech by that gnome passing himself off as a United States senator."

"I'm not going to argue with you, Detective. But, for your information, that gnome is chairman of the Senate Armed Services Committee; one of the most powerful men in Washington. The mayor obviously believes that what the senator has to say is relevant to your investigation. Be there. Or get your uniform pressed for the airport."

Click.

An hour later, after a leisurely shower and shave and after reading a chapter from Lao-tzu's book, the one I discovered on the Internet, I dressed for the evening. It no longer was raining but the night was clammy.

I figure that wearing a dinner jacket—mine is single-breasted with a peaked lapel—is a special occasion and that one should do it right. Rather than the stiff wing collar, I favor the semi-spread turndown. My shirt is a Marcella; the body is voile but the front, collar and cuffs are pique. And the front is plain rather than pleated. The black bow tie is silk barathea and I tie it myself. My shoes are not the plain black oxfords that some men favor, but rather black calf opera pumps with black grosgrain bows. Some men think these are effete. I think they are elegant and should be worn with a dinner jacket. I got them at Bennie's on sale. My socks are black silk and over the calf.

Some men believe such an outfit, all in black and white, makes them look like a penguin and they go to absurd lengths to show their flair and panache. Usually they wind up looking as if they are on furlough from a mental institution; matching the bow tie and cummerbund in some bizarre plaid is the best exam-

ple. I prefer a slight and understated note of dissonance such as a silk handkerchief in my breast pocket.
I chose a handkerchief so green it was almost black.

Tonight I would be drinking scotch. I need scotch
when I listen to politicians make speeches. And when
I drink scotch I like a good cigar. I nestled a couple
in the leather case.

I was almost ready.

The plastic ballpoint pen was eased into my sock.
Then I slid on a shoulder holster, careful not to wrin-
kle my shirt, and picked out one of my personal guns,
a subcompact nine-millimeter Glock. I looked into the
mirror and paused. "Spectacles, testicles, wallet, and
watch." Then I was out the door.

I arrived as people were wandering around looking
for their seats. It was very loud and jangled in the
way of Atlanta parties. Lots of loud shrill-voiced
brassy women and fat men in dinner jackets they must
have bought at Atlanta Tent and Awning Company.
At my table for ten were three local businessmen and
their wives, an Army colonel—a black guy—in full
mess dress, two Asian men in blue suits, and me. I sat
between the colonel and the older of the two Asian
men. I told them I worked for the city. The Army
colonel looked at me curiously.

After dinner it took about thirty minutes of civic
masturbation before Perry's introduction; mostly
about the legacy of the 1996 Olympics and the promise of Atlanta's future. Except for a new baseball stadium and several other sports facilities, I don't see
much legacy. Centennial Park was ripped up after the
games and it took more than two years before it was
finished. The bombing in the park is what people remember. None of the promise came through. People
all over the world are still bewildered about how we
ever got the Olympics.

But, as usual, chamber nabobs are talking about Atlanta as an "international city" and "world famous city" and "the city of the future."

I have never understood why we must have this daily ritual of announcing what a great city we are. I have never understood this city's need for approval. Maybe that's why so many people listen to Dr. Laura. We know we need a frequent scolding.

Tomorrow if someone from another galaxy arrived in Atlanta and announced he had a plan to save the universe, many Atlantans would become his disciples. This is a town of cement spreaders who are peculiarly susceptible to manure spreaders. In fact, manure spreaders thrive here. We stand in the ruins of old buildings and raise our eyes toward the smoke and dreams of a tomorrow that will never arrive.

Don't get me wrong. I love this city. It's just that sometimes I think I am the only person inside the perimeter highway who has a realistic view of the place.

I needed a drink. With a double shot of single malt down the hatch and another one about to follow, I could listen to the speech. The Chinese guys were nursing their drinks but the three businessmen were drinking as if they just received a secret message informing them prohibition would be declared in an hour. The Army colonel was holding his own, probably in self-defense. He was also drinking single malt. I love to see another black man enjoying the good things of life that white folk think they have a monopoly on.

The three businessmen were in the construction business. Every time someone from the chamber made a speech, they cheered and applauded as if the words had been hauled down the mountain by Moses. Then they waved at a waiter for more drinks.

The colonel seemed faintly amused. Colonel David Drumwright was about my height, very military, about ten years older than I, which made him in his early forties. He had been promoted fast. He had a trim haircut, direct gaze and a no-nonsense manner. Turned out he was from Chicago. He was stationed at Fort Gillem, a small army base about twenty miles south of town.

"I've seen a lot of that," he said, pointing at the podium.

"Lot of what?"

"Lot of that substance they're talking about."

"What substance?"

"I worked in the stockyards two summers during college."

I laughed and raised my drink. My dinner jacket gaped and his eyes widened. I thought it was because he had seen my weapon. I pulled my coat back and said, "I have to carry it."

He shrugged and leaned closer. "I'm something of a cop myself. But I was looking at the leather container. Cigars?"

"You don't look like an MP."

"I'm not."

"Yes. Cigars."

"Mind if I ask what kind?"

"La Glorias."

"La Gloria Cubanas? Where do you get those? Are they pyramids?"

"Yes. A supplier with contacts. And yes."

He rolled his eyes. "Almost as good as Cohibas, not nearly as expensive, and almost as hard to find."

"You're a cigar man?"

He smiled and shrugged.

I pulled one of the cigars from the container and stuck it in his pocket. "When this is over, why don't we go to a bar I know and have a smoke? You can buy the scotch."

He pulled the cigar from his pocket, passed it under his nose, then held it between his thumb and forefinger, placed it next to his ear and rolled it back and forth. "Deal."

"If you're not an MP, what kind of cop are you?"

"Just a cop."

Turned out the two Asian men were Chinese. Both were very quiet and both had the air of supervisors. You can usually pick out a supervisor; something about their eyes, the way they hold themselves, their voices. They look like grown-up versions of kids who throw tantrums when they don't get their way. Their suits were very expensive, tailor-made, I guessed. They were from the Chinese consulate in Dallas, which covers the southeastern United States, and were here as guests of the chamber.

A chamber mogul roamed the room during the introductory speeches, fawning over the businessmen who paid his salary. He raised fawning to a new level when he saw the Chinese. He apologized profusely for not being able to seat them at the head table.

Occasionally he raised his face to us and blessed us with his smile. Then he whispered again to the Chinese men, inviting them to a special party after the dinner. "Just a few important people," he whispered. "Senator Perry wants to meet you."

They smiled.

When he left, I turned to the man nearest me. "You are from China?"

"Yes. We are PRC. Not Chinese Taiwan." He smiled.

I noticed the spin he put on his terminology, referring to Taiwan as Chinese Taiwan, as if it were a province. I can play that game.

"Communist China?"

His smile flickered. "That is how some Americans refer to us." He paused. "We are negotiating with your city about our government placing a large business in Atlanta. They want us to locate here. It is a very large business that will employ hundreds of Atlantans."

"Will your business be connected to Universal?"

"No. It is a computer assembly plant. It would be connected to Georgia Tech." He nodded. "An excellent school. Many Chinese students attend."

"I've heard. Is there a large Chinese community here?"

He shrugged. "What is large? We have many Chinese in the southeastern United States. Not as many as in your California, but many." He smiled and leaned toward me. "We were informed that your Senator Perry will be speaking about China tonight. A very important speech. We are told it has the blessings of the State Department and of the administration in Washington." He sat back and nodded.

So that's why the chief wants me here; to get a little sensitivity training.

I always react the wrong way to that sort of thing.

I leaned closer to the Chinese guy. "You know many Chinese in Atlanta who work for your government?"

"Some. Their paperwork comes through my office in Dallas."

"How's my friend Andy Fung?"

It came out of nowhere and slapped him in the face. You know that business about the Chinese being inscrutable? Wrong.

His head snapped around and his pupils contracted. "Andy Fung?"

Repeating a question is one way to delay answering.

"A Chinese national who works for your government."

The guy was catatonic.

I wanted to help him out. "Handles very sensitive matters."

"I don't believe I know anyone by that name."

He didn't say, "I don't know." He said, "I don't believe I know." Deception.

I smiled and handed him my card. His eyes widened again. "When you run across him, tell him I asked about him in connection with a homicide case. Tell him I want him to come to my office."

He put the card in his pocket, nodded and wrapped his hand around his drink. It was as if the glass were an anchor to keep him steady. A moment later he was whispering in Chinese to his companion.

Senator Perry was introduced.

He had been in Washington five terms and was a short, paunchy, middle-aged man with a hairline that began somewhere on top of his head. The knot in his tie was a fat triangle. He managed to swagger and to look very serious at the same time. If someone poked him with a fork and all the hot air escaped, he would be no bigger than a troll.

The point of his speech was that China and the U.S. are the only two superpowers and that we must coexist. Why endanger the relationship by trying to force our values on the Chinese?

"We must rethink our human rights policy where China is concerned," Perry said. His bright little eyes roamed to our table. He was playing to the Chinese consular officials. "When we hold up our human rights policy to the world and then impress that human rights policy over our trade policy, then I believe very strongly that we Americans have a bit of a warped perspective."

The two guys from China nodded, their heads bobbing like corks in a millrace. They looked at each other and smiled.

"But even more important is the plain fact, and you as businessmen will understand this better than most, China and the former Soviet Union are the two largest potential markets in the world. You all want to do business there. You must be able to do business there."

The three construction guys applauded wildly. The Chinese guys nodded in agreement and looked around the room.

"We are now doing business with former Warsaw Pact countries, countries once our enemies but now part of NATO. Those countries are spending billions for defense. Well, I can tell you . . ." The troll paused and looked out over the audience. "I can tell you the Chinese market makes the market in those countries and in every other country in the world pale by comparison."

He hammered his clenched fist on the podium and looked out over a thousand businessmen. "China can be our salvation. I know it is one of the few remaining communist countries in the world. I know that. You know that. But by doing business with them we can demonstrate the glory of our capitalist society. We can, every businessman in this room, be examples of democracy; cheerleaders for America, and the hope of our children."

He paused and lowered his voice. "And we can all make money. More money than you can imagine."

What the chief and the mayor, and whoever is jerking the mayor's chain, want me to understand is that doing business with China is an objective worth more than two lives.

But I am not a businessman. I am a homicide detective. And I have a different set of standards.

I looked at the colonel. He rolled his eyes and leaned toward me. "I was wondering when he would bring in the children."

"Want to go smoke that cigar?"

"Leave in the middle of the speech?"

"I can lean over and pretend I'm sick—which won't take much pretending—and that you're escorting me out of here."

"We don't have to do that. Let's just leave." We pushed back our chairs. The Chinese guys stared in disbelief. The construction guys kept drinking. As we walked through the crowd, I turned toward the colonel.

"Do you know the name Henry Louis Gates?"

He broke into a wide smile. "Skip Gates? Of course. I read everything he writes."

"I thought you would know him." I laughed. "Hey, ever watch *Casablanca?*"

"I did."

"Remember the last scene?"

He put his arm across my shoulder and together we recited the line: "Louis, I think this is the beginning of a beautiful friendship."

21

David Drumwright and I leaned over a table in the back room at Manuel's Tavern, the bar at the corner of North Highland and North Avenue where Atlanta's politicians, journalists, students, nurses and everyone else gathers to celebrate the large and small things of life. It is the closest thing Atlanta has to a neighborhood pub. The place looks as if it has been there a hundred years. The dark wood walls are covered with neon beer signs and photographs of employees, customers, karate club members and former police officers.

Our table is set aside exclusively for cops. Manuel's is, most of all, a cop bar.

Thursday night is the night cops take over and civilians become a quiet minority. At the end of the day watch, dozens of detectives and uniforms rush into the smoke-filled tavern. Many on the evening watch get off early and arrive about eleven or eleven-thirty. From then until it closes, Manuel's Tavern has the greatest concentration of police of any place in the city.

This blue bedlam is presided over by Bill McCloskey, a big jovial guy who has been the night manager for decades.

McCloskey usually sticks a cigar in his mouth and

roams up and down behind the bar. But when he saw David and me come in wearing evening clothes, he could not pass up an opportunity. He followed us to a table in the back room, leaned over the table and with a straight face said, "You guys been to a costume party?"

"We're trying to show you white folk how to dress. We want to lend some class to this joint."

"God knows we need that."

"David, this is Bill McCloskey. He poses as the night manager here. But there is some doubt about what he does in real life. Bill, say hello to Colonel David Drumwright, United States Army."

Bill took in David's mess dress uniform. "Colonel." He nodded. "Damn. You guys are upgrading my bar tonight."

"Thank you," David said.

"Colonel, a lot of military people come in here. But I never saw one in a uniform like that."

David smiled. "It's called mess dress." He nodded toward me. "The military equivalent of a dinner jacket."

Bill looked at the dark blue jacket and light blue pants with a gold stripe. A design of gold braid was on each sleeve directly over the wrist and atop the braid sat the silver eagles of a full colonel.

"Mind if I ask you a question?"

"Go ahead."

"Your jacket is dark blue and your pants are a light blue. Why aren't they the same color? Army run out of material?"

"Do you recall the old cowboy movies where, when the soldiers headed across the desert, they rolled up their jackets and tied them behind their saddles?"

"Yeah, John Wayne was in a dozen of them. Loved those movies. Still watch them."

"Back then the pants and jacket were the same dark blue. The pants faded because of constant exposure to the sun. The jacket remained dark because it was rolled up. The military respects tradition."

Bill looked skeptical. "That a true story?"

"Check it out."

"Then why is your lapel still another shade of blue?"

"This shade of blue says I am in the Chemical Corps. There is a very pale blue for infantry and bright red for artillery and gold for armor. Every command has its own color."

I interrupted. "Bill, we came here to drink."

"Okay. Okay. I would ask you about your tux but we get people in here all the time dressed like you. Especially during football games." He laughed.

"We're drinking Macallan tonight," I said. "Bring us two. The eighteen-year-old stuff."

"If that's what you want."

He was back in less than a minute. He placed our drinks on the table. "Enjoy, gentlemen. You need anything, send me a fax."

David and I were quiet as we snipped the heads off the cigars, tilted the cigars downward and held lighted matches under them. Then we puffed slowly, sighed simultaneously and reached for our scotch.

"What were you doing at that shindig tonight?" I asked.

He laughed. "You didn't want to go either?"

"Nope."

"I was representing Fort Gillem. Showing the flag."

I sipped more scotch. "So what kind of a cop are you?"

He puffed his cigar and peered at me through the smoke. "Tell me, C.R., where do you work?"

"Homicide."

"I thought so."

"Do I have a sign on my head?"

"You walk like you own Atlanta. Only homicide cops do that."

"I'll have to be more careful."

"I like your cigars."

"So do I."

"I run the lab."

"What lab?"

"The CID lab at Fort Gillem." He sipped his scotch. "Only one of its kind in the world."

"CID?"

"Actually, it is the Criminal Investigation Command. Used to be known as the Criminal Investigation Division. We kept CID when we became a command." He smiled. "We can't call it CIC because it would be pronounced 'sissy' and our investigators would be called 'sissy investigators.' CID had a better ring to it. We service not only the Army but all the other branches of the military all over the world."

"What sort of lab?"

"You ever been in the FBI lab in Washington?"

"On a tour."

"Like that. Except their lab is designed to handle tours; viewing windows every few feet. Ours is a working lab. It is accredited, too. Unlike the FBI lab."

"What do you do there?"

"With the exception of toxicology, we cover every discipline you ever heard of and a few you might not have. State-of-the-art equipment. In fact, the only other place in America you will find some of the equipment we have is with the Secret Service. A questioned documents section, firearms and tool marks, latent prints, forensic imaging, drug chemistry, serology and DNA, trace evidence."

He was beginning to get my interest. "Who works there?"

"Senior warrant officers, retired warrant officers, and Department of the Army civilians. They have seen and done it all. Nothing gets by them. The best lab people in the world; bar none."

"You told Bill you are in the Chemical Corps. You a chemist?"

"A masters degree from M.I.T. says so."

My eyes widened. "Tell me about your lab capabilities. Give me some details."

He puffed on his cigar and casually looked around. Except for a few glances at our evening clothes, no one was paying us any attention.

David leaned closer.

An hour later I nodded and said, "I've got a case you can help me with."

"Does it have a green card connection?"

He saw my blank look and smiled in apology. "Someone involved in the case has to have a military I.D. card. There must be a military connection. Without that, we can't do work for a local police agency."

"Why not?"

"A little law called *posse comitatus* that goes back to after the Civil War. Basically it says the military cannot be used in civilian law enforcement."

I told him about Universal and the OSI investigator. I told him that my victim worked on a facility owned by the Air Force. Another victim, thought to have been killed by the same assailant, was killed on that same installation. That case is being investigated by the OSI. I paused. "For the sake of convenience, you might say I'm working with the OSI."

"You don't like the OSI guy?"

"Don't go there."

He studied the growing white ash on his cigar. "The

Air Force." A big sigh. "Too bad my guys are not there." He sipped his scotch, puffed on the cigar and watched the cloud of smoke. After a long moment he spoke again. "Officially, we could not get involved."

I know an opening when I see one. "Officially? But the OSI involvement, the Universal involvement, the defense contract, all this might allow you to become involved . . . unofficially?"

He pulled out a business card, wrote his home number on it and slid it across the table.

"Unofficially, if you were to come down in a liaison capacity, or a training capacity, I think we might help you use the equipment."

"What does that mean?"

"We will show you which buttons to push, what dials to turn, how to interpret the results. That is training, you understand. We could not under any circumstances be connected to your case."

"Could you do it now?"

"We're backed up maybe thirty days. But I could expedite a case involving a multiple homicide." He puffed on his cigar and nodded. "I can do more than expedite it. I can make it a priority case." He leaned across the table. "I can put you at the head of the line."

"You can do that?"

He stuck his cigar between his teeth and grinned. He held up one arm so I could see the silver eagle on his sleeve. "I'm the commander."

I leaned back and took a drink of scotch. "My crime scene is almost a week old."

"Is it secure?"

"Yes."

"At the Presidio in San Francisco we had a homicide. We went over it. The San Francisco PD and the FBI went over it. We knew who did it but we couldn't find enough physical evidence for an arrest. Eight years later we got some new technology and went back to the crime scene. We lifted a footprint and a fingerprint. The individual whom we had suspected from the beginning was arrested, charged, convicted, and will spend the remainder of his life in a military installation in Kansas; a little place known as Fort Leavenworth."

"You lifted prints after eight years?"

He nodded. "If there are latent prints, trace evidence, any evidence, at your crime scene, we have the technology and the equipment to find it."

My world was looking better. I had not wanted to go to the chamber of commerce banquet. But while there I met the man who had the horses to rescue my case. It came along when I needed it most. I'm always surprised when this happens; not *that* it happens but *when* it happens. Such things have come into my experience in the past. When you are one of God's foot soldiers, these things come about. And always at a time and a place when they are least expected.

I took another sip of scotch, looked at David and grinned.

He lifted his eyebrows. "Yes?"

"I think we have set up what white folk would call an old boy network."

He laughed. We clicked our glasses together. I held up a forefinger. "Now that business is out of the way, can we talk about something else?"

He shrugged.

"Let's talk about my man; His Skipness."

22

I did not know when I awakened Friday morning that I was entering the weekend from hell.

My plan was simple. First, I was going to Georgia Tech and shake the tree and see if Andy Fung fell out. Then I was calling the Chinese embassy in New York to do the same. I still had the gut feeling that once I opened the box with Andy Fung's name on it, things were going to come flying out that would be difficult to control; the "secondary explosions" Chuck Spinney warned me about. While the smoke was settling from these secondary explosions, I was going to call David Drumwright down at Fort Gillem to find out what his lab wizards could do for me.

That was my plan.

I called Georgia Tech. One of the secrets of life is to call early. If you have to do business on the telephone, don't wait until 10:00 A.M. when the morning has gone berserk and a caffeine-wired secretary is anxious to make you her next victim. And don't call in mid-afternoon when everyone is sleeping off a few adult beverages and the secretary is anxious to give you names of all the people—other than the one you are trying to reach—who can help you. Nope. Call at 6:30 or 7:00 A.M. and oftentimes the person you want will answer the phone.

It worked. At 7:00 A.M. I called the Georgia Tech alumni office and Elmo Clinton, the director, picked up the phone. I got the idea he spent his day in a small office surrounded by an army of assistants. I could tell by his voice he was an older guy and guessed that he was beginning to feel as if everything was passing him by; that it was not long before he would be spit out of the system.

I gave him Andy Fung's name.

"I remember a lot of names but that one doesn't ring a bell. I'll call the registrar. They have those records. When did he graduate?"

"I'm not sure, Mr. Clinton. Within the last ten years."

"Hold on a moment."

"Thank you, sir. It's good of you to do this."

He paused. "You sound like a nice young man. I bet your daddy is proud of you." He put me on hold.

My daddy? Proud of me? Not likely. I closed my eyes. My daddy never once told me he was proud. The only thing I heard from him when I was growing up was "You a sorry nigger, just a sorry nigger. And you ain't never gonna amount to a hill of beans. You gonna be just like your two brothers and wind up in Reidsville."

Reidsville is where Georgia's best-known maximum security prison is located. It is also where my two big brothers are located. Yeah, I got two older brothers doing life; one for armed robbery, one for rape. My family believes in diversity.

Until the day he died, which was only a few years ago, every time I went home to Albany I heard the same thing from my daddy. He never acknowledged my achievements as a cop or that I had become a homicide detective. He would look at me, snort and shake his head. "You just like your brothers. All my sons came from their mother's side of the family, not mine. It's just a matter of time. You got on that fancy suit of clothes and you went to that fancy school up in Atlanta but you still a south Georgia nigger and don't you ever forget it."

I wanted to say, "Daddy, I don't think that's possible."

He's dead now, but I still hear his voice. Maybe we never outgrow our childhoods.

"You hear what I said?"

I opened my eyes. "Sorry, Mr. Clinton. I was distracted."

"Well, here it is." I heard him take a sip of coffee. "Coffee's getting cold. We have had three Andy Fungs graduate from Georgia Tech in the last fifteen years." He paused. "I went back an extra five years just to make sure."

"Thanks, sir."

Three Andy Fungs?

"Hmmmmmm."

"What is it?"

"So many Asians the last ten or fifteen years. I knew we had a large enrollment, but I didn't realize how many. Judging by the records, many of them were graduated with honors."

"Any of the Andy Fungs show Atlanta addresses?"

"No. All three show towns in China as their home addresses. One from Beijing, one from Zhengzhou, and one from Shizhaishan."

"Do you have updates on those addresses? Doesn't the alumni office keep up with graduates?"

God knows the alumni office at Emory keeps track of its graduates. I get stuff in the mail from them about once a month.

"You're absolutely right. And we cross-check the updates with these records. Georgia Tech is among the best in the country at keeping track of alumni; fund-raising, you know. Hold on a moment. Let me check the computer."

"Yes, sir."

It took only a moment. "The records are up-to-date. None of these three graduates show U.S. addresses. All are from China, and according to our records, all returned there and all live there today." He paused. "They are all such intelligent-looking young men."

"Excuse me?"

"I said they all appear to be so very intelligent. But of course they would have to be to have graduated from this institution."

"You have pictures?"

"Yes. Photographs taken when they graduated are in the *Blueprint,* our annual. If they participated in sports, were members of fraternities or were active in campus activities, there are other pictures."

"Could I see those?"

"Yes."

"About an hour?"

"I'll be looking forward to meeting you, Detective." He laughed. "We might put you to work. We are about to begin Roll Call, our big annual fund-raiser. Do you have any experience in raising money?"

"My ex-wife didn't think so."

He laughed. "I don't think I'll pursue that one. See you when you get here."

Before I went to Tech—the North Avenue Trade School we called it when I was at Emory—I rang the Chinese embassy in Washington, where a very pleasant and very sharp young woman took my call. When I told her what I wanted, she said, "Let me refer you to our Mr. Lee."

Something told me our Mr. Lee was not going to be helpful.

"This is Mr. Lee."

"Hello," I said to Mr. Lee, who apparently had no first name or middle initial. "My name is Henry Louis Gates. I'm a professor at the Georgia Institute of Technology here in Atlanta and I'm trying to locate a former student."

"Yes."

"His name is Andy Fung and the last I heard he had gone to work for your government. He's somewhere here in Atlanta and I'd like to get in touch with him."

"Andy Fung?"

"Yes. He works for your government."

"For the Chinese government?"

This conversation seemed to be going in circles. "Yes."

"Where in our government?"

In for a penny, in for a pound. I took a deep breath. "Security. I don't know which branch."

"Security?"

"Yes." No doubt about it. This conversation was going in circles.

"Hold on, please."

It was three or four minutes before our Mr. Lee returned. "What did you say your name was?"

"Henry Louis Gates. I was Andy's . . . calculus instructor when he was here."

"Do you live in Atlanta?"

"Yes."

"Give me your telephone number and I will call you back when we have had time to research your inquiry."

"I don't mind holding."

"It will take a while. Perhaps several days."

"Mr. Lee, I'm going to be away for a few days. When I get back, I'll call you."

"Professor Gates, can we reach you at your Georgia Institute of Technology?"

"Have to run. Someone's at the door. Thanks."

Click.

Sometimes you eat the bear. Sometimes the bear eats you.

Georgia Tech is a few blocks from downtown Atlanta, wedged in between the Downtown Connector and the Coca-Cola building. This is not a part of Atlanta where families walk the streets; that is, unless the Papa Bear is carrying an AK-47. We are talking your basic urban combat zone. The Coca-Cola building is surrounded by a high fence and protected by numerous security guards. Tech has no fence; an oversight that allows rock stars and gang bangers easy access to the campus. As a result, Tech students manifest their high IQs by traveling in groups of three or four.

The Faculty and Alumni building is on North Avenue across from the south end of the stadium at the corner of Fowler Street; a solid brick building of the sort you expect at an engineering school. The entrance is at street level but once inside I had to descend a flight of granite-lined stairs into a large room. Off to the left was Elmo Clinton's office.

He was tall, slightly stooped, and wore a heavily starched white shirt and a tie with little bees—actually they were yellow jackets, Tech's mascot—on it. His smile was so wide that it made crow's feet at the corners of his eyes. His eyes were soft and kind, the eyes of a man at peace with himself. I liked the way he looked me square in the eye and I liked the strength of his handshake.

"Come in, come in, come in," he said. His outer

office had more than a dozen desks. Three were staffed by casually dressed people—two young men and a young woman—and one well-dressed older woman with raven black hair. "During Roll Call we ask students to come in and work the phones at these other desks," he said. "Not all of them are in yet."

He introduced me to the people in the room.

"I've pulled out the pictures and put them on my desk." He turned and motioned over his shoulder. "Come on back to my office."

At the door he pointed to his desk. "Call me if you need anything."

It took only a moment. None of the three young Chinese men named Andy Fung bore the slightest resemblance to my suspect.

Clinton was full of condolences. "Sorry we weren't able to help you." He paused. "You obviously know who you're looking for, so you are certain the young man is Chinese?"

"Yes."

Suddenly I had a thought. I remembered something from the chamber of commerce dinner; something the Chinese man at the table said.

Clinton opened the door leading into the hall. "And you are certain he attended Georgia Tech?"

I nodded, still wrestling with the idea that hit me. "Yes."

Clinton scratched his neck as we walked toward the stairs. "Then I don't know what I can do for you."

"I do."

He stopped. "What's that?"

"Let me borrow your phone book."

23

From Tech it was only a few short blocks downtown to Peachtree Center. I parked on International Boulevard—where that name came from, I don't know—crossed the street and walked through International Courtyard—there's that name again—into Harris Tower. I walked slowly when I was not in an air-conditioned space. It was too hot and humid to do otherwise. What will Atlanta weather be like in August and September if it is this oppressive in June?

The office I wanted was a small suite on the second floor of Harris Tower; the Taipei Economic and Cultural Office, the Republic of China's outpost in Atlanta.

America has had no diplomatic relations with Taiwan since 1979. We severed the relationship to please the People's Republic of China. The staff here is somewhat similar to a consular office except that no one has diplomatic status. Calling it the Economic and Cultural Affairs Office is a little side step, a way of getting around the fact China strenuously objects to the ROCs having diplomatic relations with America.

The little bit I have learned about China—the PRC—makes me wonder why we cozied up to them in the first place. But I am a homicide cop. What do I know about the subtleties of international relations?

At Georgia Tech a few minutes ago, out of nowhere, I remembered the Chinese man's phraseology
about Taiwan and I recalled the adage that the enemy
of my enemy is my friend. Taiwan has more to lose
than anyone else if China buys F-22s and a technology
exchange that enhances its ability to produce nuclear-
capable rockets. The first mission for those F-22s and
the target for the rockets very likely could be the short
distance across the Formosa Strait to Taiwan.

I could be wrong, but I figure that even if it's called
the Taipei Economic and Cultural Office, it is as much
a part of Taiwan's government as would be a consulate. No matter what their titles, the people who work
here, though they would vigorously deny it, probably
perform the same duties as would people in a consulate. And the fact the staff is so small means only that
the greatest and most pressing interests of the Taiwan
government are represented. National security has to
be at the top of the list. Which means that someone
who works in that innocent-sounding Economic and
Cultural Office is an intelligence officer.

Hey, let me tell you something. I may be up against
Universal and the State Department and the Justice
Department and China and whoever else you want to
throw in, but detective work is detective work.

They had been wary when I called from Tech and
now, when I walked into the office, the entire staff
was staring. They knew I was the cop who had called
and insisted on seeing the head man, the director.

A rear door opened and a man walked into the
room and looked at me without speaking. He was tall
for a Chinese. I'm five-eleven and our eyes were level,
though he was probably forty pounds lighter. Guy
needs to eat more than rice; put some meat on his
ass. His modest suit could not hide his squared shoul-

ders and command presence. His eyes were locked on mine as he stuck out his hand. He wore a jade ring.

"I am Sun Ming, the director of this office."

"Detective C.R. Payne; city of Atlanta." I flashed my tin but he hardly noticed.

He gave an almost imperceptible nod, said, "Please follow me" and turned and walked toward the rear of the office. The eyes of the five people in the front office all were lowered.

In his office, a slender man of perhaps thirty-five was waiting, standing in the corner, eyes never leaving me.

"My associate," Sun Ming said with a casual wave toward the man in the corner. That was the extent of the introduction. The associate made no movement to shake hands. He didn't nod. He didn't even smile. The guy was part of the furniture.

"Your phone call indicated you had an important matter you wished to discuss."

"Yes, sir. Thank you for seeing me on such short notice."

"We are always glad to talk with law enforcement officials of our host city. I trust none of our people are in any sort of trouble." He smiled thinly, as if the very idea was ludicrous. He sat in a chair in front of his desk and motioned for me to sit in a facing chair.

"No, sir. Not at all. In fact, I am here to seek your help."

"Yes?"

I explained about the homicide and told him about Universal and the F-22 contract and the side agreement. Then I told him about Andy Fung. I told him things about an ongoing case that ordinarily I would not discuss with a civilian, but I wanted him to have the incentive to talk with me. I wanted to establish a bond, a professional liaison. The cop-to-cop network is one of the most powerful in the world. It ignores politics. Cops are brothers, whether they be in Atlanta or Taipei.

When I started talking about the side agreement and the capabilities of the equipment the PRC wanted, the guy in the corner became a bit restless.

Suddenly I had that gut feeling again.

When I finished, Sun Ming stared at me and folded his hands in his lap. After a moment he spoke softly.

He looked up and to his left. "Would you please describe this person whom you call Andy Fung."

I did.

His expression did not change.

"And you believe his name to be Andy Fung?"

"Yes."

I should have paid more attention to his language. But I was too focused on something else. "Sir, forgive me, but I have the feeling that you already know about the contract and the side agreement."

"That is your feeling?"

"It is."

He stared. "You said you wanted my help. What can I do?"

This guy was tough.

"This is a bit awkward. But since yours is not a diplomatic office and I am not here officially, perhaps you will forgive me if I get straight to the point?"

"You are an American." He smiled.

"Are you a soldier?"

That got a flicker of emotion. "I beg your pardon."

"You look like a soldier."

"Is that why you are here?"

"No."

He smiled. "I am the director of what is essentially a public relations office. My associate here is a senior press officer. The official purpose of this office is to engender in your country a good feeling about my country."

Again, he sent me a signal that only later, in the light of what happened, I could look back on and recognize.

"I must find Andy Fung. That is proving very difficult. I'm wondering, since he represents the PRC on business that is not in your country's best interest, could you offer any advice? Unofficially, of course, and in strictest confidence."

After an eternity, in a very soft voice, he said, "No."

"Do you want the most advanced fighter aircraft in the world and nuclear-capable rockets pointed at your country?"

"No country wants such a thing."

"All I'm interested in is locating him. I want to arrest him on homicide charges. I have no authority in the matter with Universal."

He stared at me, weighing me. "Is it your understanding this other matter is about to be consummated?"

"A few days at most."

"And the side agreement?"

"They are joined at the hip."

Again, the guy in the corner seemed restless. Without looking in his direction, Sun Ming said, "He means the two cannot be separated; if the F-twenty-two contract is signed, the side agreement will be an integral part." He smiled. "Your colloquialisms are many."

I nodded.

Sun Ming stood up. "As I said, ours is an economic and cultural office. I regret that I cannot help you."

"We have mutual interests."

"You said the contract is about to be approved. If that is true, how can his arrest benefit my country?"

"We can take him off the street. He could be a source of intelligence. Help me now and I will see that you are made privy to whatever he says that is relevant to your country."

"This is a local law enforcement matter. Something that, even if we were in a position to help you, we could not. It would be interfering in the local affairs of a host government."

"You have more to lose than I do."

"And less authority." He nodded toward the door. "It was a pleasure to meet you and I hope you will say favorable things about my country to your friends here in America. We hope someday to again have diplomatic relations with your country."

Going down the elevator I realized the bear had eaten me again.

I had to make several quick stops on Buford Highway before I returned to Universal. I pulled into Asian Plaza up near the top end of Buford. In the first store I bought a doll, a small, multicultural sort of doll; an Asian boy. I bought an outfit for the doll, a one-piece thing that zipped up the back, but from the front looked like a suit and white shirt and tie. It fit the doll perfectly. This would go in my office at Homicide. If all went well, I would have a use for it.

My next stop was in a small but elegant little shop near the rear of the mall.

For several days, ever since I read about jade on the Web, I've been thinking about this.

I had several choices, choices in style such as medallions to be worn around the neck, or the little round medallions attached to silk tassels that are carried in the pocket. But I knew exactly what I wanted. When I left the store, I was wearing a simple jade ring set in a plain gold band. Green jade and soft yellow gold against my skin; a great color combination.

It is almost impossible for Americans to understand how important jade is in China and in the Chinese experience. We think of the Chinese predilection for things jade, if we think of it at all, as a quaint affectation. But jade occupies an almost religious significance in the mind of the Chinese.

Marvelous protective powers are ascribed to jade. There are numerous stories of people wearing jade who are protected from all forms and manifestations of evil and sickness.

Do I believe all of that?

I have my skepticism.

Do I think jade has protective powers; that it enhances one's senses, that it brings serenity and good luck into one's life?

I'm wearing it.

24

I called Pinstripe from my cell phone and told him I needed ten minutes. He didn't like my coming on such short notice but he had agreed to see me and figured he might as well get it over with.

"All right," he said. "Come on out. You can sit in on the press conference we're having."

He hung up before I could ask why Universal was having a press conference and why I would want to sit down with media slimes.

Twenty minutes later I was in the Universal parking lot along with a host of TV satellite trucks, radio trucks and several cars from *The Atlanta Constitution*. Amazing how when Universal calls a press conference, everyone comes.

A security guard escorted me to mahogany row. Pinstripe kept me waiting fifteen minutes; he was playing mine-is-bigger-than-yours.

Pinstripe's outer office was different from that of J. Stanford; it was a cubicle farm with four secretaries, each of whom stuck her head up when I opened the door. I introduced myself to one, who motioned for me to sit down. The four women were like a colony of prairie dogs, their heads occasionally popping up over the top of the cubicles to look around.

A phone rang and a moment later one of the secretaries prairie-dogged up to say, "You can go in now."

She sat down quickly. I knew from her manner that Pinstripe had not spoken highly of me; nor had he conveyed any great interest in my visit. She felt it was okay for her behavior to approach rudeness.

I knocked on Pinstripe's door.

"Come."

He was behind a desk big enough to land airplanes on. He did not stand up. He motioned for me to have a seat in one of the leather chairs in front of his desk. I looked around. "No FBI agents? When I talked to Mr. Godbey, FBI agents were there."

He leaned back. "I don't need FBI agents."

"I forgot my manners, Mr. Vandiver. Thank you for seeing me on such short notice." I reached across his desk to shake his hand. He ignored my hand but he did stare for a moment at my jade ring before he motioned again for me to sit down.

He tossed his head to the side. "Let's get something straight at the beginning, Officer—"

"It's detective."

"Yes, well, Detective. Let's get something straight. This is my office. I will sit at my desk and you will sit in that chair. You will stay in that chair. If at any time you exhibit any of the behavior you did when I was at your office, I will call a Universal lawyer as well as my personal attorney. If there is a subsequent interview, which, by the way, I shall resist by all available means, it will be scheduled at the convenience of both lawyers and will be in one of their offices. I will smoke as often as I like and if I need to go to the bathroom or to adjust the thermostat I will do so. Do I make myself clear?"

He tossed his head again.

"Yes, sir."

"Proceed."

Sometimes I am amazed that my professional role

models are people such as Pinstripe. He puts up one hell of an appearance. But now that I know he has the personal morality of a ferret in heat, I am not so impressed. Skip Gates is a far better model. His Skipness is a beacon of intellect, is on track, focused and, so far as I know, keeps his pants zipped.

I was wrong in the way I interviewed Pinstripe when I had him in the Box. The techniques I used, while effective, are outdated and left Pinstripe embarrassed and defensive. I let my anger get in the way of my judgment.

Even so, when I think of him puking into the wastebasket it makes me feel good.

I looked around his office. Cherry bookcases containing models of every aircraft Universal built. Furniture of soft leather. Deep wool carpet. "Mr. Vandiver, you have one of the nicest offices I've ever seen. I can understand why you would rather talk to me here than in my office downtown."

I had to roll over and show him my tummy, let him see I was no threat. Hell, all I wanted to do was put him in Reidsville for the rest of his life. I had enough information now that I could begin asking direct, specific questions.

He looked at his watch. "Are you here to admire my office?"

I looked at the wastebasket at the corner of his desk. Varnished wood, looked like maple, with a plastic liner. Wonder if he's ever puked in it.

"Big waste can."

There I go again.

His face flushed and he leaned toward me. He lit a cigarette and blew the smoke toward me. "If you have nothing to ask me about . . ."

"Sorry, Mr. Vandiver. I'm here to talk about Richard Morris."

"I'm told you're making little progress on that matter. Too bad. Richard Morris was one of this company's brightest young executives. He had a great future here. My relationship with him was close."

"Did his change of heart about the Chinese contract jeopardize that relationship?"

He tossed his head. Then he puffed on his cigarette and studied the smoke as he expelled it from his lungs. "Officer . . . Detective, I don't know where you get your information. I have to be very careful what I say, because some aspects of that contract involve national security issues. But I can say to you that to the best of my knowledge, Morris had no change of heart. He was responsible for that contract. That contract was about to bring him the largest bonus any executive at that level has ever received in this company. He was about to be promoted. He was about to be given a substantial increase in salary. He was being groomed for upper management." Pinstripe leaned across the desk, hands spread wide. "What is there in all of that to indicate he had a change of heart?"

"Perhaps I was wrong. After all, you knew him well."

"Very well indeed. My wife and I . . ." He glared at me as if daring me to say anything about his family status. "My wife and I have been to dinner in his home. We knew his family. He had no change of heart about that contract."

"He wanted to press on with the contract even though the Pentagon opposed it?"

Pinstripe made a grimace of distaste. He leaned back in his chair and flung his arms wide in exasperation. "The Pentagon did not oppose the contract. Why would the Pentagon oppose it? China is potentially our biggest trading partner." He paused. "Which reminds me. I saw you walk out of the chamber banquet

the other night in the middle of the senator's speech."
He shook his head as if in disbelief.

When you interview someone, you have to understand how they are wired. Pinstripe is missing part of
his wiring. The component that contains morality and
ethics was not installed. This makes it easy for him to
lie. He lies with the ease of a prisoner who's been in
jail twenty years. It's natural. But the signs are there;
mostly in how he throws his head around. Gestures
above the neck or below the waist are largely unconscious. And most people have a default gesture they
go to under stress or when they are being deceptive.
With Pinstripe it is how he tosses around that impressive head of gray-tinged hair.

"Did his job, his position as point man in the contract with China, put him in a vulnerable position?
With anyone?"

"On the contrary. It put him in a position of power
within this company."

"Who do you think had reason to kill him?"

"My God, he was found in a cheap motel on Buford
Highway. I wouldn't say anything like this around his
wife, but you have to ask yourself what the hell he
was doing over there. He had gotten so wrapped up
in everything Chinese that he probably was looking
for a Chinese woman. I don't know. Anyone on Buford Highway, I suppose."

He looked away, staring at the wall.

See what I mean about missing a component? This
man, with his record, is accusing Morris of looking for
a Chinese woman.

"You think he was doing business with a Chinese
prostitute and was murdered?"

"He made a good salary."

I didn't mention that Morris's wallet contained several hundred dollars, that nothing had been taken, or

about the jade pieces. I figured the feeb and the dweeb
had passed along everything I sent them. But Pinstripe
was giving no indication he had read my reports.

I nodded as if I agreed. "It's happened before."

Pinstripe spun in his chair and faced me. "Tell me
this, Payne. Was there anything there that night to
lead you to think it was anything other than robbery?"

I wasn't touching that one. And I wasn't going to
allow him to turn this around and ask me questions.
"You don't think his death had anything to do with
his work?"

"No. I know what Stan Godbey told you about that,
but I disagree. I think it was robbery, plain and
simple."

"He have any enemies that you know of?"

Pinstripe laughed. "He had no enemies here." He
paused, took a final puff of his cigarette and ground
out the butt in a crystal ashtray.

I wonder if he knew how he emphasized the word
"here."

He studied me as he blew smoke toward the ceiling.
"Let's be frank, shall we. I know what you think of
me. You made that abundantly clear. But I'm telling
you Richard Morris was as close to being universally
liked as anyone I've ever known."

"So you are convinced it was a random thing connected with whatever he was doing on Buford
Highway?"

"I don't know how random it was. But I think he
was looking for a woman and was killed. That composite picture you released to the media. Was that guy a
pimp? He looked like a pimp to me. Who is he, by
the way?"

I sighed and stood up. "We're not sure."

He smiled up at me. When he spoke, he made no
effort to hide the glee in his voice. "You're not mak-

ing any progress at all, are you? You have absolutely
no idea who killed Richard Morris. You don't know
if it was that guy whose picture you released or someone else?"

"The investigation is continuing, Mr. Vandiver. I
know you are busy. But I hope that if I need to, I can
talk with you again."

He waved a hand in dismissal as I walked toward
the door. He liked the way this interview went. He
felt more in charge. "Of course. This company wants
to find out who killed Morris. In fact, I've discussed
this with Stan Godbey and Universal is going to offer
a fifty-thousand-dollar reward." He looked at his
watch. "Stan is announcing that to the press in about
ten minutes." He smiled. "We want to help you,
Payne. Maybe this will flush out your murderer from
Buford Highway. And that, by the way, is where you
should be instead of here at Universal. Your man is
on Buford Highway."

"I'll keep that in mind."

At the door I turned around. "How well do you
know Andy Fung?"

His head dropped and he tucked his chin in as if to
protect his throat. Even from across the room I could
see his pupils contract. Whatever was about to come
out of his mouth would be a lie. He stood up, half-
crouched behind his desk. "Andy Fung? Who is he?"

"I just wondered if you know him."

"Is he the person whose composite was in the
paper?"

"Thanks, Mr. Vandiver."

I shut the door.

The secretaries were prairie-dogging as I walked
out.

I wondered if being a pathological liar is a prerequi-
site to being a Universal executive.

*   *   *

Kitty was leaning against the door of my Explorer when I walked out of the guard shack. "You must be here for the press conference. You better hurry. You'll be late."

"You've been holding out on me," she said.

"Oh."

"You were in black tie the other night at the chamber of commerce dinner?"

I motioned for her to move away from my door. She had sources all over town. I guessed one of the uniforms pulling a second job at the hotel that night had told her.

"Yes, I was."

"Homicide detectives don't usually go to the chamber of commerce annual banquet."

"You're right." I opened the door and pressed the button to roll down the windows. It was hot.

"What were you doing there?"

"Kitty, I don't report to you. I report to a major in the Atlanta Police Department."

"Come on, Payne. Tell me what's going on. You went over to Manuel's with an Army colonel that night. What was that about?"

I shrugged. I did not want her calling David Drumwright. I leaned inside, turned on the ignition, then switched on the air conditioner and turned the fan on high. "He is a friend. Don't you have more to do than waiting for me out here in the heat?"

"You were talking to Ray Vandiver, weren't you? How is he connected to the homicide? You can tell me. I need it for background so when the story breaks I can do it right."

I took off my jacket and climbed inside the Explorer. I closed the door.

Kitty leaned against the door. "Come on, Payne.

We're friends. I need this. I can do a story, you know. I can say you were at the chamber dinner listening to Sam Perry talk about China and . . ." Suddenly it registered. "China? You mentioned China several times when you were talking with Chuck Spinney." She stared as all the possibilities boiled in her brain. "Tell me what's going on, Payne. I'll sit on it. I swear by the balls of John the Baptist."

I laughed and reached up to slide the gear selector into Drive. She saw my ring.

"That's jade. It's new. Why are you wearing a jade ring?"

I slowly began to move forward. She followed, holding onto the door. "It wards off evil spirits."

She released the door and stopped.

"I'll find out, you know. I'll find out."

I smiled and waved and then raised the window.

She probably would.

25

She could barely control her voice.

"Something has happened. You must come now. Right now."

I looked at my watch. It was 7:10 A.M. Saturday.

"What is it, Mrs. Morris? Are you okay?"

"*I'm* okay."

"Are your boys okay?"

"Yes. Please come now. I'll explain when you get here."

"Fifteen minutes."

"Thank you."

She was standing in her front yard, right arm clasped around herself, left hand over her mouth, her body twisting back and forth.

I jumped out of the Explorer and ran up the walkway. Her eyes were stricken. She didn't say anything. She pointed toward the flower bed at the front of the house.

Many of the flowers had been pulled up and tossed aside, leaving a bare patch of ground. What appeared to be a small crumpled pile of hair lay there. Beside the hair the dirt was dark and wet. Etched into the dirt was a drawing.

I walked closer. There was something vaguely famil-iar about the pile of hair. It was black and brown and . . . I turned to her.

"Is that . . . ?"

She bit her lips and nodded rapidly. "It's Annie. My God. I came out to get the paper and I find . . ." She turned away. "My dog. What's left of her."

I leaned closer. The dog had been skinned. Only the hair was here. I looked around. "Is there . . . ?"

She shook her head, keeping her eyes averted. "No. Look at the drawing."

It was a bird. It resembled a fighting rooster. Even as a simple line drawing in the wet dirt there was a tenseness and aggressive energy about the bird. One foot was in the air and its head was drawn back as if its curved beak was about to strike. The tail was long and looped back over the top of its head and was far out of proportion to the body. The bird was angry and dominating. I remembered it from my computer research about jade.

"What is it?" she said, horror in her voice.

"In Chinese mythology it is the red bird. The phoenix. It symbolizes the south, a direction honored by the ancient Chinese. It is a bird of prey, the ultimate raptor."

She turned.

We stared at each other.

I broke the silence.

"Mrs. Morris, I'll have this moved. But first . . ."

"No. That is . . . that was my dog. Annie will be buried here. In the backyard."

"All right. I have to have this photographed. I'll call our tech people and have them come out. They will put the remains in a box for you. I'll dig the grave if you show me where you want it."

"No. Thank you. That is something my sons will do." She turned away again and shook her head. She wiped her eyes. "Not now. Not now. Not so soon after Richie."

There was nothing I could say.

Then the front door was flung open and one of her sons, the older one, was there.

"Richard, I asked you to stay inside. You close that door this instant and look after your younger brother."

"Mom."

"Please. Do as I ask."

"Mom. It's the phone. They want to talk to you."

"Ask them to call back."

"I did. He said it was important. He wants to talk to you."

"Who is it?"

"I don't know. He sounds funny."

"What do you mean?"

"His accent."

"What?"

I interrupted. "Mrs. Morris. Perhaps you should take it."

She looked at me, confusion on her face. Then it registered.

"I'll come with you," I said.

She nodded. "Richard, please go back inside. I'll be right there."

As I walked with her toward the door, I made a quick call on my cell phone and got things started from my office.

A moment later she was in the kitchen, leaning into the phone, her body tense, eyes narrowed in concentration. "I'm sorry, I don't understand."

She shook her head in bewilderment. "A special? Your restaurant is having a special? Perhaps some other time."

She pulled the phone away from her ear and I heard the voice of the caller raised in anxiety. "No, no, no.

He say call you for special. One day only." It sounded like an old man.

She pulled the phone closer. "Who said for you to call?"

She listened. "I don't know who . . . I don't understand."

Then her eyes widened in horror and she dropped the phone, stood up and rushed from the room, hands over her mouth, retching.

I picked up the phone. "Who is this?"

"This Saigon Joe's Restaurant on Buford Highway. Special today. One day only."

"Not interested."

"Dog, mister. Today, dog."

26

The Vietnamese guy was about fifty and looked as if he had worked eighteen hours a day every day of his life. Short, skinny, rumpled old clothes. He was not very helpful. He showed me the carcass of a dog hanging from a hook in the kitchen. A small dog. Said a man brought it to him early this morning; the man was waiting when the restaurant opened and gave it to him and told him to call Mrs. Morris later. The man said she would like to know that dog was on the menu.

That was all he knew.

I pulled the composite of Andy Fung from my pocket, opened it and showed it to him. "Is this the man?"

He looked at the picture then looked at the ceiling and backed up two steps. I reached out and pulled him closer.

"No." He was nodding his head up and down.

"You know this man. Who is he?"

He shrugged.

I looked around the restaurant. "I can have the county health department here in about an hour to give you an inspection you'll never pass. They will close you down."

"No. I work hard long time."

I don't like to lean on people. Especially old guys like this. But he was lying to me about not knowing Andy Fung. And the son of a bitch was selling dog meat in his restaurant. You can't do that, even on Buford Highway.

"I'll have you deported to Ho Chi Minh City. You can eat dog there every day."

He shrugged and looked away. He was more afraid of Andy Fung than he was of being closed down. Whoever Andy Fung was, he had a lot of juice in the Asian community. Mr. Hot Wok here would tell me nothing.

I clapped him on the shoulder and smiled. "Okay, my friend. I understand. No problem. No health department. No deporting. But I want you to do something for me."

He was nodding and smiling. "Yes? Yes?"

"Take the dog off the menu."

"No dog?"

"No dog."

He shrugged. As soon as I left, he would put Annie back on the menu.

"If you ever need anything, you let me know." I gave him a card.

He stared up at me. "You no close me?"

"No."

He studied the card. He looked around. We were in the restaurant alone. Even so, he locked the front door. He tapped me on the breast pocket.

"Picture."

"You want to see the picture again?"

He nodded.

I opened the composite.

He looked around the empty restaurant, stepped closer and almost reluctantly pointed at Andy Fung. *"Tai zi dang,"* he whispered.

"*Tai* what?"

He tapped the picture and looked up at me. *"Tai zi dang."*

That was all he would say. I asked him how to spell the words, and wrote them down in my notebook. I looked at him.

"One more thing. I have to take the dog."

His eyes were big as saucers and he was all innocence. "You want dog?"

"Yes. Wrap it up in . . . Do you have heavy brown paper?"

He nodded.

"Good. Wrap it in heavy brown paper then put it in a plastic bag. Can you do that?"

He nodded and smiled. "You want takeout."

27

The tech people were through by the time I returned. Annie's remains, both sets, were put into a box. Mrs. Morris had a long talk with her two boys then gave them the box and suggested the three of them go to the backyard, where the boys would dig a grave.

"Mom, we will do it by ourselves," Richard said. "David and I will do it. You stay here."

She looked at him for a long moment, realizing his need to be the man of the house. "Call me when you've finished so I can say a few words about Annie. Then we will bury her."

Richard nodded and walked away carrying the box. David hung back.

"What is it, son?"

He looked at the ground. "Mom, we've been to a lot of funerals."

She bit her lips and kneeled down and put her arms around David and pulled him close.

"We will be okay. The three of us will be okay."

He nodded and walked away, his head still down.

"I'll be there soon."

She looked at me. "I forgot to turn on the security lights last night."

I didn't say anything.

"This was a warning." Her voice was flat. "Just as his following me after the funeral was a warning."

I nodded. Not many people realize the significance police put on crimes involving animals. If a person threatens to kill his neighbor's dog, we send the SWAT team to deal with the person. If a person threatens to kill a dog, he will threaten to kill a person. And if he does kill a dog, he might kill a person. She was right. This was a warning.

But one thing bothered me. Andy Fung wasn't the sort to give warnings.

"He knows I talked to you." Her voice turned harsh. "I am no longer part of the Universal team." She spat out the word "team."

Again, I did not respond.

"Tell me more about the red bird," she said.

"Books have been written about the red bird. It is very significant in Chinese mythology. It symbolizes aggression and power. It prevails over all; it is the ultimate raptor."

"Is it identified in Chinese as a raptor or is that how it is translated?"

"In the little research I have done, it was translated using that word."

She looked away and sighed. "I'll never be able to work in that flower bed again."

"Maybe, as time goes on . . ."

"What is he doing?"

"Who?"

"Andy Fung. Why is he doing this to me? Is he going to kill me?"

I took a deep breath. "He is creating chaos. Out of chaos comes order. Fundamental to Chinese thought is the idea that order can come only from chaos."

"I asked you a question. Is he going to kill me?"

My conversation with Elmo Clinton suddenly began replaying in my mind. It was urgent that I see him.

"No, Mrs. Morris, he is not going to kill you. I'm

having a twenty-four-hour guard placed on your house."

She shook her head. "No. No, you're not. I won't live that way, Detective Payne. You have to find Andy Fung and bring a stop to all this. That is your job."

"It is. And I will. But until I do, do you have a gun?"

"Yes. And I know how to use it."

"I have to go now. I want you to remember your security lights tonight."

She nodded.

As I turned toward the driveway, I saw the dark red spot where Annie's skin had been found. If it didn't rain today, perhaps the sun would dry the ground. But it would be a long time before flowers again bloomed on that spot.

I got in my Explorer and headed downtown.

Then I picked up my radio and called the major. Like it or not, Mrs. Morris was going to have police protection.

28

I tracked Clinton down at home and asked him if I could meet him at his office. He laughed, that great booming laugh of his, and said, "We're getting ready for Roll Call and I was coming down later to work a few hours." He laughed again. "More than twenty-five thousand alumni, faculty, students and parents participate in this thing. It's the one time of the year when I have more people working for me than does anyone else on campus. I'm a big wheel." He lowered his voice. "All this rain we've been having has made the weeds grow. My wife has got this big wheel working in the yard. You are giving me a good excuse to leave."

He didn't ask what I wanted, just said, "Give me about forty-five minutes then come on down. Always glad to see you."

I grabbed a quick lunch at the Varsity, the fast-food emporium across the expressway from Tech and the place where generations of Tech students have discovered the haute cuisine of glorified steaks, dressed dogs, Varsity oranges and peach pies. If you like fat and cholesterol, this is the place to go. If you believe that eating healthy is bad, come to the Varsity. An occasional visit here keeps you in tune with the celestial verities. Curb service is part of the Varsity experience so I sat in my Explorer and looked at the menu painted on a big board hanging in front of me. I wasn't in the mood for a dressed dog or a naked steak, so I got a couple of pimento cheese sandwiches on wheat and an old-fashioned chocolate milk shake; one made with ice cream.

You think all milk shakes are made with ice cream? Wrong. About six months ago a group of us were having that discussion so we took milk shakes from five different fast-food restaurants to the Georgia Bureau of Investigation crime lab and had them analyzed. You know what one of the main ingredients was? Kaolin. That's right. Clay. The white stuff dug out of the ground down in central Georgia. Thick, slimy, gooey dirt. They put it in milk shakes to give it body and to impart that slick taste that ice cream has. Let me tell you something. You want a real milk shake made with ice cream that is about twenty percent butter fat, you come to the Varsity. And if you ask them, they will give it only a short twirl in the blender, leaving it with big lumps of ice cream and so thick you have to eat it with a spoon. That's the way a milk shake should be made.

From the Varsity it was a one-minute drive up North Avenue to Clinton's office.

I believe Richard Morris was telling the truth when he told his wife that Andy Fung had gone to Georgia Tech. From what I've learned about Morris, he wasn't the sort of man who would lie about anything, much less something so trivial. No, when he told her that, he believed it. For him, it was true. Therefore, either he was wrong in his belief or I have been overlooking something. He was an engineer, very detail 'oriented and methodical, so I don't think he was wrong. I think I know what I overlooked. That's why I'm returning to Tech.

I banged on the upstairs door.

"Hello, young man. Good to see you again," Mr. Clinton said when he came to the outer office. He had the warm smile that some older men, if they are lucky, manage to have. A no-regrets-about-life sort of smile. "How can I help you today?"

I looked around at the empty office.

"The staff is coming in later."

"Can we go back to your office?"

"Sure can."

We sat in two chairs in front of his desk. He looked at me, eyebrows raised. "Yes, sir?"

"Mr. Clinton, you said a couple of things the other day that took a while to register."

He gave me a lazy smile. "Most of what I say never registers. Especially at home."

"You said a lot of Asians went to Tech."

He turned serious. "A bigger and bigger percentage every year. I asked several of our Asian students about that. Several work in here part-time. You know what they told me?"

"No, sir."

"Very interesting. They said Asian students in America almost always study medicine or dentistry or engineering; they're usually somewhere in the sciences. The reasoning is simple: immediate hires upon graduation and guaranteed levels of income. Look around. Almost never will you find an Asian student majoring in history or English or wanting to be a writer or teacher. The rewards are too iffy and take too long. Asians, whether they stay here in America or go back home, want a job and they want money." He nodded. "A degree from Georgia Tech guarantees both. Pretty practical, huh? These kids know what they want. Very focused. Extremely goal-oriented. Not like American students."

I nodded. "I believe you said students are photographed for the annual when they graduate."

"Yes."

"Is that mandatory?"

"No. We want a photographic record of our students but we can't force them to have a picture made. If they elect not to, for whatever reason, we simply list their names in the *Blueprint*."

I nodded. "What I would like to do is look at the class graduation pictures of every graduating class for the past . . . say, fifteen years. Is that possible?"

"Of course." He turned to a bookshelf behind him. "Easy." He picked out a stack of yearbooks and turned. He pointed to the chair behind his desk. "You want to sit here?"

"If it's not inconvenient." I pulled the chair out from behind his desk. It slid easily on the waxed floor, so easily that I inadvertently banged it against the wall. "Sorry."

"Don't worry." He stacked the yearbooks atop the desk, turned and pulled down another stack, and another. "There. That is the last fifteen years. While you're looking through those, I'll be in the next office. Let me know if you need anything."

"Thanks."

I pulled out the composite of Andy Fung, laid it atop the desk, and began leafing through the yearbooks.

In the yearbook for the graduating class of eleven years ago I found a photograph of a student who resembled Andy Fung. It was hard to tell because the picture was taken of a group of Asian students at a football game and his face was partly hidden by the head of the student in front of him. The only reason I stopped was because of his eyes; or, I should say, his eye. Only one eye was visible and it was dark and bottomless and flat. He appeared to have seen the photographer and tried to move out of the picture.

I stared at the photograph a long time. I was not sure. Under the picture, I ran my finger along until I found his name: Wu Hsieh. From Beijing. I looked at the class picture for that year. There was no picture, only the name.

I walked to the door.

"Mr. Clinton, when the photographer takes these candid shots, does he take only the one?"

Clinton laughed. "Heavens, no. He takes dozens. In every class there are clowns who make certain gestures—I think it is called a digital salute—who grimace, close their eyes, who turn aside, who are laughing. These kids are graduating from a very tough school. They're full of piss and vinegar. The photographer has a motorized camera and he points and snaps off a dozen or so exposures."

He paused and stared at me. "Did you find the person you want?"

"The name is wrong."

He walked toward the desk. "May I?"

"If you would."

I passed the book toward him, my finger on the name.

"Oh, my," he said.

He was not looking at the yearbook. He was looking at the composite atop the desk. "This is the person you're looking for?"

"Yes."

"I should have known," he murmured.

"Should have known what?"

"A police officer interested in an Asian student who was graduated about ten years ago. I should have known."

I tapped the composite and then the yearbook.

"You are telling me that the person in this composite, a man by the name of Andy Fung, and this student named . . . ," I checked his name again, "Wu Hsieh. They are one and the same?"

"The person in the composite is Wu Hsieh."

"You remember him."

"Yes. But you can't be looking for him. He—"

I interrupted, which is the most common mistake a detective makes when he is interviewing someone. But I was hot on the trail of whatever his name was. "Are you absolutely certain, Mr. Clinton? You know this Wu Hsieh?"

He paused. "I knew him. But—"

I interrupted again. "Do you have other pictures of him?"

"I don't think so. We had to . . ." He stared at me for a moment, shrugged and said, "Let me call the telephoto department." He picked up the phone. "We have a photographer who has taken these photographs since the beginning of time. He's almost as old as I am. But I don't think . . ."

He spoke to someone for several minutes. He told them the year of the *Blueprint* and the page number, then he waited a moment. He looked at me. "He has some contact sheets."

"That's fine."

He spoke into the phone again, then hung up and turned to me. "Five minutes. He's just across the way."

"You were going to tell me about Wu Hsieh."

He nodded. "I don't know what good it will do. The other Chinese students said he was a *tai zi dang*. Do you know the expression?"

I froze. That was what the Vietnamese restaurant owner said when he looked at the composite. "What does it mean?"

"As it was explained to me, originally it meant a prince or a princeling; the son of wealthy, well-connected and influential parents. But in modern China it has come to mean the corrupt offspring of China's aging rulers." He looked at me. "Essentially hoodlums. Gang members. But with very powerful protectors."

I waited.

"Wu Hsieh's grandfather was a hero of The Long March. He was in the caves with Mao. The two men were very close. And his father is . . . By the way, none of this came from Hsieh. It came from a Chinese student who worked in this office."

I nodded.

"Wu Hsieh's father is a senior official in the Chinese government; the head of something called MSS."

"What is that?"

"Ministry of State Security."

"A Chinese student told you that?"

"Yes."

"Is that like our FBI or CIA?"

"I asked the same question. He said it was like both of those plus a lot more. We have no equivalent, no government agency with the sort of powers he ascribed to the MSS."

"What do you remember about him?"

"Not that it matters now, but I have two memories. First, every Asian student on campus, particularly those from China, was terrified of him."

"Was he violent?"

"Not that we ever saw. But Asians are very close, very tightly knit. They do not open up easily to non-Asians about discord in their midst."

"Did Tech ever take any disciplinary action against him?"

Clinton smiled. "No."

"There's more?"

"There is nothing in his record to reflect . . . to reflect the fear and, we suspect, and even though he . . . Well, we have very rigid privacy laws about our students but I suppose it's okay to tell you this now. We believe he was responsible for the death of one student and the withdrawal from Tech of two others."

I stared in disbelief. "Why couldn't you do anything?"

He turned and looked at the wall. "The first time Hsieh got into trouble—I forget what the offense was, but he was about to be suspended—we had a visit from the Chinese consulate in Houston, Texas. They represent the southeast from there. They have a lot of influence in Washington."

I nodded.

"The consul went to the president of Tech and said his government was interested in funding research in areas that, coincidentally, we thought at the time, Tech wanted badly to get into. He even offered to fund the work of four Chinese graduate students."

I thought about what Spinney had said.

"Did they make it a quid pro quo?"

"Heavens, no. The Chinese are never so direct." He paused. "But the president felt that was the subtext. And, I am ashamed to say, we took their money and let the incident slide."

"Bad move?"

He nodded. "Very. Hsieh had a disregard for others that I considered sociopathic. Two students, both Chinese, who had the temerity to disagree with him over something, I don't know what, were beaten, they said by muggers who came on campus. They both withdrew from this institution."

"You think he did it?"

"One of the Asian students told me he was quite adept at some arcane martial art."

"You said he was involved in a death?"

"The student who told me that Hsieh's father worked for the Chinese intelligence agency." Clinton turned toward me. "He died in a hit-and-run accident crossing North Avenue. The driver was never identified."

"Wu Hsieh?"

"We had no proof. But that is what an Asian student told me."

I thought for a long moment.

"You said there were two things you remember?"

"The second is the experience he had when he went out for soccer. Remember all I told you about him, his . . . supreme self-confidence, shall I say, the great deference shown him by Asian students, and put it in the context of a young man who goes out for the soccer team the year we happen to have the best team in memory. He was humiliated by American boys who were bigger and faster, was called a gook, and was so outclassed that he didn't make the team. Not even close. He was humiliated as I have rarely seen a student humiliated." Clinton shook his head. "In the locker room they laughed about the size of his penis. The athletes called him 'little fellow.' "

There was a knock on the door. Clinton looked up. "Come in," he boomed.

An older man in khaki pants and white shirt and white athletic shoes entered, nodded at me and placed a large manila envelope on the desk. He pulled a loupe from his pocket and placed it atop the envelope.

"Call me when you're done or have a student return them," he said. He nodded again and was gone.

"No-nonsense guy," I said.

"He's that way." Clinton pushed the envelope

toward me. "I don't think you'll find anything, but you're welcome to look."

I saw what Clinton meant about students hamming it up for the camera. They were gawking, had their eyes closed, were wearing sunglasses, their mortarboards pulled low across their eyes—everything you could think of. In the first five pictures, the student known as Wu Hsieh had most of his face covered. But in one of the prints he was peering around the head of the student in front and was clearly recognizable. The man I knew as Andy Fung was staring up at me, caught like a deer in the headlights. The resemblance to the composite was remarkable.

I stabbed the picture with my forefinger. "That's the man."

I looked at Clinton. "Didn't you see his picture in the paper or on television the other day?"

He smiled and shook his head. "This time of the year I see nothing but fund-raising reports."

"I need the other pictures of him, the individual pictures. I know about the privacy restrictions so I'll get a court order for his academic records and everything else you have on him."

I clenched my fist and jabbed toward the ceiling. "I'm about to nail this guy."

Clinton was shaking his head.

"What is it?"

"That's what I've been trying to tell you. There are no other pictures. I'm surprised we had this one. There are no records. No application. No academic records to show he was here. Nothing." He pointed at the annual. "They would have bought all those if they had not already been distributed."

"I don't understand."

"Two years after Hsieh was graduated, we were informed he died in a hiking accident in the mountains;

somewhere in the interior of China. We received a phone call from the undersecretary of state for Asian Affairs who asked us, on behalf of the U.S. government, to lend all possible assistance to a Chinese official who would be calling us. Then the consul from Houston called and made an official request on behalf of the Chinese government. He asked for, and was given, all of Wu's records, everything, and all known photographs. They were disturbed about his name in the yearbook, but there were hundreds of those printed and distributed, so there was nothing they could do about that. I don't think they saw this partial picture at the football game."

I had to let that soak in for a minute. "You mean Tech expunged every record of his ever having been here?"

"Yes." He paused. "Not long afterwards, the Chinese government gave Tech a ten-million-dollar grant and funded the research for another six Chinese graduate students. The research was classified, so the grant was never publicly announced." He looked at me for a long moment. "We are not alone in this. China exercises extraordinary influence in many universities here in America; usually engineering institutions such as this, and, to a lesser degree, some medical schools."

"Can you tell me what the grant was for?"

"No. I know it went to the Aeronautical Engineering Department, but I have no way of knowing the specific nature of the research."

I stared at the class picture and the composite. "And this guy is dead?"

"According to the Chinese government."

"To hell with the Chinese government. I saw him in a bar last Saturday night. I saw him again a few hours later at Universal. I think he was driving a car I saw two days ago. This composite was identified by a Vietnamese restaurant owner several hours ago. He's very much alive."

Clinton nodded. "I know."

"What do you mean, 'I know'? You just said he was dead."

"No. I said the Chinese government said he was dead."

"Then how . . . ?"

"I saw him, too."

I waited.

"Last week I was on Buford Highway in a Chinese restaurant. Wu Hsieh was having lunch. Our eyes crossed and he looked away."

He paused. "Detective, those of us at colleges and universities are like parents. We are reluctant to let our students grow up. I shouldn't have said anything further to Hsieh. But as I was leaving, I stopped by his table, called him by name and reminded him we had met when he was here at Tech. Very calmly and in that precise way of speaking he has, he said, 'You are mistaken.' When I registered disbelief, he glared at me with the blackest and most impassive eyes I've ever seen and he said, 'We don't all look alike, you know.' "

Clinton shook his head. "I knew his voice. His face has hardly changed. It was him."

29

I was exhausted when I got home. Too tired to eat.
But then a Varsity meal lasts a long time. I opened
my briefcase, took out my notes from the day and
tossed them on the bed. I carefully hung up my suit
and took a quick shower.

No matter how tired I am or how late it is when I
get home, I read for a half hour or so before I go to
sleep. I glanced at the books by the side of the bed
and picked up Lao-tzu. Then I noticed the blinking
light on the answering machine.

Kitty had left a message saying it was urgent that I
call her, no matter how late. She had, to use her
words, "big fucking info on your homicide."

I sat on the edge of the bed and dialed her number.

"Hey, stud man, you see the bulldog?"

"What bulldog?"

"The first edition of the Sunday paper; the one that
comes out about noon Saturday."

"No, I didn't. Kitty, it's been a long day. Tell me
what you got."

"I got a front page story in the bulldog that will
knock your hat in the creek. Universal has offered a
fifty-thousand-dollar reward for information leading to
the arrest of whoever shot Richard Morris."

"I thought they announced that Friday. Why wasn't
it in the morning paper?"

"How'd you know they announced it Friday?"

"Kitty."

"They embargoed it until Sunday."

Only Universal.

"I quoted the president of Universal as saying the reward would help the police solve the homicide. He said the investigation has dragged on a week without any significant progress being made and that the young investigator on the case needs assistance."

"You quoted him on that?"

"That's not all of it. He talked about Atlanta's image, how the police need help, same old stuff. Hey, I have to play it straight. My boss is meaner than seven hells." She paused. "Do you like your boss?"

I was thinking about what Godbey said and mumbled, "Yes."

"Well, I don't like mine. Here's a news flash for you. The word 'cunt' is a despicable word that women rarely use and that men cannot use at all. But sometimes it is the only word that fits. Say you wanted to corner the market on the worst bitches in the universe. Say you spent a million dollars and bought a train and fifty boxcars. And say you shopped the entire world and filled every car with the worst shrews, bitches, sadists, arsonists, disease-ridden, husband-killing, child-beating women in the universe. The train pulls up and there is only one boxcar. And in that boxcar there is only one woman. That woman is my boss. She is such a cunt that you would have gotten your money's worth."

"Uh huh."

Why would Godbey publicly criticize me? He doesn't want this case solved.

"The day she dies I'm buying a video camera and installing it in her casket. Then I'm buying a case of beer, taking off two weeks and planting myself in front of a monitor so I can watch the worms eat her rotting corpse."

"Godbey told the Atlanta press I needed help?"

She was silent for a moment. Then she sighed in exasperation. "That's what he said. I called your major and got a response."

"Which was?"

"You want his response or you want what I quoted him on? His response was that Godbey could stick a C-one-thirty up his ass sideways and still have room for a pickup truck, two caraway seeds and the mayor's heart. For the record, he said he appreciated Universal's cooperation. He said he had every confidence in you and that the investigation was proceeding to a rapid conclusion."

"That's why he's the major."

"Payne, why would they offer this much money to help solve a case that you're going to solve anyway?"

"You working or we just talking?"

"Payne," she yelped in pretended indignation.

"Well?"

"I've never burned you."

"Which is it?"

"We're just talking."

"One, Universal is playing politics. This was for Washington's benefit. Two, they don't want this case solved. But people who read your story don't know that and they will think Godbey is a fine man and that Universal is a great company."

"Godbey is turning up the pressure on you."

I laughed. "Kitty, I'm a black man up against a company whose very presence here is a manifestation to everyone in this city that God Almighty Himself has singled out Atlanta for special blessings."

I didn't mention Andy Fung or Wu Hsieh, or whatever his name was, and the Chinese government.

Throw all that in there and then you're talking pressure.

"Guy at the Pentagon help you?"

"He did. And I thank you."

"Just keep me in mind when this thing breaks. I want the story and I want it on my time. Fuck a bunch of television airheads."

"Sometimes it is hard to believe you won a Pulitzer Prize. Your vocabulary . . ."

"Lot of toilet mouths have Pulitzers. No inconsistency there, big stud."

"When the story breaks, I'll do what I can."

"Payne?"

"Yes."

"I think I'm getting old. I don't like my job as much as I used to."

"Are your shins shiny?"

"What?"

"You're not old until your shins get shiny. That happens to white people."

"You're as fucked up as I am. Except mine is on the outside."

"Could be."

"Want me to bring you a copy of the paper?"

"I'll buy one tomorrow morning."

"It's no trouble. I'm sitting here drinking beer, reading. Only five minutes away."

"No, thanks."

"I was out riding up and down Ponce de Leon today. I saw the Monkey Man. Thought of you."

The Monkey Man hands out fliers on the street corners. He is a burned-out case from the sixties; long stringy blond hair, sleeveless T-shirts and tight jeans. The guy has the biggest penis in captivity. It's there in his jeans like an enormous Polish sausage. Women from all over Atlanta ride up and down Ponce looking for the Monkey Man and thinking impure thoughts.

"I'm tired. Good night, Kitty."

"Okay. Call me if anything happens."

I read about the Tao for a half hour. Then I picked up the case notes. Sometimes, the last thing I read before going to sleep percolates in my unconscious during the night. The next day I have sudden insights. Maybe that will happen tonight.

I was asleep when my former wife called.

Let me tell you something. I do not believe in speaking ill of a former spouse. It doesn't matter what happened before, during or after the divorce. What is important is that there was a time when she and I knew the days, when our time together was magic, when we chose each other as a partner for life. We have a daughter. Three years of my life I spent with this woman. That means that when I come to the end of my days and look back over my span of life, she will be one the people who was important to me.

I've only been divorced once. Most of my cop buddies have been divorced at least two, three times. To hear them speak of their former wives, you'd think they married the cheapest, sleaziest bunch of bimbos in the Western world. I can't join those conversations. To speak ill of my former wife would be a refutation of her, our marriage, my judgment and that time in my life. I'm not going to do that.

However, that does not mean my heart is a wide-open bundle of throbbing receptivity when she calls. I haven't heard from her since the divorce and then she calls twice in less than a week.

I don't know why she called. She said, "Caesar Roosevelt, I'm out here in California drinking a lovely bottle of Pouilly-Fuissé. I'm all alone and I thought I would ring you."

"Where's Kimberly?"

"Asleep. She's a baby."

"She okay?"

"I called to talk to you about something else."

"Tell me about it."

She did. She talked and I listened. She told me all about her and what it was like living in California, visiting the wine country on the weekends, problems she was having decorating her house, how she had met several famous actors, about several white guys she had dated—all serious, substantive stuff. She never asked anything about me or what I was working on.

I try not to use any interview techniques with my friends, only with witnesses or suspects. But sometimes I can't help noticing things. The pitch and volume of her voice was normal, but the rate was accelerated. She was anxious about something.

It could be guilt over that fax she sent three years ago.

After she talked for about an hour she said, "I did so enjoy our conversation."

She is a very confused woman. Her inheritance was not enough to buy the one thing that would help her the most: a compass.

In my dream, my daddy was standing in front of a big room, a classroom. I sat on the front row. Each time he asked me a question, I shook my head and said, "I don't know." Question after question. Then he began lecturing the class, all those people sitting behind me whose presence I could only feel, about the case I was working on. They stared at the back of my head. I felt their disapproving stares. Each point he made, always a critical point about my performance in this case, he rang a bell to emphasize what a dummy I was. The bell rang and rang and rang.

Struggling up through layers of fatigue, I realized a bell was ringing; softly but insistently, somewhere in my house. It was not the telephone next to the bed. It was a softer ringing that sounded vaguely familiar, a distant bell, like the bell in my dreams.

I sat up, puzzled, and listened.

It was my cell phone. I left it in the open briefcase in the living room. Muttering to myself, I stumbled out there, picked up the phone and growled, "Hello."

"C.R., this is Lee. Listen carefully and do exactly as I say. I want you to say 'You have the wrong number' and then start bitching about wrong numbers and then take this phone to your bathroom. Shut the door, turn on the water, then talk to me. Do it. Don't say anything. Just do it."

"You have the wrong number," I said.

"Son of a bitch," I grumbled as I headed toward the bathroom. "Wrong number in the middle of the night when I'm tired. I'm getting rid of this stupid phone."

In the bathroom I did as Lee suggested, then put the phone to my ear. "What's going on?" I whispered.

"The FBI has tapped your phone. Did it two days ago. It's one of those taps where the phone itself is the bug. Anything you say in your house, on or off the phone, can be monitored. You read me?"

Now I was awake. "Why?"

"Hell, I don't know why. Because they want to know what you say, that's why."

"What are they doing with the information?"

Lee laughed. "Right now, they're asking each other who is Skip Gates."

I thought for a moment. "My call to the Chinese

embassy?" I laughed. "They don't know His Skipness?"

"They got two agents trying to I.D. him and figure out why he is interested in Andy Fung." Lee laughed. "They didn't recognize your voice."

"Lee, I owe you."

"They went ape when they heard Andy Fung's name. They're curious about Georgia Tech."

"Whatever you can pass along I'll appreciate."

"It won't be much and it won't be often."

"I know. But thanks anyway."

"You know what to do about this? Pay phones near your house."

"I do."

"Flush the toilet and go to bed."

I did.

30

When the phone rang, I bolted upright. One-fifteen
a.m. by the bedside clock.

"Payne?"

"Kitty."

I groaned and fell back in the bed, hand over my
eyes.

"I'm at a homicide at Georgia Tech. You might be
interested in this one."

I'm being notified of a homicide by a newspaper
reporter? What happened to the police? I sat up and
turned on the light.

"Who's the victim?"

"White male. Late fifties. Name of Elmo Clinton."

Not that nice old man.

Wu Hsieh did this.

And I thought it was Mrs. Morris he was stalking.

"Damn him to hell."

"Damn who to hell? You know who did it and you
haven't even seen the crime scene?"

I threw back the covers, stood up and began reaching for my clothes. "How'd he die?"

"The uniform doesn't know. Homicide is on the
way. No obvious stab or gunshot wound."

"When did it happen?"

"Who the fuck knows? The M.E. will tell us. He's

just lying there on the floor. The campus police said he sent his student helpers home about nine P.M., called his wife and told her he would be home about ten or ten-fifteen. She went to sleep. Awakened at twelve-twenty and he wasn't there. She called the campus police, they entered the building, found his body and called APD. A uniform responded and called Homicide. That's it."

"No, that's not it. What are you doing there?" I reached for a pair of pants.

"I have a scanner. Heard the uniform call Homicide. I was still up, drinking alone since you wouldn't come over. I was out the door before the uniform quit talking to Homicide."

"He let you on the crime scene?"

"He knows I won't contaminate anything. Besides, he didn't have a choice."

"What does that mean?" I slid on a white shirt.

"Let me tell you a story, Payne. I was down home several weeks ago. You might not know this, but they are building cotton gins all over southwest Georgia. Cotton is coming back and is a bigger crop than ever, far bigger that it was back in the fifties. You know why?"

She didn't wait for an answer. "Because they finally got rid of the boll weevil. And you know how they did that?"

Again, she didn't wait for an answer. I was tying my bow tie and trying to hold onto the phone at the same time.

"They got him by his dick, that's how. They put these little traps at the end of the cotton rows. Look like little green milk bottles but they smell like boll weevil tootie. All the male boll weevils come flying in from miles around, get into the bottles and can't get out. They are trapped by tootie. Tootie will do it every time."

"You are coming to the point?" I slid my holster on and stuck a ballpoint pen down inside my sock.

"The point is, I'm not wearing a bra. The young uniform would let me roll old Elmo up in a ball and bounce him down the street if I wanted to. Kid can't keep his eyes off my boobs. He needs to get some." She paused. "I might fix him up. Good-looking guy."

I looked for my briefcase. It was in the other room. "Why do you think I'd be interested in this homicide?"

"Because of what brother Clinton is holding in his hand."

I froze. I knew what it was but I had to ask. "What is it?"

"A carved pig." She snorted. "Uniform didn't know what it was. I had to tell him."

I was right; it was Wu Hsieh.

"You didn't touch it."

"No, dammit, I know better than that. It's lying there in his open hand."

"How do you know it's a pig?"

"I'm from Edison, Georgia. I know what a pig looks like."

That was my response to the DeKalb major a week ago tonight, almost to the hour. Three people killed in a week, all holding pigs in their hands and nobody knows they are pigs. Were all these people born on concrete? Granted, the pigs have exaggerated stylized features. But even so, anyone who ever saw a pig would recognize them. What's happening to America? Nobody knows what a pig looks like.

"Why would a carved pig interest me?" I slid on my shoes and leaned down to tie them.

"Payne, you should know better than to try to blow

smoke up my ass. You're not the only person I know in Homicide. I know about the jade pig in the security guard's hand. I know there was jade at your crime scene on Buford last week."

"Dammit, Kitty. That hasn't been released. You shouldn't know that. If I find out whose been talking to you—"

"Lighten up. I've known this for days and you haven't seen it in the paper, have you? I can wait until you catch the perp. But if TV gets this story first, I—"

"I know. I know."

"Homicide is coming up now," Kitty said. "It's Peep Sight." I heard her say, "Morning, Peep. How you doing?"

Peep Sight, so named because he is always squinting; should have bought glasses years ago but refuses to do so. He's one of the middle-aged white guys who have more time at homicide crime scenes than I have with the department; the closest thing I ever had to a mentor. Sharp dresser, like most the Homicide guys, a little on the quiet side, eyes that reveal a great sense of humor.

"What the fuck you doing on my crime scene?" I heard him ask.

"Waiting on you, Detective."

"Get your ass outside and wait there," he said. Then a moment later, "Who you talking to on that cell phone?"

"Sergeant Payne."

"Let me talk to him."

"Let me hang around. I won't contaminate your crime scene."

"Sergeant, you briefing the press? Where are you?"

"I'm leaving my house now. Should be there in ten minutes. Look, Peep, this one might be connected to my Universal homicide."

"Since you were talking to Kitty, I guess she told you everything."

"She did."

Peep laughed. "Come on down. You'll get a chance to see a great police officer at work."

"Kitty said the uniform doesn't know the cause of death."

"That's why he's a uniform."

"You might take a look at his throat."

"I'll do it, buddy. Now I got to go be a policeman. See you in ten. Here's the fearless reporter."

"You coming down?" she asked.

"Kitty, thanks for calling me on this one. I needed to know about it tonight." I hung up, grabbed my briefcase and walked toward the door.

As I got into my Explorer, I remembered something. My house was bugged and the FBI had heard the conversation.

31

I cut over to Ponce de Leon, turned west and raced across town toward Tech. I picked up my cell phone, keeping an eye out for traffic. Even at this hour on Sunday morning Ponce is busy, a favorite of the city's night crawlers.

I called the FBI regional office, gave my cell phone number to the agent on duty and asked him to contact Special Agent Streighton Harde. It's not that I am trying to make the feeb's job easier; I'm trying to make my life easier. My house is bugged. Not contacting the feeb now, especially after Kitty mentioned the jade connection, would result in both the feeb and the major chewing me out.

Harde called as I was crossing the Downtown Connector on North Avenue. "Special Agent Harde with the FBI returning your call, Detective." His voice was strong and showed no sign that he had been asleep. It also showed what a tight ass he was. Can you imagine identifying yourself to a person you've seen a half-dozen times the past week as "Special Agent Harde with the FBI"?

"I'm responding to a homicide that may be connected to my homicide of last Sunday and to that of the Universal security guard. It's at Georgia Tech."

"Georgia Tech? How is that connected?"

It is belaboring the obvious to say that when you tap a telephone you don't reveal to the owner that his conversations are being recorded; not if you want to keep listening. So he has to pretend he's hearing all this for the first time and I have to pretend that I don't know he's listening to everything that goes on at my house.

"I'm told that a jade pig was found in the hand of the decedent."

"Who's the victim? How did he die?"

"Alumni director at Tech. Name is Elmo Clinton." I was thinking fast, trying to remember the conversations with Kitty and Peep Sight and everything we had discussed. "The uniform who was first on the scene said there was no obvious gunshot or stab wound. I asked the detective to check the victim's throat."

Harde was silent for a moment.

"How can the Alumni director at Georgia Tech be connected to an engineer and a security guard who worked at Air Force Plant Six?"

It is difficult for me to be civil with Harde. The only reason he is awake and sharp this time of the morning is that he was awakened earlier to listen to a tape of my phone calls with Kitty and my former wife. Or maybe he is still trying to figure out who is Skip Gates and why was he calling the Chinese embassy from my house to ask about Andy Fung. If all cops were as obnoxious as he is, I'd go into another line of work. And if all white people were such pains in the ass, I'd go back to Africa and change my cologne.

"I don't know. As I said, I'm en route to the crime scene. You're welcome to observe."

"I don't need to be there. Just copy me on the report. This is a timely call, Detective. The FBI appreciates your cooperation." He paused. "It's a good thing you don't have house guests. They wouldn't appreciate your hours."

I almost laughed. He wanted to ask me who was Henry Louis Gates. "You're right.

"I'll fax the reports to your attention as soon as they are typed." I drove to the Alumni office and waved at the uniform standing by the door.

"Detective, based on what you know at this time, what do you think happened? Is it the same perp or a copycat?"

I stepped out of the car and walked toward the uniform. "I don't think it's a copycat. Not too many perps in Atlanta leave carved jade pigs in the hands of their victims."

"You're right," Harde said reluctantly. "So you think it is this person whose composite you are circulating?"

"Could be."

"I understand you interviewed Raymond Vandiver Friday."

"That's correct."

"We weren't told of the interview."

"Somebody told you. Otherwise you wouldn't be asking about it."

"You didn't tell us."

"I didn't tell you about the interview with Godbey either. But you were there. I assumed that Vandiver didn't feel your presence was needed."

"You should have let us know you were interviewing him."

All the feebs want to do is pick and nag and argue.

"Agent Harde, I was told to cooperate with you. This phone call is proof positive I am doing that. But I don't think anyone, and I include the chief, expects me to check in with you before I take a step. The city of Atlanta has primary responsibility in this investigation.

You will be notified of whatever happens. You got a problem, you get your A.G. to talk to the mayor again."

"You asked Mr. Vandiver about a Mr. Andy Fung?"

"I did."

"Is that the name of the man in the composite?"

"That's the name of the man who killed Richard Morris's dog. Or rather the dog belonging to Morris's children. Nice guy. You'd like him."

Harde was silent for a moment. "You're telling me that this Andy Fung killed a dog belonging to the widow of Richard Morris?" His voice was filled with disbelief.

"Then the son of a bitch skinned it, took the body to a Vietnamese restaurant and had the owner call Mrs. Morris and tell her there was a special on dog that day."

I knew what he was thinking: Anybody who kills a dog is out of control.

"And he's the perpetrator you're looking for?"

"There's no record of him anywhere. What can you tell me about him?"

"What can you tell the FBI about him?"

"Do you have anything on him?" I stopped at the door of the Alumni building.

"I'll check."

"Do that." Not many people are perfect. But I'm beginning to think FBI Special Agent Streighton Harde is a perfect asshole.

"I don't understand the connection this newest victim has to your investigation. Have you interviewed him recently?"

I put my hand over the receiver. "What was that? I'm going inside the building over here and I'm losing you."

"I said . . ."

I turned the phone off and put it in my briefcase.

Cooperation with the FBI only goes so far.

32

"You were right about his throat," Peep Sight said. "The M.E. said it was crushed. This old boy died slow and hard." He shook his head and squinted down at Clinton's body. "You'd think someone who worked at a university would die at home in bed. Man, this is a great town we live in."

I sighed. There was something childlike about Elmo Clinton with his white hair and his gentle face, lying there, arms outstretched, the carved pig in his right hand. It was as if he were lying down to sleep with a toy in his hand.

Something about the angle of Clinton's body on the floor of his office bothered me.

"How many we got for this year?" Peep asked.

"How many what?"

"Homicides, Dude Man. How many bodies we had so far this year littering the streets of our fair city? I lost count."

"Hmmmm. What, more than one hundred?" I moved around to get a better angle.

"This one makes one hundred and thirty-four," Kitty said from the door.

"Look," Peep ordered in stern voice. "You can stay there but you can't step on my punch lines."

With a warning glare at Kitty, he turned back to

me. "I'll tell you exactly how many. This guy makes one hundred and thirty-four. Not the end of June yet and we got a hundred and thirty-four bodies. I think we'll hit two fifty this year. I'm starting a pool. You want to pick a number?"

I didn't answer.

Peep tilted his head and squinted at me. "What is it?"

"Peep, look at the angle of his body in the room. Does anything strike you strange about it?"

"Well, he's got a pig in his hand. That's worth two in the bush." He and Kitty laughed.

When I did not, Peep squinted again and said, "He's a tall guy. He needed room to stretch out."

Peep stopped, looked at me and then back at Clinton's body. "That's not a coincidence. A perp is not interested in where the body falls."

"This one was."

"Peep, which way is north?"

"You want to navigate somewhere?"

I looked up, thinking, orienting myself, and pointed. "That's north. That's the way his head is pointed."

"So?"

I closed my eyes and thought rapidly, turning my body as I remembered, then again orienting myself to north. "My homicide on Buford Highway was in a bed that had been turned sideways in the room. The victim's head was to the north. And I remember the crime scene shots from Universal; the security guard's head was pointing north."

"What the hell difference does it make?"

"It was in the book about jade, about funeral jade. Now I remember. The ancient Chinese oriented the bodies of the dead so their heads always pointed north."

"The ancient Chinese? What has that got to do with anything?"

"I was right about the perp. He is living in the glory days of China. He wants to recreate the time when China was the greatest civilization in the world; when it was the only true power, when the Chinese court was the center of everything considered important, whether it was military power or education or the arts. He is a man out of time."

"You got that right, dude man. He's out of time."

"My perp did this one. We'll work it together."

"You the sarge."

I remembered what David Drumwright told me about some of his equipment. I remembered what his team needed in order to do the job. This was a fresh crime scene where he could work his magic.

I turned to Peep. "I want this crime scene locked down tight. I'm bringing in a special crime scene unit. You and I will process the body but not move it. Have the uniform keep our tech people out. My authority. No one gets in this building. We'll establish an outer perimeter several blocks in each direction. Get on the radio and have North Avenue blocked at the expressway and at Northside Drive. Nobody gets in."

Peep nodded. "You're putting yourself way out on a limb, Sarge."

"Lend me your cell phone."

"Yours broken?" He reached into his pocket and handed me his phone.

"The feebs have bugged my home phone. Probably my cell phone, too."

His eyebrows rose as I dialed the number. There was an answer on the first ring.

"Colonel Drumwright."

"David, C.R. Payne here."

After a pause, his voice came back strong. "Where are you?"

"Crime scene downtown. The equipment you told me about the other night? Is it portable?"

"Usually evidence is sent to us. We rarely go out on a crime scene. But, yes, the equipment can be packaged. We have a crime scene team."

"The liaison and training thing we talked about the other night. Can we do that now?"

"I can have my team assembled and ready to go in less than an hour." He paused. "The body still there?"

"Yes."

"Don't move it."

"You got it."

David is crisp and sharp. No time-consuming irrelevant questions, no speeches, no nothing except whatever it takes to get the job done.

I gave him directions on how to get to Tech. "And when you pass the stadium on your right, slow down. At Fowler Street turn left and then an immediate right into the parking decks. Your vehicle will be out of sight there."

"Good. There will be a car and two vans. We can't be visible. Clear out everyone whose presence is not crucial and who can't maintain security."

"They will all be gone by the time you arrive. I'll alert the uniforms to let you through."

"I'm on the way."

"Waiting on you."

I clicked the phone off and smiled at Peep Sight.

"Who the hell was that?"

"Peep, we got the U.S. cavalry riding to the rescue. Just like in the movies."

"You're kidding me? For what?"

"The best forensics lab in the world is right down

the road at Fort Gillem. The Army's CID boys are lending us assistance."

He shook his head and looked at me in amazement. "You can call in the U.S. Army?"

I showed him my ring. "Jade. Good things happen when you wear jade."

"I want a suit of the stuff."

"And I'm wearing Mormon underwear."

"I'll wear jade. But I'm not wearing Mormon underwear. I don't know where it's been."

"Mormons don't drink, don't smoke, don't use profanity."

"Yeah. They just drink orange juice and fuck everything that walks, crawls, creeps and flies."

I grinned.

The U.S. Army was on the way. Universal was throwing the U.S. government at me. So I go through the back door and bring in the U.S. Army. There's something circular about that. It appeals to my sense of humor.

"What are you smiling about?" Peep asked.

"Let's finish up here."

He nodded toward Kitty. "What about her?"

I stared at her. If I ordered her away, she would wait outside the perimeter. Knowing her, she would try to stop David Drumwright and interview him before he got here. Or she would follow him back to Fort Gillem. It's better to have a camel inside the tent peeing out than to have one outside the tent peeing in.

"Kitty, a special U.S. Army team is coming here. It is a training and liaison activity between the Army and the APD. You cannot write about it, even when everything is over. If you do, you will have to change jobs. Because I will personally poison the well for you at this department. You read me?"

"After it's all over it won't matter."

"There will be no discussion on this, Kitty. Unless you agree right now, I will charge you with interfering with a police investigation and I will put you in jail. You'll be out tomorrow and I will catch hell. But you will not write about the Army."

"Goddammit, Payne, you can't—"

"No discussion."

"What about the fucking First Amendment?"

Peep Sight turned to Kitty. "Fuck the fucking First Amendment."

"Can I say a special forensics team was here?"

At that moment I realized a police officer can never truly be friends with a newspaper reporter. Ultimately, it comes down to this. And if the story is big enough, the reporter will burn the cop. I have to distance myself from Kitty because, ultimately, there will be a serious conflict. She thinks that what a newspaper does is far more important that what a homicide cop does, while I think newspaper people are scavengers who will feed on living flesh.

"No. You cannot. If they find evidence and that evidence helps us to charge and convict a perpetrator, you can talk about that evidence. But there will be no mention, no hint, no clever innuendos, nothing about their assistance. These people are going out on a limb for me. The person in charge is a good man. He is my friend and you will not burn him. Kitty, I'm up against the U.S. government and I don't want to be up against the media. But I will."

I walked over to her. "Kitty, you are my friend. And I hope you will stay my friend. We are southwest Georgia buddies."

She looked at me for a long moment. "And that's all, isn't it?"

I nodded.

She shrugged and smiled. "Then that will have to

be enough." She nodded. "No mention of the Army. Only the evidence." She stuck out her hand. "Friend."

We held our hands together far longer than we should have. Both of us knew something had just ended and it saddened us. "Friend," I said.

"When this goes down, I get it first."

"Kitty, what you just did was very hard for you. If this works out as I hope, tomorrow or the next day I'm going to give you an exclusive on the best story you've had since you won the Pulitzer."

She looked at me, eyes glistening. "That's not as exciting as I thought it would be."

"You okay?"

She threw her head back. "Well, I'm not about to join the Hemlock Society, if that's what you mean."

I laughed and turned to Peep Sight. "Lock this crime scene down. The buffalo soldier is on the way."

33

They rolled up in a white van and two unmarked cars and parked by the side door on Fowler Street, the narrow street that runs off North Avenue and along the side of the Faculty and Alumni building. Colonel David Drumwright and his men alighted and swiftly began unloading a series of large plastic containers. They wore civilian clothes but they moved with the erect bearing and confident professionalism of career military men.

The colonel and several of his technicians quickly filed in through the side door while two others drove the car and the vans into the underground parking lot next door. The colonel waited in the hall until the two men ran across the road from the parking lot, then he looked at me.

"What have we got?"

I briefed him on the location of Clinton's body and the layout of the building. "The perp might have come in this side door, but I doubt it. I don't think he has ever been here before, which means he came in the front door." I pointed up and to our left and then across the hall. "He knocked on the door, the victim walked up those steps and met him, they came down the steps and into the office."

"Do you have the traffic log for the crime scene?"

Peep Sight stepped forward. "Sir, I can answer that. The campus police who found the body came in through this door. So did the uniform officer who first responded, the homicide officer, the M.E., one civilian and me. I walked around earlier to check the main entrance. It was unlocked. Crime scene tape blocks off the sidewalk and the front door. A campus policeman is up there to keep people away."

The colonel nodded. "Good. First, we photograph everything, then we process the body so it can be moved." He nodded at two men. They picked up suitcases and moved toward Clinton's office.

"First man is Runion, our photographer," he said. "Senior guy. Former agent so he knows what to shoot. Guy behind him is Flohr, our forensic chemist and trace evidence expert."

The colonel nodded at two other men. One went out the side door while the other walked to the foot of the stairs and looked upward. He opened a plastic box and took out a piece of equipment I'd never seen.

"That's for electrostatic lifting of evidence," the colonel said.

We walked across the large center room and stopped at the door to Clinton's office.

The colonel looked at the heavily trafficked carpet. Hands by his side, he studied the office for a full three or four minutes, examining Clinton's body without saying a word. He looked at Clinton's desk.

It took Runion almost a half hour to get his photographs. Then the trace evidence guy nosed around another half hour.

"Flohr, picking up anything?" the colonel asked.

"Yes, sir. Adhesive lifts picked up both hair and fibers from the victim's clothing. I still have a few lifts to do off the walls and furniture."

A moment later he was finished.

"Anyone go behind the desk?" David asked.

"No, sir. I told them to stay on the carpet on this side of the desk."

David nodded approvingly then turned to another one of his men. A stocky middle-aged man stepped forward. "Detective Payne this is Paul Llewellyn. You need latent prints lifted, he's the best."

We shook hands.

The colonel pointed behind the desk. The carpet ended at the desk and behind it was a linoleum floor, heavily waxed. "The floor behind the desk. RUVIS."

Llewellyn nodded.

"What's roovis?"

"Reflected Ultra Violet Imaging System, one of those pieces of equipment I told you about the other night. The Secret Service is the only other agency in this country that has this equipment. It's a modified night vision device that magnifies ten thousand times. It's hooked up to a camera with a quartz lens."

"Why quartz?"

"Doesn't have the water content of glass."

"What does it do?"

Llewellyn had the camera pointed toward the floor near the chair.

"It works in the shortwave end of the spectrum. When you look at that waxed floor with the naked eye, you don't see anything because the wax is transparent. The UV makes the wax look like hot tar. Reveals handprints, footprints, anything that's touched it. Better than laser technology."

"Looks expensive."

"About ten thousand dollars." He watched a moment then said, "Llewellyn, would you get the victim also? Neck and arms."

He looked at me. "When you photograph human skin with RUVIS, the outer layer of the skin becomes transparent. It shows up like the Tin Man in the Wizard of Oz. We can get prints, bite marks, whatever we need."

We waited.

"They're here," Llewellyn said from behind the desk.

"What have you got?"

"Footprints. I'd guess a nine or ten. They're on top of everything else. If none of the city detectives came back here, I'd say the prep left them."

"Any distinguishing marks?"

"Yes, sir. The way the sole is marked. I'm almost certain it's a Cole-Haan shoe, a perforated summer-resort-type shoe. I've seen it in my exemplars. Near the left toe is an accidental characteristic that occurred during the wearing of the shoe. A cut. Probably stepped on something sharp."

"How much longer you need?"

"Ten minutes."

"Flohr, how about other parts of the office?"

"Yes, sir. I'm going up the steps to the front door. The wall by the steps is granite. A lot of people have brushed it so I don't know about the evidentiary value of what I find. I'll get everything and sort it out later."

The colonel nodded and turned back to Llewellyn. "Alternate light source for the walls and floors."

"Yes, sir."

The colonel turned toward another one of his men. Slender, wore glasses, almost academic. The guy had eyes bright with intelligence and brimming with experience.

"Detective this is Ed German. Twenty years ago he liberated a bit of technology from the Japanese and brought it to America. One day I'll tell you that story. Everyone is supposed to know about it but we find that even today very few agencies use it." He nodded toward German. "Tell him."

"Cyanoacrylate fuming," he said.

"What?"

"Super Glue fuming. Latent prints on nonporous surfaces sit on top of the evidence surface. They do not soak into the surface like they do on, say, paper. Fuming locks in those prints. It's like setting them in concrete."

"I know about superglue fuming. But you're right. Our tech people rarely use it; say it's too much trouble."

German smiled. "If crime scene people don't fume nonporous evidence before they put it into plastic bags, they might as well wipe the evidence clean."

"I'm not arguing."

"Do you have any reason to suspect a DNA exchange?"

"No. But if your trace evidence man found hair samples anywhere, I want to go for DNA." I remembered the cigarette butt I found in the Universal parking lot. "And I have a piece of evidence for DNA testing."

"Okay. When everyone else is finished we'll fume the entire suite of offices."

"Everything?"

"You'll be amazed at what it reveals. But it will leave a white haze over everything."

I nodded and pulled the colonel aside. "David, when you're through here, how about coming up to the first crime scene?"

"How far away?"

"Ten minutes."

"Is it still secure?"

"It is."

He looked at his watch. "My guys will be through

in about . . . It will be daylight when we are through up there." He nodded. "You got it."

"I'm buying you some good cigars."

"La Glorias. Pyramids."

"I said good stuff. I'll get you a half-dozen Partagas one fifties."

He stopped and stared. He was curious. "Those things cost forty bucks a piece."

"My supplier?"

He waited.

"His mother was killed in a home invasion. I caught the perp. He's sitting on death row. My supplier sells to me at cost."

"In that case I'll take them." He smiled. "But let's finish here first."

About ten a.m. the colonel and I stood in the parking lot of the Han Motel trying to talk over the traffic noise on Buford Highway. The colonel's men waited in the vans. They were weary but they had a look of anticipation. They were anxious to return to the lab and process all they had found.

"I can't believe they got that many new prints here," I said.

The colonel nodded. "Civilian law enforcement works under the theory that prints rarely are found below two feet or above six or seven feet. They work a zone. We work a crime scene."

"And the trap in the sink. We missed the hair samples."

The colonel nodded. "You ready to go?"

"I'm ready to go home and sleep."

"You have to come to the lab with us. We will take you into the different departments and show you how to process the evidence. This is a training and liaison exercise. It has to be that way."

"Can you have one of your men drive your car?"

He looked at me for a moment then turned around and spoke to one of the men in the van.

"What is it?" he asked.

"I need to talk to you."

34

I had not told David of my belief that Washington did not want this case solved and how I believed the FBI and OSI were shielding the Chinese perp.

Now I had to tell him. He had gone out on a limb to help me and I couldn't saw off that limb behind him.

As I followed the Army vehicles toward the expressway, David watched me from the corner of his eyes. He knew I was wrestling with something. Finally I organized my thinking and was about to begin. He reached over, squeezed my arm and said, "Are you about to tell me something that I shouldn't know? Think about this."

"The implications could—"

"Think about this." His voice was emphatic. "Should I know what you are about to say?"

It took a moment for me to understand what he was saying. "Maybe not."

"Then don't tell me."

"But—"

"We are going to have the results of these tests before anyone can tell us to stand down."

I wheeled onto the expressway ramp and picked up speed. The three government vehicles ahead of me were pulling away. "Will you get in trouble?"

He shook his head. "Negative. There is a green card

connection. The OSI is involved. One of the homicides took place on a GOCO facility. And—"

"GOCO?"

"Government owned, company operated. Plus this is legitimate liaison with a local law enforcement agency. We will be training you in the use of some rather specialized equipment. I'm covered. And since I don't know whatever it was you were about to tell me, I can be truthful when my boss calls."

The government vehicles were still pulling away. I picked up speed.

"Detective, may I make a suggestion?"

"Of course." I kept my eyes on the road as we made the sharp turn on the Downtown Connector.

"Stay off your radio until we are finished at the lab. Do you wear a pager?"

I reached for my belt. "I got up in the middle of the night and forgot it."

"Good. Cell phone?"

"In the briefcase."

"Turn it off. Consider yourself incommunicado for the next few hours."

"You can do—"

"Not *you* can do. *We* can do."

"We can do all this in the next few hours?"

"It's Sunday. Our off day. We have the lab to ourselves."

"I think I'm going to throw in a bottle of scotch to go with those cigars."

David nodded. "We can drink scotch, smoke cigars and talk about Skip Gates."

I laughed. "His Skipness."

"Do you have the crime scene pictures and the detective's report from the Universal homicide?"

"In my briefcase. Plus a cigarette butt I need tested for DNA."

"May I?"

"Of course." He reached over the seat and pulled the briefcase into his lap, opened it and pulled out the cell phone. "May I?"

"Go ahead."

He turned it off. Then he picked up a large manila envelope. "This it?"

"Yes."

For several minutes he thumbed through the report and did not speak. He began going through the photographs. Suddenly he stopped. "Do you know what this is?"

I glanced over. He was holding a blown-up shot of the face of the watch found at the Universal crime scene. There was also a picture of the inside of the back cover of the watch. He was pointing to the mark inside the cover.

"The Cobb guy and I couldn't figure it out. Neither could the FBI. The Cobb guy and I finally decided it was some sort of manufacturer's mark; one of the assembly line guys etched it in there. It's done professionally."

David grinned. "You didn't pursue this?"

"Nothing to pursue."

He tapped the photograph. "This is the sign of the jeweler who once did work on this watch. They do that so if someone comes in later complaining, they can open the watch and know at a glance if they ever worked on it."

"You mean . . ."

"I mean this is an expensive watch that he took back for repairs. I'm guessing he took it to the place where he bought it."

"That's an expensive watch. It came from a high-end store."

David nodded. "And that means . . . ?"

"Security systems. Video cameras."

"Give the man a cigar."

"Do jewelers know each other's marks?"

"In the same city? You bet."

"So once I identify the jeweler who made the mark, we check his records for the repair date, look at the videotape for that day and we have the owner of a watch found at a homicide."

"Unless he says he lost or sold it."

"Possible. But strong circumstantial to go with everything else I have."

"He had to deliver the watch and he had to pick it up."

"Shots of him both days. I hope the shop, if they had a camera, hid it well. My guy is very camera shy."

I thought for a moment. I knew exactly what I would do to track down the watch. Then I pursed my lips and thought. I glanced at David.

He broke the silence. "You want to ask me something else, but you're afraid you've used up all your favors."

"Do I give away that much?"

He laughed. "What is it?"

"The lab you run? You're part of a larger command?"

He paused, trying to figure out where I was going. "It's what we in the military call a stovepipe organization. The line of command goes from me to a two-star at Fort Belvoir. He reports to the Army chief of staff."

"Inside that stovepipe, is there some cosmic records division or counterintelligence division?"

This time his pause was longer. When he spoke, his voice was cautious. "The Army Crime Records Center is part of this command. Counterintelligence is not part of the Army law enforcement structure. It's a separate command."

"Okay, so you have a Records Center. You know people there. You talk to them?"

He nodded. "From time to time."

"Ever do liaison with Counterintelligence?"

"I thought you were a homicide detective."

"I am."

"Occasionally."

"I need you to make a couple of phone calls for me."

For a long time I thought he was not going to answer. Then in a noncommittal voice he said, "We'll see."

I laughed and slapped my hand against the steering wheel. "David, I don't know if it's this new jade ring or my Mormon underwear. But I feel invincible. The Big Guy is on my side today."

"Tell it all, preacher."

Fifteen minutes later we drove through the main gate at Fort Gillem. This place is old. It looks like an abandoned movie set. Everything here appears to have been built circa World War I. At the second MP station, we turned right and followed the military vehicles down a long road. On the left was warehouse after warehouse. Behind each I could see railroad tracks where, at some time in the distant past, supplies were put on boxcars for shipment to Army bases around the world.

At the end of the road we turned left, passed one building and then parked under the overhang of what once had been a loading dock. David's crews were already unloading the plastic containers and rushing up the steps.

I looked at the decrepit building. It had the dingy sagging look of very old buildings. Even the bricks seemed tired. "The Army must not think much of its great laboratory; not if they put you in this place."

He opened the door. "We have a first-rate lab and first-rate people, both of which are in a facility that is not first-rate."

"This is an overgrown outhouse."

"The Army has its priorities. We have asked for a new lab. But the Army also needs day-care centers, a new gymnasium at West Point, other things."

"You're competing with day-care centers."

"Kwajalein got three point four million for a day-care center."

"Where?"

"Kwajalein. An island in the Pacific."

"And West Point got a new gym?"

"They got twenty-nine million for the second phase of their gym."

"Twenty-nine million? What sort of gym are they building?"

"One befitting West Point. Maybe it's the granite. I don't know."

"So what would a new lab cost?"

"Twenty-five million."

"You do forensic work, investigations into major crimes for all of the U.S. military all over the world. And day-care centers on Kwajalein and gyms at West Point take precedence?"

"We do our job."

The door at the top of the loading dock opened and the Army guys picked up the last of the plastic containers and rushed up the stairs.

"For a bunch of old guys, they move fast."

He nodded. "Every one of those guys is a legend. Other labs, cops all over the world, use their work as the benchmark. When my guys write papers, those papers have ecclesiastical weight."

"They are all in their forties or fifties. I thought guys that age were edging into burnout."

"That is a comment only a young man would make. Evidence from the most serious crimes committed in the U.S. military is sent here. It might be a once-in-a-lifetime case for the investigating officers who sends the evidence. That means that almost every case my men work is a once-in-a-lifetime case for someone. That's all they do. They are challenged every day. They get better and better." He paused. "You should hope, young detective, that you grow in your profession as much as they have in theirs."

"Should I go stand in the corner? Or do you want me to write on the blackboard one hundred times that I will not do it again?"

He opened the door. "Let's go. You're about to earn a postgraduate degree in forensic technology."

It was 7:40 P.M. when I came out the warehouse, stood on the loading dock and took a deep breath. It had rained again while I was inside but now the air was clean and soft. Even though I was standing in the middle of one of the biggest warehouse complexes I had ever seen, there was no sound. It was as if the world has paused for a moment. The air was tinged with orange and seemed to cradle everything in a soft glow. It was that time of the evening that photographers call "magic time," when the shadows are long and the light is soft and everything seems to glow with an inner fire.

I held a stack of papers in my right hand; a stack of photographs plus the results of all the lab work. I shook my head in amazement at what RUVIS had revealed, at what electrostatic lifting had provided, at the DNA comparisons.

I had all I needed to put the Chinese guy in jail for a long time.

I have to make one stop before I got home; a stop that will get everything rolling on arresting him. Then it's home and bed. This has been an eighteen hour day.

I rubbed my ring. If this really brings luck, my ex-wife won't call tonight.

But I don't know if even jade is that strong.

As I drove out the main gate, I turned on my police radio. I had just turned onto I-285 when I heard my call sign.

"This is forty-one twenty-four. Go ahead."

"Stand by," came the dispatcher's voice. He sounded almost surprised.

A moment later the major was on the air. "Detective, I've been paging you and calling you for hours. Why have you not responded?"

"Sorry, sir. I was awakened in the middle of the night and forgot my pager. And this afternoon I was . . . I was on foot outside my vehicle and left my radio in the car. It was turned off."

"The FBI has been trying to reach you all day."

"I'm en route to my residence. They can meet me there in a half hour."

"I will so advise them." He paused. "You have one other call."

The major was sending me a message. "Yes, sir. I'll find a land line and call the dispatcher and get the number."

"Keep your radio on."

"Yes, sir." I would catch hell about this from other cops.

At the next exit I pulled off and found a pay phone and called the dispatcher. Lee, my friend at the phone company, had called. I returned his call.

"C.R., you remember why I called the other night?"

"Yes."

"The same thing. Another unit. Hand held."

I was right. My cell phone had been bugged.

I hung up then thought for a moment. Wu Hsieh wanted chaos; I would give him all the chaos he could handle.

I called Kitty and talked to her for a long time. She was very happy about what I told her.

Then I drove to a phone store downtown. Competition is so tough among cellular phone providers that stores are open around the clock. I badged the manager and told him what I needed. He turned me over to a young woman at the front desk. She was all perky and bouncy and liked to toss her long red hair as she talked.

"And what name will this phone be in, sir?" she asked. "Last name first, the first name, then the middle initial."

"Gates. Henry L."

She completed the paperwork in a rapid fashion, handed me the telephone and said, "We appreciate your business, Mr. Gates."

"Please. Call me Skip."

35

A familiar car was parked in front of my house; the gray G-car driven by the feeb and the dweeb. I didn't see their pointy heads sticking up so either they were having a close personal relationship or they were sitting on my porch.

They were on the porch.

I was almost disappointed.

Let me tell you something. I have observed that as a man gets older his aversion to eating crap slowly disappears. I've seen guys in their fifties and sixties eat whatever was shoveled their way with no more than token resistance. Sure, they bitch and moan. That's why we think older men are cranky. But they are bitching and moaning because they remember how they used to be, and because they have become the men they swore they would never be; old men living lives of quiet desperation. I hope I never get to that place. I know I am not there now. I had enough crap when I was a kid. My father ladled enough for a lifetime. Maybe that's why I'm still angry at him. Anger keeps my crap detector on full alert.

I've had enough of the FBI and the OSI and City Hall and J. Stanford and the Chinese guy with two names. I am breaking out. And if I get sent back to the airport, so be it. There are some things more important than working in Homicide. Like keeping my dignity.

I picked up my briefcase, made sure it was locked—everything I had on Wu Hsieh was in there—then stepped from my car and walked up the walkway. At the foot of the steps I stopped and stared at the two guys sitting on my front porch.

Special Agent Streighton Harde, whom I am beginning to think of as a real prick, finally broke the silence. "Well, Detective," he said. He made the word "Detective," which is a word I worked very hard to have attached to my name, a word of which I am very proud, sound like profanity.

"We want to talk to you," said his faithful companion, the former black man.

I walked up the steps. "Make it fast. I'm tired."

Harde motioned toward the door. "We'll talk inside."

"If I ever see you in my house, I will consider it a home invasion and shoot your sorry white ass. Now say what you have to say and get off my property."

Harde came a step closer. He clenched his fist. "Why you . . ."

I dropped the briefcase and met him nose to nose. "Say it and we will go to war. Right here. Right now. Say it. Say it."

Little Maynard, the former black man, bounced up against my elbow, clenching his teeth and trying to be a tough guy.

"He was about to call me a nigger. What the hell are you doing in my face? Back off."

"I wasn't about to call you a nigger."

The feeb had a quick vision of the FBI image and what a public relations problem he was about to create. He could see the attorney general hanging him out on the line and using him as an example of how enlightened the Justice Department had become.

"The hell you weren't."

He backed up a step, ducked his head and held his hands toward me, palms up. "Okay. Okay. Let's calm down. We have business to discuss."

I waited.

"Look, I don't want to stand out here on the porch. Can't we go inside?"

"No. You," I turned to Little Maynard, "and you, will not come inside my house. Not without a search warrant." I looked at each of them. "I'm not choosy about who I let in my house, but I do have limits."

Harde squeezed his Baptist lips into a paper-thin line. "If that's the way you want it, Detective."

"That's the way it will be."

"Then you don't mind if I sit." Without waiting for an answer he sat in one of the straight-backed chairs on the front porch. Little Maynard sat. Harde studied me for a moment. "Detective Payne, you are not keeping us fully briefed on your progress in this investigation."

"My aching ass. Not that again. What are you, a one-trick pony?"

He stood up and pointed his bony Baptist finger at me. The dweeb stood up and glared. "You were on Buford Highway this morning talking to men in vehicles with U.S. government plates. Who were they? And why haven't you notified us? We've been trying to reach you for hours. What have you been doing?"

"You want to back up and give me those one at a time."

Harde sat down and bit his lip in frustration. Jackson sat down. "Who were the federal people you were talking with and what were you doing on that crime scene? The manager said you were in the room several hours. You and maybe a half-dozen others."

"She told you that?"

"She did."

"She speaks better English with you than she does with me. Must be that FBI thing."

"Who were they?" He stood up. Faithful Companion stood up. These guys were bouncing up and down like they were at a Catholic funeral.

"Am I under surveillance?"

"No."

"Then who reported to you I was at the crime scene?"

Harde bit his lips again. I could almost hear machinery grinding between his ears.

"That's not important. You were seen."

"By whom?"

"What agency do those men represent?"

From his questions, whoever saw me, and I'm guessing it was Andy Fung or Wu Hsieh or whatever his name was, who, like a dog returning to its vomit, was riding up Buford Highway when he saw the government plates but could not read the small numbers. Which meant that Harde was groping in the dark. He was scared, too. It was in his eyes. Andy Fung or Wu Hsieh was out of control. Richard Morris had to be killed because of the eighty-billion-dollar contract. But not the security guard. And not the alumni director at Georgia Tech. And the dog sure as hell didn't have to be killed, skinned and taken to a Vietnamese restaurant.

Andy Fung had roamed way off the reservation.

Harde had to bring him back. I'm guessing Harde's pension was on the line.

"This may be your world, Special Agent Harde, and I may be just walking through it. But that is my crime scene. I not only have the right but the obligation to return as often as I think necessary."

"What agency do those men represent?"

"I'm betting you called DEA, Customs, ATF, the Secret Service, INS, IRS and every other federal agency represented in Atlanta. Including the National Park Service."

His thin lips told me I was right.

Time to stress this puppy a little more. "I found out the real name of the perp. Wu Hsieh."

Harde blanched and sat down. There went his pension.

The former black man sat down. Maybe his too.

"He is a known agent in China's Ministry of State Security. He has represented his government in negotiations with Universal; specifically a side agreement to the F-twenty-two contract."

Harde looked up at me and shook his head. He was in shock.

Little Maynard spoke. "The details of that contract are classified by Universal and by the Department of Defense as Top Secret."

"So what are you going to do? Shoot me?"

I picked up the briefcase. I wasn't going to tell Harde anything that Wu Hsieh could alter or change, such as the fact he wore Cole-Haan resort shoes and that I had documented evidence those shoes were to two homicide crime scenes—behind the bathroom door in the motel room and behind Elmo Clinton's desk. I also had black cashmere fibers from the granite wall near Clinton's office and from under the bed where Morris's body was found. I needed Wu Hsieh's black coat for a positive match. There was also DNA evidence. Hair the lab had identified as coming from the head of an Asian male had been found in the sink trap in the motel room as well as on the carpet in

Clinton's office. It matched DNA in the saliva of the cigarette butt I found in the Universal parking lot.

But I could tell him about the fingerprints. Wu Hsieh couldn't change those.

"He left latent prints on the frame of the bed where Richard Morris's body was found and at the Georgia Tech homicide scene."

Harde stood up. He was shaking his head. "You don't understand what you've done."

Faithful Companion stood up.

"I'll tell you something else. Wu Hsieh lost his watch when he killed the Universal security guard."

"You think the one found at the crime scene was his?"

"The mark inside the back cover? Remember?"

Harde's eyes widened. He did remember. He also remembered that he didn't know what it meant.

"The shop where it was repaired has been identified and the manager contacted. By tomorrow I'll have video of Wu Hsieh delivering and picking up the watch. I'm told it is very good video."

"Nobody but the federal government has this sort of resources. Who were those people with you this morning? The Federal Bureau of Investigation is the lead agency on this investigation."

I got in Harde's face. "Wrong, Special Agent Harde of the FBI. I keep telling you I have jurisdiction in two of these homicides but you don't listen. So listen up. I'm putting Wu Hsieh's ass in jail."

Harde collected himself. "I want every bit of evidence, everything you have found, on my desk tomorrow morning. I am exercising federal supremacy in this matter. You are relieved, Detective Payne."

"That won't do you any good."

"The attorney general of the United States may have something to say about that."

"You didn't let me finish. I put out an APB on Wu Hsieh." I looked at my watch. "By now every local, state and federal agency in the country has been notified. A narrative was attached listing all the evidence, all we suspect him doing—including the dog—and advising everyone he is considered extremely dangerous."

Harde looked at Jackson. "Can you have that withdrawn?"

Little Maynard shrugged. "It won't do any good. Not if everyone has received it."

Harde ignored me. "But we can send out a corrective notice saying the first one was in error. It can be expunged. We can stop the search."

I don't like being ignored. "He's in Atlanta," I said. "The APB was just to get all this on the record." I smiled. "You're not keeping up with me, Special Agent Harde of the FBI."

Harde stared. "There's more, isn't there? I can tell by that shit-eating grin. What have you done?"

"Nothing you can stop." I thought of the story Kitty was writing that would appear on the front page of *The Atlanta Constitution* tomorrow morning; the full story of Wu Hsieh and Universal and the side agreement. Plus how evidence found at three homicide scenes made Wu Hsieh, an agent of the Chinese government, the prime suspect.

It was thoroughly documented. David's phone call to a contact in Army Intelligence had been a gold mine.

I looked at Harde. "Do you understand the theory of chaos as espoused in Chinese thought?"

Harde and Faithful Companion looked at each other. Faithful Companion shrugged.

"Let me give you the American version. Some people work in the dark like roaches. Put a little sunshine on them and they panic." I gave the two feds my mule-eating-briars grin. "Tomorrow morning you will see panic." I held up a finger. "But out of that panic will come order." I paused. "All the roaches will be in a roach motel; locked up."

The same story I gave Kitty will be picked up on the morning news of all the local stations, plus CNN, and, if I am lucky, on the three big networks' morning news. I think I am about to pull a hat trick plus one— a story on all three networks plus CNN.

"What the hell are you talking about?" Harde's face was red. His eyes were bulging. He kept making hacking motions in the air, motions of frustration.

I unlocked the front door. "Gentlemen, if there's nothing else, I have to get some sleep. Tomorrow is going to be a big day." I looked over my shoulder. "Wu Hsieh is about to become a very popular man."

"What does that mean?" Harde snapped.

"It means get your ass off my porch."

36

At 10:40 P.M. the phone rang.

"Payne."

"Detective Payne, I am calling for somebody we both know."

It was a man's voice. Middle-aged. Trembling slightly. Speaking slowly with restrained indignation. Not a voice I recognized.

"Who? And who are you?" Shouldn't have asked that one; not with the feebs listening. I sat up.

"I can't give you the person's name. But this concerns Universal and the person you know as Andy Fung."

"Stop right there." The FBI agent monitoring the line would be going ballistic. He would be contacting Harde. I thought rapidly. "Hold on one moment please." I opened my wallet and pulled out a piece of paper. "I'm about to give you a telephone number. Call me there in . . .," I calculated rapidly, "four minutes."

The voice paused. "Give me the number."

I did.

"Four minutes," he said.

The FBI had monitored the call and heard me leave the house. But it would take them a half hour to gear up and put a wire on the pay phone. They are supposed to get a court order, but when they bug phones for intelligence purposes they often forget.

Three minutes later I jumped from the Explorer and was high-stepping my bare feet across the empty parking lot of a Mexican restaurant on Ponce de Leon. Fifteen seconds later I was standing by the phone, stuffing my shirt into my jeans and muttering about my bruised feet.

Fifty-seven seconds later the phone rang. I picked it up before the first ring was completed.

"This is Detective C.R. Payne. Identify yourself."

After a brief pause, the voice said, "Felix."

"Felix who?"

"The important thing is why I'm calling. The person I mentioned earlier wants you to know something."

"I don't like mysteries. Who's the person?"

"It's the information that is important. I've been asked to tell you that Andy Fung is getting out of town tomorrow morning. Early. You lit a fire under his ass."

Now I was picking up other things from the voice. He was not a well-educated person. A bit gruff. I figured him for a blue-collar worker.

"Where is he going?"

"He's on a Delta flight to New York. First one out. Then he's flying to China until the flap over the killings settles down."

"Then he'll be there a long time."

"I've been asked to tell you that the paperwork on the F-twenty-two deal will be signed in the next few days."

"Out of my jurisdiction. I'm after a killer."

"You're going to have to get up early."

"How do I know this is good information; that this is not a diversion?"

"It's solid, buddy. You be at the airport if you want this guy."

"I will. Thanks . . . Felix."

"Good-bye."

37

I drove east on Ponce for three blocks and stopped
at the pay phone in front of the Majestic Diner. Ponce
was beginning to throb and pulse with nocturnal energy; night creatures were beginning to stir, to emerge
from their dens and seek sustenance before going
forth to mug and rape and rob. This is a seedy part
of Atlanta trying to pass for funky, or, in the case of
nearby Virginia-Highlands, genteel.

Grafters and muggers, whores, pimps and snake
charmers, along with drug-numbed refugees from the
sixties, own this part of town at night. They ooze up
and down Ponce de Leon like a big oil slick waiting
for some unknowing soul to come around a bend and
become locked in their evil embrace.

From the three little coin holders between the front
seats of the Explorer, I pulled a couple of quarters
and stepped up to the phone.

A half-dozen homeless people stood in front of the
Majestic trying to cadge money from passersby. They
didn't know what to make of me; a barefooted black
guy with a gun stuck in his jeans.

My first call was to the drug task force people working at the airport. They have a direct hookup to airline
computers and it took only a few seconds to tell me
that the morning flight to JFK was full and that no
one name Andy Fung or Wu Hsieh was listed.

"You know he's going to JFK?" asked the DEA guy on the task force.

"He's departing New York on an international flight; to China probably."

"Then he should be coming to JFK. But the name he used when he bought a ticket doesn't mean a thing. He could be traveling as Mickey Mouse. If you think he's on the flight, be at the gate."

I thanked him.

"Word is," he said, "you might be coming back out here full-time. When's that?"

"The word is wrong."

Then I called my major at home.

"Dammit, this better be important," the major said. That passes for "hello" when you are a major and you answer your phone late at night.

I told him about the message from the unknown caller.

"How you want to handle it?"

"No uniforms. Metro Fugitive can do it. I don't know how he is arriving at the airport, whether he is coming in the north or south terminal. He's not listed as a passenger, but this guy changes names like I change shoes. I'll have detectives at the adjacent gates and when he checks in we'll take him down."

"This is good information?"

"I don't know. I can't afford not to follow up on it." I paused. "Major, we have one problem."

"The FBI?"

"I know you got people over you. But this is an Atlanta case."

The major did not speak for a moment. "Call me when you get to the airport. I'll call the FBI and tell them the arrest is going down. That will give you about an hour before they get there."

"Thanks."

"How many Metro Fugitive people you need?"

"A half-dozen. I don't think he can get a gun through security. But if you could call and ask them to tighten up the screening procedures tomorrow morning, it would help. If he's not armed, there shouldn't be a problem. We'll take him hard and fast."

"I'll make the call. The officers will meet you at the airport precinct." He paused. "You do remember where that is?" I sensed he was smiling.

"Yes," I snapped as I hung up.

It was going to be a long night. I looked inside the Majestic. A good cup of tea can be had in there. Suddenly I was hungry. Hot toast. Grits and eggs and bacon; an early breakfast that will fortify a person all day. I took a step toward the door. But the manager was standing there shaking his head. He pointed down.

"No shoes, no service."

The homeless people snickered. "Why don't you take that goddamn gun out and shoot the son of a bitch?" one asked. "We'll be behind you all the way. We can all fill up."

For a moment I was tempted.

I entered my house slowly and quietly. The FBI had heard me leave but I didn't want them to know I had returned. I was still hungry but I couldn't go to the kitchen. They would hear me. I tiptoed slowly into the bedroom. The light on my answering machine was blinking. I hit caller ID. Two calls from the FBI and one from Gwendolyn. Both of them would call back if I didn't return their calls. I sighed, picked up my alarm clock and walked back into the living room. I closed the door and lay down on the sofa.

I wondered as I drifted off to sleep if the FBI could hear my stomach growling.

38

People from a big part of America east of the Mississippi River, people who fly often, say that when you die, no matter whether you go to heaven or to hell, you have to change planes in Atlanta. The Atlanta Hartsfield International Airport—there's that international word again—was jammed at 6 a.m. as the first push of the day began; dozens of aircraft maneuvered in the skies overhead to fit into the landing pattern, and dozens more taxied around the vast taxiways waiting to take off. The chaos is compounded today because of the weather—surprise, more thunderstorms. Every departing flight is delayed and aircraft waiting to land are backed up and stacked up.

Both the north and south terminals are wall-to-wall people; every train is full and every concourse is crowded. Many people have that vacant thousand-yard stare as they jockey through the crowds, annoyed that there are several thousand other people in the airport.

I briefed the Metro Fugitive squad an hour and a half before the Delta flight to New York was scheduled to depart.

We sat around the airport zone police station, a place I do not like at all. The stay was made a little more pleasant by the content of the morning papers. Kitty's story was on the front page of *The Atlanta*

Constitution. The New York Times and *The Wall Street Journal* had picked up her story off the wire and run it on their front pages. We flipped television channels and found the story on all three network affiliates and CNN. Wu Hsieh was getting his fifteen minutes of fame. So were Universal and China. I made a mental note to tell Chuck Spinney how Universal and China were getting hosed.

One of the uniforms came in, said he had been out on the concourse and the story was running on the airport channel. I never figured on the airport channel; that was the best one yet. Travelers and airport workers would be checking out every Asian male they saw.

I grinned. By the time he was in the airport ten minutes, Wu Hsieh was going to be one angry puppy.

It was almost show time. After going over the plan again, I sent the four men and two women from Metro Fugitive to the A Concourse. Two team members rode a Delta tractor across the flight line to the end of the A Concourse and walked back up to Gate 17 where the flight was to board. Two others rode the train out to B Concourse then caught another train back to A and walked up the escalator as if they were catching a connecting flight. The two women arrived separately and sat across the concourse at Gate 18. The squad members wore everything from jeans to suits. All had their police ID on chains around their necks under their shirts ready to pull out. All carried guns and radios. The guns were hidden and the radios were turned off. The plan was for everyone to arrive at Gates 17 and 18 an hour before departure time, read papers or books and look bored. I was to sit against the wall at Gate 18. I suspected Wu Hsieh would arrive at the last minute. The crew at the Delta counter had been asked to delay any male Chinese passenger long enough for me to identify him. When I stood up,

members of Metro Fugitive were to produce their ID
and fall on Wu Hsieh like a ton of bricks.

It was a good plan.

It fell to pieces because of unexpected events.

When I arrived at A Concourse and turned right
toward the gate, a hell of a furor was taking place at
the entrance to the men's washroom adjacent to the
Delta Crown Room. Uniforms were running into the
bathroom, hands on their weapons, radios to their lips.
I heard one of them say a person was down and to
expedite the EMTs.

I had a bad feeling.

No one resembling Wu Hsieh was at the gate or
visible on the concourse.

I stuck my ID into the breast pocket of my suit so
the badge was visible and ran into the bathroom.

"Homicide," I said. "Step aside."

The uniforms parted.

The face of the man on the floor was covered with
blood. But I could tell from his neck and his hands
that he was Asian.

I kneeled down. "How bad is he?" I asked one of
the uniforms.

"He'll live. But he's going to need a doctor to re-
work his face."

Something about the man on the floor was familiar.

"Hand me some paper towels."

One of the uniforms ripped off a handful from a
dispenser on the wall and passed them to me. Very
gently I wiped away the blood on the victim's face.
His eyes opened. It was the guy from the Taipei Economic and Cultural Office; the young guy who had
stood against the wall while I was interviewing the
director, the one identified to me as a senior press
aide.

"What are you doing here?"

He tried to smile but couldn't. The pain from the broken bones in his face must have been considerable. He motioned for me to lean closer.

"You said we have more to lose in this matter than anyone else."

"You came here to stop Wu Hsieh?"

He nodded. Blood bubbled from his crushed nose. "We know about him."

"You found him here in the bathroom?"

"He found me."

"And since you are a press officer you couldn't handle yourself very well." Sometimes I am sarcastic.

"You understand."

"I understand that I was right about you guys." I looked around. "Where is he?"

The Taiwanese man tried to shrug. But the pain was too great. He was slipping into shock. "He ran away."

I looked up as two EMTs ran into the room. I held up my hand. "Just a second. I have one more question."

I turned back to the victim. "How did you know?"

"We tapped your phone and discovered someone else was interested in you. My superior said you were smart, that you probably knew about the tap. So we tapped the half-dozen pay phones nearest your home."

I stood up and motioned for the EMTs. It's a good thing I don't go up against the Chinese every day. Communist China or free China, PRC or ROC, China or Taiwan, I don't care what you call them—they are a sharp bunch of guys.

I looked at one of the uniforms. "Witnesses?"

He pointed to two middle-aged white guys standing wide-eyed against the wall. They wore golf shirts, Sansabelt polyester slacks and those god-awful white loafers that look as if they have been dipped in some kind of shiny liquid. Who dresses these guys?

"These two saw it." He pointed to another group standing across the room. "They were in here but didn't see much. Happened pretty fast."

"I'll talk to them in a minute. What else you got?"

The uniform grinned. "I got two suitcases."

"Belonging to the subject?"

"Yep. He checked one. The other he left with a Delta attendant when he went to the bathroom. I have them both. He was traveling under a fictitious name."

"I'm beginning to wonder how many names this guy has." I thought for a minute. "Hold those suitcases for me." I patted the uniform on the back. "You did a good job."

"Thanks, Detective."

"You're not through. This guy has probably left the airport." I handed him a picture of Wu Hsieh. "Make copies real fast. Get on the airline computer and see if anyone looking like this got a last-minute booking on any flight leaving Atlanta in the next hour. An APB is out on him." I thought for a moment. "I believe he is still in town. Gone to ground, but still in town."

The uniform nodded.

I walked over to the two witnesses and introduced myself.

"What happened?"

They both tried to talk at once. I pointed to the one on my left. "You."

"We're from Birmingham. On the way to North Carolina. Play some golf up at Pinehurst. Our wives are out at the gate. God, wait until their hear about this."

"What did you see, sir?"

"Oh, yeah. We got about an hour between flights.

Came in here to take a leak. We're standing there at the urinals pissing away." He pointed to the victim. "This Korean guy—"

"Chinese," I interrupted.

"What? Oh, yeah, Chinaman. Anyway, this Chinaman is down there in the corner washing his face when another one, another Chinaman comes in."

I showed him a picture.

"That's him. That's him."

The other guy from Birmingham leaned over, looked and nodded. "Yep, that's him."

"Anyway, the second guy never slows down. He was mad about something when he came in. He walked in the door, sees this guy here at the sink, runs across the room and kicks the dog shit out of him. Right in the face. Guy never had a chance."

"What happened then?"

"Second Chinaman picks him up, turns him around and runs him full speed into the door of that stall. I heard his bones break clear across the room. Chattering in Chinese the whole time. Sounded mad. Kicked his legs out from under him, kicked him again in the face and walked out just as calm as you please. The whole thing was over in about three seconds."

"He say anything to you?"

"No. He just looked at me. I didn't move. That guy had eyes that would freeze the Sahara Desert. He put a handkerchief up to his face like he was blowing his nose and walked out. Not in any hurry at all. I sure as hell wasn't going to stop him."

"See which way he went?"

"Shit no. You think I'm going to follow somebody like that? I told the people at the Delta counter and they called the police. Asked me to stick around since I was a witness." He smiled. "I kept a bunch of people

out who tried to come in. Told them this was a crime
scene and to go piss somewhere else."

"You did the right thing. Thank you, sir." I turned
to one of the uniforms. "Get the names and addresses
and phone numbers of these gentlemen, please."

I talked to the group of men across the bathroom.
But the uniform was right. Everything happened so
fast, by the time they turned around it was all over.
They had seen Wu Hsieh leaving and they identified
his picture.

The leader of the Metro Fugitive squad came into
the bathroom. I waved.

"What we got?" he asked.

"Zip."

He smiled. "I don't know about that."

"What do you mean?"

"Two feds out here say they are working this case.
They want to come in."

"Feds?"

I looked at the door. The feeb and Little Maynard.
I motioned for the uniform to let them pass.

"Well, well, well, Detective Payne," said Agent
Harde. He had a supercilious smirk on his face. "At
least you are consistent. You fuck up everything you
touch."

39

As I drove toward town, I wondered how Wu Hsieh would try to leave Atlanta.

When people are stressed, they revert to predictable behavior; to the basics of what they are. Wu Hsieh was a *tai zi dang;* a prince of the Chinese upper class with a powerful government position. He was used to privilege. Now his picture was in the biggest newspapers in America and on the major television channels. He was exposed, out in the sunlight, options narrowing, feeling the pressure. He was on the run and the best way out was by airplane.

He will be afraid to use Hartsfield again. Perhaps the general aviation airports. I made a radio call and asked that requests be made for officers to be assigned to Fulton County Airport, DeKalb-Peachtree, McCollum Field, Lawrenceville and a half-dozen other airfields around Atlanta.

I hope I'm right. The guy could get in a car and drive, but I don't think so. He wants out the quickest possible way.

But how will that be? Where will he go?

The radio on the seat blared my call sign.

"Be advised we have a male on the radio who says it is urgent to speak with you. Says it is in connection with your current case."

"Who is it?"

"Felix is the only name he will give us. Says you know him."

"He still there?"

"He's holding. Want me to patch him through?"

I gave him my new cell phone number.

Whoever Felix is, he has good information. My cell phone and the phone on my police radio are being monitored by the FBI. I don't have time to stop and find a pay phone. My only option is the Skip Gates cell phone.

The phone rang.

"Payne."

"This is Felix. We talked last night and—"

"You had good information. But—"

"He's at Universal. The company airplane, a C-one-thirty, is being refueled on the south side of the field and is about to be moved across the flight line to the Administration building to pick him up. They would have gone before now but the weather has slowed getting the clearance. The man you want is the only passenger. Universal is flying him to California; to our facility at San Francisco. From there he will be taken to the international airport, where a ticket is waiting for him to fly to Beijing."

He said "our facility," which means he works for Universal. "How do you know this?"

"Like I told you, we both know somebody."

"Who?"

"You're going to have to hurry to get to Universal before the aircraft takes off. Come in the Air Force side off Highway Forty-one and drive down the flight line. You'll be cutting it close."

He hung up.

I was still on the south side of Atlanta, about thirty miles from Universal, and running out of time. I reached under the seat, grabbed the blue light and slapped it on the roof. I pressed hard on the accelerator.

Then I called my major.

He did his job. When I rolled up to the gate at Dobbins Air Force Base, a blue car with a flashing red light was parked to the side. A captain in a dark blue raincoat was standing beside the car.

When I rolled down the window, he stuck out his hand. "Captain Baldowski, provost marshal for Dobbins Air Force Base. I understand you wish to apprehend a civilian suspect in a triple homicide. Where do you want to go?"

"I have to stop a C-one-thirty from taking off. I believe it's on the ramp in front of the Administration building."

He nodded. "I know where that is. I'll escort you to the Universal ramp and stand by as backup."

I could get used to working with the military. These guys know how to do a job in a professional manner.

"Let's go."

"Do you want me to call the tower and stop the aircraft from taking off?"

"It won't stop them. All it will do is warn them."

The captain nodded. "I'll go to the front of the aircraft and block it. The C-one-thirty boards passengers from a forward door on the left side. You take the door."

I nodded.

"Follow me. And stay close. It's foggy on the flight line and we have lots of jet aircraft on the ground."

He jumped into the blue car. We turned left, drove between two big hangars, between lines of aircraft, and suddenly were on a taxiway that paralleled the main runway. We turned right and raced toward the Universal complex about two miles away.

The fog and rain were so thick that I had to keep my eyes on the flashing light atop the captain's car. I hoped he was on the radio talking to the tower. The last thing I needed was to be inhaled by a jet.

We were almost on top of the C-130 when it popped out of the fog and I saw the navigation and clearance lights strobing on the wing tips and atop the tail. Then I saw the name "Universal" on the side and a distinctive paint job. The props were turning.

The bird was ready to fly.

A white car was pulled up near the left front of the aircraft. I parked in front of it and jumped from my Explorer. Just as my feet landed in the middle of a big puddle, J. Stanford appeared in the open door of the aircraft and stared, probably one of the few times in his life when he was speechless.

It was a Kodak moment.

I ran to the door of the aircraft.

"What are you doing here?" J. Stanford shouted over the noise of the screaming props. The thunder of the four engines combined with the banshee shriek of the propellers surrounded us and pummeled us. The downward blast of the exhaust splatted exhaust fumes against the concrete parking apron, blowing up a torrent of water and a mist thicker than the fog. The fumes washed over us, filling our nostrils with the acrid sweetness of burning kerosene.

J. Stanford grabbed my arm and tried to push me away from the aircraft.

"This is government property. You have no jurisdiction here."

He jumped to the ground, turned and made a motion to someone behind me. A crewman stood there. He wore a helmet with a microphone in front of his mouth. The helmet was attached to a long line, I

guessed a radio line to the pilot. He stepped forward
and began to swing the door closed.

I badged him.

"Get away from that door."

The crewman paused.

"Is this aircraft going to Burbank?" I shouted.

The ramp was a scene from hell: fog and rain, strobing lights on the aircraft, flashing lights on my car and
that of the captain, the cloying odor of burning kerosene and the relentless scream of four powerful
engines.

J. Stanford was a bit befuddled. His raincoat was
flapping as if he were trying to take off himself. He
was losing his command presence. He stepped closer
and shouted. "This is a courier aircraft carrying papers
and equipment to our home office." He pointed his
finger at me. "No one but the crew is on board."

"I didn't ask you who was on board."

"No one."

"Then you won't mind if I have a look."

"This is a military installation. You have no authority here."

All this shouting was hurting my throat. I stepped
closer until J. Stanford and I were nose to nose.

"I'm in pursuit of a fleeing felon; a man I believe
to have killed three people, including one of your security guards. The provost marshal will hold this aircraft until it runs out of fuel or until I get a warrant."

"You can't go aboard."

"Fuck you." I shoved him aside.

I'm definitely getting over this intimidation thing.

I pulled my weapon and stepped into the C-130.
The crewman moved aside. The small windows were
covered with rain, leaving the unlighted interior a
darkened tube. The noise was thunderous, a high-

pitched scream that caused the floor or deck or whatever they call it to tremble under my feet.

Wu Hsieh moved fast. He came out of the shadows and attacked before my eyes were used to the darkness. I sensed a blur of motion as he kicked the gun from my hand. I crouched as the hatchetlike edge of his hand sliced overhead. That one would have given me a sore throat of the worst kind.

Wu Hsieh was confident. He had relieved me of my weapon. I heard him laugh as he advanced toward me, arms up, fingers rigid, crabbing toward me like a chop suey version of Chuck Norris.

He faked a kick and in the darkness I did not see his right hand until it exploded against my ear. The ringing he put in my ear made the four engines so silent and knocked me against the bulkhead and hurt the hell out of me.

"Hey," the crew member shouted. He was wandering around the cargo compartment with his helmet on and speaking into a microphone. "What's going on in here?"

I shook my head to clear the ringing and pulled myself off the bulkhead. "Tell the pilot to shut down the engines," I shouted. I think that's what I said. I couldn't hear anything.

By now my eyes were adjusted to the dim interior. I backed up as Wu Hsieh advanced.

"No," he shouted. "We take off now."

"Shut down the engines."

The young crewman was confused.

"I'm a cop. You tell whoever is running this thing to shut down the engines or I'll put his ass in jail and impound the airplane."

I wondered how I could impound a C-130. But the crewman, being a good patriotic American with a healthy respect for law enforcement, pressed a little button on the cord and chattered away.

Wu Hsieh was sliding toward me again, acting as if he had all the time in the world, smiling as his hands sliced circles in the air.

He was about to strike again. I don't know where. But it probably would have put me away. At the precise second he was about to throw his punch, the pilot pulled the throttles and all four engines began spooling down in a dying whoosh.

For a split second Wu Hsieh paused. I ducked under his arms and jammed my ballpoint pen into the large muscle of his thigh. I shoved it in hard then pushed on it again.

He screamed and collapsed on his other knee, holding the injured leg with both hands. Then he reached for the pen. This guy didn't know when to stop.

I kicked him behind the ear as hard as I could. He flew across the cabin and collapsed on the deck. Immediately I was there, twisting his arms behind his back and cuffing him before he could get up. This guy could slice me into chocolate noodles.

He was groggy, lurching and staggering, when I marched him out the door. Blood was running down his leg and oozing between the woven leather of his Cole-Haan shoes.

Oh, my.

The provost marshal stood by as I stripped Wu Hsieh down to his shorts to search for concealed weapons.

I reached into the back pocket of Wu Hsieh's discarded trousers, pulled out a handkerchief and tied it around his leg. Then I pulled the pen out. He never flinched.

"Captain, you have a tarp or a piece of canvas?"

"How about plastic raincoats? We keep several in the car."

I opened the back door of my Explorer, holding Wu Hsieh's arm all the time. He was still groggy. "Mind speading them out back here? I don't want this individual bleeding on my personal vehicle."

"Not at all."

"You have a pair of cuffs?"

He handed me a set.

I shook Wu Hsieh. "You want to get inside the car or you want me to put you there?"

With his good leg under him, he gingerly climbed into the back of the Explorer and lay down. I put the second set of cuffs around his ankles, looped his belt around the handcuffs on his wrists, then tied the belt to one of the cargo hooks. I don't want this guy attacking me while I'm driving through Atlanta traffic.

"Now relax and be a model minority until I get you downtown." I jerked on the plastic raincoat. "And try not to bleed."

The pilot and copilot watched through the open cockpit windows. The crew chief, or whatever he was called, stood in the door of the aircraft.

"Where are you taking this man?" J. Stanford demanded. "You can't just toss him into the back of your car and haul—"

"You said there was no one on the airplane."

"You have no authority here. The FBI is investigating this case."

"Sir, I suggest you call your lawyer."

I was thinking of the possible charges: Hindering apprehension or punishment of a felon, that's good for one to five; then there's criminal responsibility of corporations, a felony. I might go the civil route and initiate forfeiture procedures against the C-130 since it was used to aid and abet a fleeing felon. The stockholders will go bananas. But all that can wait. I need to put Wu Hsieh in the Box and see what he gives up.

Wu Hsieh was lying calmly when I crawled into my Explorer.

"My ears are still ringing. I got Excedrin headache number thirty-five," I said.

He didn't answer. I suspect that my foot had given him number thirty-six.

Captain Baldowski walked to the door and leaned over. He was smiling. "Detective, pleasure working with you."

"I'll return those cuffs soon."

"I'll escort you to the gate."

I looked in my mirror as I drove away. J. Stanford was standing in the rain there on the tarmac, frozen, watching me drive away with the key man in his eighty-billion-dollar contract tied up like a sack of salt. The fog and rain were so heavy that I quickly lost sight of him, but I knew he was there.

Sometimes these old white guys take a while to absorb reality.

40

The squad room at Homicide was filled with cops. They knew a big case, the biggest since the missing and murdered children's case almost twenty years ago, was going down and that the suspect was in the office getting medical treatment and about to go into the Box. A video camera had been set up behind the smoked glass of the room adjacent to the Box. The audio came from a microphone hidden in the ceiling. Homicide detectives were jostling over who would get the half-dozen chairs in the little room. They knew this interview would be one for the books.

Word had gotten out that the suspect was an agent in Chinese intelligence and my fellow homicide detectives were taking bets about the outcome. There was agreement that even though I was the best interviewer in APD that the Chinese agent was going to hand me my head.

I came out of my office and turned to a detective, a new homicide investigator, a muscular young black guy, and said, "Let me borrow your knife."

The detective looked at me, looked at the Asian doll in my hand, and said, "For what?"

"Don't you have a knife?"

He pulled a knife from his back pocket, pressed a button, and a four-inch stainless steel blade flicked open. "Every cop in Atlanta has one. Why don't you, Sarge?"

"I'm a walking supervisor. I don't need a knife." I took the knife and walked into the Box. I held the doll tightly and cut away most of the face on the right side. The Asian features still were identifiable. Then I perched the suited-up little doll in the window.

I returned the knife. "You got potential for promotion, young detective."

"So when I get to be a sergeant I can cut the faces off dolls? I really got something to look forward to."

"A smart ass, too. I like that. You get a seat in the observation room." I looked around the squad room. "Hey, Peep Sight. Where's my prisoner?"

"EMTs are about finished with him," Peep said. He laughed. "That ballpoint pen of yours must have hurt like hell but it didn't do much damage. Two stitches and some antibiotics. He will limp for a few days and be as good as new."

"Did you tell them I said no painkillers? I want him wide awake and alert. If he's drugged, his confession will be inadmissible."

"They gave him a couple of Advil; that's all." He paused. "You're pretty confident."

"Put your money on me, Peep."

He smiled. "Already did."

I clapped my hands and spoke loudly enough that everyone in the squad room could hear. "Okay, people, listen up. We got a major case here and I'm about to take the suspect into the Box. When the light goes on I want silence in the sanctuary. Especially from you people in the observation room."

"What makes this a major case?" one of the older guys asked.

He knew the answer to that as well as I. But a good homicide investigator questions everything and everybody and has a bone-deep problem with authority. The very qualities that make a person a good homicide detective also make him a pain in the ass, a manager's nightmare. I know. My major says I'm that way. He's tolerant and understanding with me so I'm tolerant and understanding with my people.

"It is a major case because it will keep me away from the airport and bring me back here to be your loved and revered supervisor."

Everyone applauded and hooted with laughter.

"You hope," said a quiet voice.

The ranks parted and my major was there, solemn and foreboding, glowering from under the brim of his hat. Two uniform sergeants flanked him. The major looked around. "Don't you people have work to do? What the hell is this? Recess?"

The detectives scattered for their offices.

The major stared at me from across the room. "I want to talk to you."

I opened the door to my small office. He walked in and turned around. I shut the door.

"The feds are on the way," he said. "The FBI and the OSI."

"What do they want?"

"The suspect. They want to conduct the interview at the FBI office. They say national defense issues are involved. They're claiming federal supremacy."

I bowed up like a tomcat. "Major, this is a homicide case. Give me four or five hours and I'll have a confession. They can still interview him about whatever they want."

He looked at the floor. My major was on the edge of getting a bad case of the wobbles. It suddenly occurred to me that if I didn't get a confession, the feds would pee all over him.

"You got the physical evidence you need for a conviction."

"Yes. But I want the big mule. I want the president of Universal."

The major shook his head. "What makes you think this Chinese guy will confess?"

"The recency of the arrest. His injury. His type personality. He considers the arrest a personal defeat by an enemy who is an inferior. The probability of his confession is upwards of eighty percent."

The major looked away and made a grimace. "You haven't even put him in the Box and you're sounding like a confession is a done deal."

"The only way this guy can regain his ego control is to reveal the truth. He has to confess to save his ego."

"I don't understand that weird shit."

"You don't have to; not if I get you the results you want. Atlanta has to keep this case. Major, we're talking a triple homicide."

"Can't give you four or five hours."

"I've got to set him down, desensitize him and then move very slowly. I want him to give up everything, including the president of Universal. This guy knows interrogation techniques. It will take a while for me to get the truth."

"A minute ago you sounded like it was a foregone conclusion. Now you want several hours. Can you get him to talk or can't you?"

"Yes. But I need time."

"You got one hour."

I stared in disbelief.

He dropped the other shoe. "Max. It may be less."

I exploded. "An hour? I need that much time to set him up."

The major stepped around me and opened the door. "Stop whining, Payne. An hour is all I can delay the

FBI. When they start making phone calls to Washington and it begins rolling downhill, the chief will order me to pull you out."

He walked into the squad room and pointed to the two uniform sergeants. "Outside. The FBI does not come in."

The older uniform looked at the major. "The FBI, sir?"

"The FBI will be here in a half hour, maybe twenty minutes. If they get past you two, both of you will be busted to patrolmen working morning watch at the airport with Tuesday and Thursday as your off days. That's how you will retire."

The two sergeants swallowed hard. "Yes, sir," said the older one.

"They will tell you to get a message to me. Do it, but don't be in a hurry. Delay them. Tell them I'm in a meeting."

"Yes, sir."

The major turned to me. "Go to work, Detective."

41

I did some fast thinking.

Wu Hsieh is a psychopath. That means he is bright, egocentric, feels no guilt or remorse, is an actor-deceiver, has no loyalty to people or organizations, is quick to anger, aggressive, does not learn from experience and rationalizes his mistakes.

His bizarre crime scene behavior comes from one of five possible motivations.

First, he was laying a trail of confusion to cover something obvious. That was what Jeffrey McDonald, the Special Forces doctor, did in the murders of his wife and children.

Second, he was following instructions from someone whom only he can hear. Charles Manson is a good example.

Third, he could be acting out some unconscious conflict, as do psychosexual criminals.

Fourth, it could be a ritual in which the bizarre is commonplace to him but holds no real personal significance. Remember the scene in *Apocalypse Now* where Robert Duvall left "death cards"?

And finally, he could be leaving a message, communicating something of importance to another person.

I believe it is number five: Wu Hsieh was leaving a message. Now, in such cases, the message is not intended for the victim or the public or the families of the victim. These people rarely if ever know of the message. The message is for the investigating officer. The public doesn't understand this, but it is the police officer who is the intended psychological victim of serial killers. The perpetrators want to challenge the cops, to play games with them.

That's what Wu Hsieh has been doing. Only marginally was he acting as an agent of his government. I thought it was killing the dog that first revealed his lack of control. But the jade showed he was out of control from the get-go. He was throwing down the gauntlet to the stupid American cops when he placed jade in Richard Morris's body and in the hands of the other two victims.

He knew within hours of the first homicide, when I went to Universal the next morning, that the investigating detective was a black man. Few people are more contemptuous of blacks than are Asians, particularly if they, like Wu Hsieh, consider themselves elite and urbane intellectuals. Wu Hsieh feels utter contempt for Americans in general and black Americans in particular. To him, I am a mongrel.

The time is now right for me to claim ownership of Wu Hsieh's messages; to give him credit for his creations.

He will not be accustomed to or prepared for either an elegant interrogation or to persuasion techniques. But my approach cannot be obvious. I must come at him from two directions; simultaneous moves against the conscious and the unconscious mind. I have to be a magician; to pull a David Copperfield and use misdirection and confusion to hide what I am doing.

I motioned for Peep Sight to come close. "Call the EMTs and get them to hold off bringing in the suspect

for about two minutes. When he arrives, here's what
I want you to do." I whispered rapid instructions.

He looked at me, confused.

"Just do it, Peep."

"Okay, Sarge."

Quickly I pulled an old chair out of my office and
put it in the Box. All the other chairs save one I took
from the Box and placed against the walls of the squad
room. Now that the major had gone into the lieutenant's office, the detectives had cautiously emerged into
the squad room. They looked at me curiously.

"Why the hell is he moving furniture around?" one
of them said.

"Shut up and listen," Peep Sight said. He told the
detectives what to do. Their brows wrinkled in bewilderment. "Get Gigi in here now," he added.

It was time for the perp walk.

I motioned for Peep to bring him in.

A moment later the prisoner, wearing only a pair
of shorts and a small bandage on his leg, was led into
the room. His hands were handcuffed behind his back.

Peep Sight pointed and laughed. "That *little* son of
a bitch is supposed to be such a bad ass? He's a *little*
pip-squeak."

Wu Hsieh's eyes flashed.

Gigi, one of the female detectives, laughed. "Look
at that *little fellow.*"

"Doesn't look like he's carrying much in that *little*
set of drawers he's wearing," said another.

Wu Hsieh's eyes were locked somewhere in the
distance.

"I see why the Chinese make good Ping Pong players," said another. "They ain't big enough to play a
real sport."

"Yeah," said Peep. "How many Chinese football

or basketball players are there?" He paused. *"How about soccer?"*

Wu Hsieh's body was rigid.

"Detective," I said to Peep Sight. "Please escort the prisoner into the room and give him a seat."

I took off my weapon and locked it in a desk drawer. Then I stepped down the hall, washed my face, snugged up my tie and made sure my suit was riding smoothly on my shoulders. I popped a lozenge in my mouth, closed my eyes and took a deep breath.

Time to do it.

I flipped the switch that turned on the red light over the door. I took a sheet of blank paper from my pocket, then took a cigarette and a lighter from Peep.

I walked into the Box.

Wu Hsieh was sitting in an old straight-backed wooden chair. His right hand was handcuffed to the rungs. About three quarters of an inch had been cut off each of the front legs. The seat had been heavily waxed.

Let me tell you something. Being paraded through an office filled with detectives wearing guns while you are wearing only a pair of shorts is unbalancing for anyone. Add a woman who laughs. Add belittling comments. And someone with Wu Hsieh's psychological makeup is on the way to Jell-O city.

I handed the cigarette to Wu Hsieh. He took it with his left hand and without even looking at me leaned forward for a light. I took my time, making him hold the cigarette steady with his left hand. He lit it. Then he pushed with his feet. He was sliding forward in the chair.

As I sat at the table across from him, he pulled the cigarette from his mouth with his left hand and blew smoke in my face.

Truth is a right-brain function. I want to appeal to that area. By making him use his left hand, the right brain is activated. And by seating him in a slick-bottomed chair, he is constantly slipping and read-justing himself. Physically he is off balance. That means that psychologically he is off balance.

Now he is sitting here blowing smoke in my face and feeling superior. He doesn't know I have opened the door to his unconscious.

He looked around the room again, his eyes stopping on the doll in the window.

I began doodling on the piece of paper in my hand, drawing a circle that contained two smaller circles.

"The thing with the doll is supposed to signify losing face? How obvious." He blew smoke in my face again. "And how amateurish."

I nodded in agreement. He was not concerned with losing face. He was concerned with losing ego. He is also aware of Chinese icons, which is why he is staring at the drawing, a subliminal suggestion of a faceless image.

I'd waited for this moment for more than a week. And I had thought about it almost daily. Guilt would not be a suitable motivation for this guy. There is such a thing as a noble purpose lie. Say you came upon a car wreck where the mother and father were killed and the child was injured but tossed free. You pick up the child and he says, "Are Mommy and Daddy okay?" You tell him, "Yes, everything will be fine." It is okay to lie under those circumstances.

And it will be okay for Wu Hsieh to lie to me today. He will lie to me with the greatest of ease.

But I have several advantages. The Chinese know nothing of NLP. Another advantage is that cops are pretty much the same around the world. Many cops are Rambo types who believe that screwing a gun into some guy's ear is the best way to get a confession. Either that, or they are eight-to-five types who are more worried about whether or not they have week-

ends off than they are about someone committing a
crime on their beat.

Still another advantage I have is that most people,
no matter how heinous their acts, think of themselves
as decent people. Hitler was proud that he was good
to his dog. I arrested a serial killer who boasted about
how good he was to his mother. No matter how tough
a man tries to be, that unconscious and uncontrollable
battle goes on within his soul.

The big question with Wu Hsieh was whether I
should conduct the interview as if he were Chinese or
Western. I have no time to explore his psyche. This
has to be done quickly and it has to be done right. If
I come at him from the wrong direction, I will learn
nothing and the FBI will take him away.

This is a man who was educated in America and
spent most of his life here. He speaks flawless English.
He dresses Western and knows how we in the West
think. But he also is a man who left jade in the orifices
of his first victim, one of the most ancient of Chinese
burial practices. He left jade pigs in the hands of his
two other victims. He oriented the bodies of his victims to north and south, another ancient Chinese practice. In Mrs. Morris's flower garden he called on the
symbology of ancient China when he drew the
phoenix.

I believe his adherence to ancient Chinese tradition
is based not so much on reverence for the past as it is
an anti-Western sentiment. After all, he is a psychopath.

"First, I'm going to read you your rights."

He smiled. "You Americans and your rights."

He listened as I read his Miranda rights. I was trying
to move along without giving any appearance of haste.
Ordinarily I would ask a lot of administrative type
questions—name, age, DOB, address—to desensitize
someone to the Box. Then open questions of a non-

interrogative nature, then direct questions, then random recall. I would have flipped back and forth between various interview techniques, experimenting to see which worked best: SCAN, NLP, cognitive techniques, behavioral analysis, pupilometrics, proxemics, kinesics, mirroring, voice—whatever worked. I would have asked a lot of open-ended questions, as information received from open statements is far more reliable than information that comes from direct questions.

But today I had to remember I was one of God's foot soldiers, bore in and hope for the best.

The feeb and Little Maynard were on the way.

I smiled at Wu Hsieh.

"My friend, it would appear you made a very poor career choice," I said.

He smiled and adjusted himself in the chair. "Your interrogation techniques lack a great deal."

I was beginning to feel good about my decision. "This is not an interrogation. We're just talking. There is plenty of time."

His eyes again were attracted to the drawing. It's not very profound but it appears to be having some effect. Every little bit helps.

The psychological defenses dealing with deception are conscious. Therefore they must be occupied with a diversion, the general-to-specific technique known to trained interviewers. Wu Hsieh has prepared for and expects direct questions concerning his assault on me in the Universal aircraft. He cannot deny that happened. So I will ask a few questions about that incident.

Wu Hsieh will put up a defense. But he's rearranging deck chairs on the *Titanic*.

I rubbed the side of my head where he struck me. "You're pretty good with your hands."

He blew smoke in my face.

I don't mind. Every time he lifts the cigarette to his

mouth he is accessing his right brain and that's where truth resides.

"Is that a martial art?"

He smiled. "Your question indirectly goes back to the reason you brought me here."

He saw where I was going and did his countermove. Again, that's okay. It occupied his conscious mind.

"Your people back in China didn't give you very good directions, did they?"

The pause as he put the cigarette in his mouth was almost imperceptible.

"You did very well. You made the best of a bad situation."

He adjusted himself in the chair, puffed on the cigarette and looked at me.

"I've got enough physical evidence from the crime scenes to convict you of two homicides. But you probably won't be in prison very long. Considering your connections, the political pressure that can be brought to bear."

He nodded.

"Besides, not much to those people you killed."

He looked at me curiously.

"A salesman and an old man. And we mustn't forget the dog. It took a top-notch agent to kill a dog."

His expression hardened. I was saying to him that he was nothing special, just another hood, a common killer. This challenged his ego. He didn't know it yet, but he wanted to defend himself, even if it meant confessing to murder.

Most people believe self-preservation is the strongest motivator. Wrong. The strongest motivator is preservation of the self, of the ego.

I leaned across the table. It was important I show no emotion. "I know a great battle is tearing at your spirit."

Confusion, bewilderment, the desire to agree with me—all these were in his eyes.

I leaned closer and very softly said, "The Tao is disturbed."

He flinched and his pupils slammed down to pinhead size.

I figured the people in the observation room were holding their sides trying to keep from laughing. The were in there watching the master interrogator take on a Chinese agent and they wanted fireworks, flashy technique, something they could write down and remember and practice. Not a one of them understood what I was doing or where I was going. And all at once I come out with "The Tao is disturbed."

That's only one step away from saying "May the Force be with you." They are probably rushing outside to roll on the grass in hysterics.

But it got Wu Hsieh's attention. He straightened up in the chair.

"What do you know of the Tao?"

I remembered Lao-tzu. "The universe must be in balance. Our activity must be in tune with the rhythm of the universe. Right now, the universe—the Tao— is out of balance. We must find harmony."

"You are of the West." He spat it out. Contemptuous.

"Followers of the Tao know not to use force. What you do comes back to you. Weeds grow where armies have camped."

He looked past the doll, out the window.

"You don't see the Way of Heaven by staring out the window."

The Way of Heaven. That must have put them in snicker city inside the observation room. I was afraid to turn and look at that mirrored glass.

Wu Hsieh's head snapped toward me. "Memory tricks. You do not know the Tao. You do not understand. You can never understand." He looked me up and down in contempt and then spat out: "You are a nigger."

In an ordinary interrogation, if a suspect said that to a black detective, the suspect would find his blood on the wall and his ass on the floor. But this was not an ordinary interrogation.

I nodded. "But I understand that there is already a supreme executioner in charge of doing the killing. You put yourself in his place. You wielded the ax of a skilled woodsman and you ended up injuring yourself."

He shook his head.

"You never intended for things to get out of hand, to go this far, did you?"

He moved his head a fraction of an inch.

"The man you work for should have helped you, should have called you. It was his fault all this happened."

His head moved again.

I leaned toward him. Our eyes were locked and our noses were almost touching.

Then Wu broke eye contact, lowered his head and slumped in his chair. He stayed there this time. He gave me everything I wanted and more. The detectives in the observation room heard things that would cause the feds to threaten them with life inside the slammer if they ever breathed a word of it.

When I exited the Box, the two uniforms came in and stood across the room from Wu Hsieh.

The door to the observation room opened and the detectives spilled out, looking at me curiously, but saying nothing. They were not sure what had happened or what I had done. But they heard the confession.

One of the uniform sergeants who had accompanied the major walked over. He pointed at the lieutenant's office. "The FBI is in there raising hell. The major instructed us to take the prisoner out to Douglas County Jail and hide him. He says for you to get out of here and do what you have to do."

"Was he in the observation room?"

"No."

"Then how does he know I got a confession?"

"He never had any doubt."

I turned away for a second.

"The videotape . . ."

"Doesn't exist for right now. It will take several days to have a copy made. The feeb will be in the dark until then."

I nodded toward Peep. "Get some clothes for the prisoner."

One of the detectives spoke up. "What the hell was all that mumbo jumbo in there? You playing with him under the table?"

Another detective, a black guy, looked at me. "Man, you let him get away with calling you a nigger." He shook his head. "You should have—"

I smiled at them and remembered another line from the Tao. "Do not strain to see through muddy water. Be still, and allow the mud to settle."

The black detective spoke over his shoulder to the room filled with detectives. "He's flipped his fucking wig."

I headed for the front door. The uniform sergeant spoke up. "The major thought you might be going out to Universal."

"He's right. Tell him I'm arresting the president of Universal. And you can tell the two feds if they try to interfere, I'll arrest them, too."

42

I flashed my tin at the security guard and told him I had official police business with J. Stanford Godbey. I refused to wear the visitor's badge. "I can find my own way."

He studied me. "You the Atlanta homicide guy investigating Bill Brumby's death?"

"I am."

"We heard you had a perp; snagged him off the ramp a few hours ago."

"You heard right."

"Now you're going up to Mr. Godbey's office?"

"You're three for three."

He pursed his lips and nodded slowly as he added up the possible reasons I was going to see Godbey. It didn't take long.

"You know the way?"

I nodded and turned to go.

"Detective?"

I paused.

"I never liked that son of a bitch Godbey anyway."

I took out my I.D. and hung it in my coat pocket so the badge was visible. My suit was still damp and rumpled. It didn't matter. The badge is all that matters.

Pinstripe was entering his office as I walked down

the hall. He stopped, hand on the door. He had to have heard about the incident on the ramp. Now I was back. And usually I brought bad news.

"You aren't wearing a visitor's badge and you have no escort."

"You're a sharp guy, Mr. Vandiver. You should be president of this place." I tapped my tin. "This trumps your visitor's badge."

"This is a federal installation. An escort is required at all times."

"I'm a homicide detective. I don't need an escort." I brushed past.

His eyes were on my back, following me.

J. Stanford's secretary, the middle-aged and elegant woman who had served tea the last time I was here, was in the outer office when I opened the door. A few other secretaries bustled about.

"Oh, Detective Payne," she said as if we had talked five minutes earlier. "How are you today?" She walked toward me.

"I'm fine." I paused. "I'm afraid I'm here on official police business."

"Well, of course you are."

She was so nice that I wanted to caution her. Civilians can get upset when they see someone they know being arrested. "I have an unpleasant duty to perform."

Actually, it wasn't unpleasant. I was looking forward to arresting the son of a bitch. I don't know when I've looked forward to anything as much. But I said that to help her.

She stepped closer. In a soft voice that none of the other secretaries could hear, she said, "It concerns Mr. Godbey?"

"It does. I'm here to arrest him."

A flicker of what I could have sworn was a smile

passed across her lips. She didn't say anything for a moment. "You know, Detective Payne, I've been thinking of retiring. This might be a good time." She smiled. "My family has been involved with Universal for many years. In fact, my brother retired about six months ago."

After the encounter with Pinstripe and the anticipation of putting the cuffs on J. Stanford, my adrenaline was pumping. I was anxious to confront the big mule. I wanted to brush past her and push my way into Godbey's office and slap the cuffs on him. But she was telling me something. I had to listen.

"I didn't know you had a brother here."

She nodded. "Oh, yes. In fact, I believe you know him."

"I do?"

"His name is Felix."

I stared.

She smiled and waved me toward the polished wooden door across the office. "Just go right in."

43

Two days later Kitty ran a story saying Pinstripe had been promoted to president of Universal. She rehashed the earlier story about J. Stanford's being in jail on a half dozen state and federal charges. The federal charges were tacked on after the FBI realized they could not stop J. Stanford from going down; charges involving procurement fraud, heavy-duty stuff.

I hope the state gets first crack at J. Stanford. He could end up at Reidsville and get to know my brothers.

Pinstripe's wife filed for divorce the day he was promoted. I suspect with what she knows about his behavior and his desire to avoid any further problems in his personal or professional life that the settlement will be generous.

I did not get to put an ass-whipping on Little Maynard, as he and the feeb left town as quickly as they had arrived. On the way out of town they turned their investigation over to Cobb County Homicide. I told the detective up there he could stand in line; that I didn't think Wu Hsieh was going to get out of jail for a long time, maybe ever. Because of the Universal contract, his people back home denied he worked for the government. They cut him loose, which means he is facing homicide charges in Atlanta and, if convicted, will enjoy the hospitality of Reidsville for many years. If Wu Hsieh thinks China is a worker's paradise, wait until he gets to Reidsville.

I'm driving down there soon to visit my brothers. This might surprise you, but convicts are patriotic people. My brothers will spread the word about Wu Hsieh.

Universal and China won, just as Chuck Spinney said they would. Kitty had a story this morning in which Pinstripe announced that the largest defense contract in history had been signed with the Chinese government. She also explained about the side agreements, which the State Department and Universal described as "insignificant codicils, standard in these sorts of things."

The secretary of Defense was quoted about the importance of the contract to America. There was even a quote from the President about how the contract had cemented a trading relationship with the largest emerging market in the world.

China is our friend.

But are we China's friend?

The President didn't say.

As a citizen, the contract bothers the hell out of me. But as a cop I did my job.

And that means the Atlanta airport is only a bad dream. I have been reassigned to Atlanta Homicide, day watch. I'm back where I belong.

Kitty's stories, and the way television picked up everything she wrote, made me look like a hero. That made the chief and the mayor happy. Right now, I'm the flavor of the month. The major told me not to relax; things change quickly at APD.

One of the tidbits Wu Hsieh spilled during our little chat I quietly turned over to Kitty. She confirmed that the good Senator Sam Perry had a lot to do with the

Universal deal, that he has been hustling every branch of the military to do business with China and pushing for the State Department to grant unheard of concessions to the PRC. Turns out he should have been registered as an agent of the PRC. He's up for election next year and I suspect he will find some reason not to run. He probably will get a job with a big Atlanta law firm and become a rainmaker, a man who puts American businessmen in touch with government officials in China.

I called Mrs. Morris. She asked me to come out one night and have dinner. I told her maybe in a month or so when things settle down and her life is back to normal. But I know something Mrs. Morris doesn't. In a case like this, when the perp is caught the family is so grateful that they cannot do enough for the investigating officer. But time eases their wounds and soon the presence of a homicide cop in their lives is only an unpleasant reminder of what happened.

I'll probably never see her again.

Gwendolyn called again last night and we had a long talk. She mentioned that she might be returning to Atlanta. I was very nice to her but I think she accepts that we will never be back together. Although with her, you never know. I could change my phone number. But she was my wife and is the mother of my daughter. Maybe one day, when my daughter is grown, she will seek out her dad. I'm going to make sure she knows I am always here.

I'd like to be married again. And one day I will. But it will not be to Gwendolyn. And it will not be to Kitty or to any other white woman.

The Chinese are right about one thing: Out of chaos comes order. My life has fallen back into an ordered existence and I am happy.

There is only one thing left to do. I called my new

bud and role model, Colonel David Drumwright, United States Army, commander of the CID laboratory at Fort Gillem, and told him it was time to go to Manuel's Tavern, smoke a Partagas 150, have a few drinks of the Macallan and talk about His Skipness.

Being a man of eminently good judgment, he agreed.

"Good. But we have to do something first. I saw how you work. Now you need to see my side of law enforcement."

"Oh?"

"Meet me at Homicide about four-thirty."

"What are we doing?"

"David, it's a beautiful day. The rain is gone and the air is clean and the sky is blue. The good weather should hold for a while. It's a day made for celebrating. The first part of our celebration is to go up on Buford Highway for a come to Jesus meeting."

"I'm not from the South. What is a come to Jesus meeting?"

"The umbrella man is going to make a final appearance. I'm going to close down a sleazy bar, arrest several dope dealers and a half-dozen prostitutes, roust the owner, and impress upon him the majesty of the law."

"By yourself?"

"Hey, one redneck bar, one Atlanta detective."

The colonel laughed.